ARIZONA DREAMS

BOOK ONE OF THE ARIZONA SERIES

MARSHA DEFILIPPO

CHAPTER ONE

From the first time she'd been in Arizona, she'd felt the familiarity of returning to a place she'd been before. She'd always believed in reincarnation and the thought of it not being a given was stranger to her than that it might all be *woo woo*. That was ten years ago and ever since, Sharon Peterson had known that someday she would be living there.

Her entire body thrummed with anticipation upon arriving at the Tucson airport. The wait for her baggage seemed interminably long but she kept reminding herself that there wasn't the hurry this time to make sure every minute was spent getting in as much as she could because two weeks go by very quickly when you are on vacation. This time she'd be staying and her new house was waiting.

The years between her first visit and today had included several short vacations checking out the usual tourist spots but she'd known that any permanent location had to be where the winters would be warm. Living in New England most of her life and suffering through the six months of cold and snow had convinced her that she was meant to be elsewhere—somewhere

where the winters did not include snow or the humidity of Florida where most of the northeastern snowbirds spent their winters. But it was more than that. That sense of familiarity on her first visit had grown to a longing to return *home* even though she'd never lived in the Southwest before. At least not in this lifetime.

And now she was coming home, literally. Being self-sufficient had always been second nature so it was no surprise that her choice for her house here was one that was self-sustaining and eco-friendly. She'd sworn she'd never build another house after having gone through two projects before but this seemed worth it. And perhaps it was a good omen that unlike the others, this construction had gone surprisingly well. She would now truly be able to be on her own and independent of any outside influences---the 21st century pioneer. Sharon had never been much of a social butterfly and although she wasn't anti-social, being alone was well within her comfort zone.

She found the cab stand and gave the driver the address to the dealer where her new car was ready to be picked up. She'd made the arrangements by phone and internet after having driven a similar model at her local dealer.

After finally picking up her car and clearing the Tucson traffic, a sense of peace flowed through her as she drove along Interstate 10 towards Wilmont. She was going home. She smiled at that—going *home*. Yes, it was that and a new beginning, too.

It hadn't been easy to make this decision in spite of the knowing in her heart that this was where she should be. She still had connections to Maine. Her children were there and that carried some guilt at abandoning them. That wasn't quite true as they were grown and had lives of their own but the societal conditioning she'd grown up with still brought that twinge of guilt when she thought about not being there, at least in the same time zone. Her second husband for the past 25 years, Tom, had recently passed away. Her former job could be done mostly online and would have allowed her to move at any time but his kept him tied to Maine. They'd planned to become snowbirds in the Southwest as he'd also had that affinity to the area and had begun planning their house and having it built before he became too ill to participate in the process. Perhaps they'd both had past lives here together—that felt right somehow and she'd always thought they'd be returning together when they retired. Fate had other plans, however, and she was making the trip alone. Her happiness at being here turned to sadness as she thought of that. *You're here with me in my heart*, she whispered softly.

An hour later she arrived at the town of Wilmont. She'd chosen it primarily because she'd been able to buy a sizable tract of land for a reasonable price but had grown to love its natural beauty. Convincing the local authorities that her unconventional house wouldn't violate any building restrictions hadn't been as difficult as she'd feared. She'd known from her experience living in a semi-rural town in Maine that dealing with small communities was often a lot easier which was another reason for choosing this town. She'd looked at several parcels of land but this one spoke to her with its hills rather than the flat desert landscape of so many others that she'd found while spending hours searching through realtor.com's listings. Had to love the internet!

She parked her car in the driveway and sat there for a few minutes taking it all in. She resisted the urge to pinch herself but let the feelings wash over her. *I'm really home. This is my house and I won't have to leave here in two weeks or three or at all if I don't want to.* That brought a huge smile to her face and with that, she couldn't wait to get inside. She checked her key ring for at least the hundredth time since leaving Maine and, of course, it was still there. A part of her kept thinking this was all a dream as she flew West but now it was right in front of her. There was still a lot to be done she realized as she surveyed the grounds around her house. She wanted to plant a small garden and some trees--- never in her life had she thought that she'd be living in a place where she could have fresh oranges and avocados growing. The thought of planting a garden gave her hope that there was a future waiting for her. Those first few months after Tom died had been incredibly hard and there were times when she wasn't sure she wanted to go on. So many dreams had died with him. But maybe, just maybe, there were still new dreams and a life to live. It was time to put passion back in her life.

She unlocked the door and stepped in. *Honey, I'm home!* she called out. That she'd said it out loud both surprised and delighted her. It surprised her even more when she mentally heard the response *Welcome home, I've been waiting for you.* After a slight start, she smiled as it was a friendly rather than malevolent greeting and with it a feeling that she was going to be okay.

She'd put off decorating most of the house except for a few basic necessities—a bed, living room chair, a small kitchen table with two chairs, dishes and the most essential item, a coffee pot —which she'd arranged through a service that set up houses for people who were relocating. It was important to make this a fresh start and she wanted to take her time making it her own. It was the first time in her life she had a house that was completely hers. She planned to take a trip or two to Tubac. There was a shop there that carried Mexican imports at incredibly reasonable prices and she'd known on previous visits that she'd be returning there to hunt for treasures to furnish her home *when*, not *if*, she finally had one in Arizona. After putting her suitcases in the master bedroom, she walked through each room in the house soaking it all in, mentally making a shopping list of things she'd need to buy. She was glad she'd chosen an SUV as she would need the extra room for all the things she'd be buying. First, though, was a trip to town to pick up a few groceries—at least the necessities—coffee, sugar, and half-and-half. A nearby grocery store had also been on the must have list when searching for property so that wouldn't take long.

That feeling of wanting to pinch herself came over her again as she drove to town. *This is where I live now.* It was a simple, ordinary sentence but it carried such implications. The pundits called it a geographic cure and maybe there was something to it because she hadn't felt this kind of excitement for a long time.

CHAPTER TWO

As sleep came over her later that night, it was as though she'd been there for years. In the morning, she recalled a dream she'd had, which was unusual for her. She knew everyone dreamed but seldom remembered hers. This one had come with such clarity that she'd remembered every detail, though. In it, a young Native American girl was playing with her childhood friend, a young boy about her age perhaps a couple of years older. She sensed that they were kindred souls -- the connection between them had been there for more than a lifetime and they were meant to be together.

"Running Deer, come here. See what I found!"

He followed her call to the stream. "What is it, Shy Dove?"

She pointed to a stone that glinted in the water near the shore as the sunlight hit it. She reached in and took it out. It sparkled in her hand, glistening with the water and sunlight.

"Isn't it beautiful?" She smiled as she held it up for him to inspect.

"You should put it in your medicine bag to bring you luck. You never know when you may need good luck."

A slight shiver came over her when he said those words as though he spoke a warning of things to come.

CHAPTER THREE

*S*haron frowned as she thought of the dream and the feeling it had carried. *That was weird* she thought, but the smell of the coffee brewing and all she had to do that day overtook her musings. She'd made a to-do list while she was on the plane to distract her from the monotony of the trip. A more in-depth shopping trip was next on the list. Although Wilmont had a small grocery store, it was more of a convenience store so it made more sense to find a larger store to do the full-scale shopping for all she'd need to stock the pantry. She'd fought an internal battle over that. It would be so easy to fall into a routine of frozen dinners or take-out now that she was only cooking for one. But part of Sharon's reason for this move was to start again and to live again. She'd always enjoyed cooking and making sure she did it, even if just for herself, was a way of nurturing her soul as well as her body. It reinforced that she was worth the time it took. *And now I can cook all those things I avoided because Tom didn't like them.* She felt a bit guilty about the plea-sure that brought her—as though she was somehow dishonoring his memory by being pleased that he wasn't there to keep her from doing something she and only she wanted to do. She knew intellectually that there was no reason why she couldn't have done that while he was alive, but it had been her nature to put other people's feelings and needs before her own. *Well, that's not gonna happen now, baby!* A strength and resolve she hadn't known she possessed rose in her.

She finished her breakfast, showered and dressed—jeans, a tee shirt and sandals—not her typical January attire. Again, she smiled. Sharon was beginning to think her face would be sore from all the smiling she'd been doing since she arrived. It was a 60-mile drive back to Tucson and she wanted to get on the road.

She'd done some searching on the internet to find a grocery store but decided to make a detour in the same shopping mall for some kitchen implements. It wouldn't do much good to have groceries without any way to cook them. It didn't take long before she was on her way with the basic four-piece starter set. She didn't need a lot and could always add on later. After what seemed like an exhausting trip through the grocery store—it had never been her idea of a good time and meant backtracking several times to find all she had on her list—she was finally on her way back to Wilmont. Finally! Her earlier good humor had taken a hit but was returning now that she was on her way back home.

After unpacking her groceries and new dishes and running them through the dishwasher, she was overcome with exhaustion. A siesta seemed perfectly natural here although she rarely napped in Maine. After a brief internal discussion about the pros and cons of succumbing to the need for sleep and all the things she still needed to do, the rationalization that she'd be better able to do those things if she was rested won out. The clincher was telling herself it must be jet lag. Although she normally would have tossed and turned for half an hour before sleep overtook her, she was out almost as soon as her head touched the pillow.

CHAPTER FOUR

"*You can't catch me!" Running Deer called out over his shoulder.*

Shy Dove replied, "Wait! Wait for me!"

He slowed down to let her catch up to him before once again running ahead. It was a game they played often and one which irritated Shy Dove. Why did she always follow him? One of these times she was going to just turn around and let him run on for miles before he realized she wasn't there. Maybe then he'd be sorry and not taunt her. *She slowed down to catch her breath. Maybe today was that day. She sat down on a boulder and watched him sprint away. Her eyes saw him in a new way as she noticed that his body was taking the shape of a young man. His waist was slimming and his shoulders broadening. His legs were long and lean but well-muscled from the running he so loved to do. She hadn't been aware that he had been noticed the changes in her as well.*

He turned to see if she had caught up and realized she was no longer there. A momentary panic overtook him but then he caught sight of her sitting on a boulder several hundred yards behind him. He must have gone too far this time, both literally and figuratively.

"Shy Dove, are you alright?" he called out.

"I'm fine but I'm not going to chase you anymore," she called back.

He sprinted back to where she was sitting.

"I'm sorry. I wanted to surprise you. I found something I wanted to show you when I was out tracking the other day."

Running Deer would soon be old enough to be included in the hunts and was expected to spend more of his time learning to track and hunt than playing. Shy Dove was also being trained for her duties as an adult. Learning to cook and weave had taken on a more serious nature.

"Come on it's not far now. I promise I won't run ahead."

"Okay, but if you start to run away, I'm turning around!"

"I promise and you'll be glad you changed your mind!"

CHAPTER FIVE

*S*haron woke with that groggy feeling she always had after a nap. It was one of the reasons why she usually avoided them. Like that morning, she awoke remembering every detail of her dream. *What's this place doing to me?* she wondered aloud. She thought it might be worth finding her notebook to write them down. Even though she remembered the details now, if past events were an indicator, they'd be gone tomorrow. She reread her notes several times. The dreams had felt real—more than just an overactive imagination, they felt like memories.

She decided to give her daughters a call to let them know she was okay and had made the trip safely but also to shake off the effects of the dreams. Talking to them would reconnect her to the present. *Definitely need a reality check here, girl.* It was still early enough to reach them both even with the time difference. After chatting with each of them for the time it took to exchange the obligatory Q&A *How was the trip? What's the weather like?* and ending with the *I miss you already,* she wasn't sure if she felt better or not. She did miss them more than she thought she would so soon and the fact that she was really alone hit her.

"What were you thinking? This may have been the biggest

mistake of your life. It was one thing to do this when you were going to be with Tom but are you sure this is really what you should be doing at this point in your life?" she said aloud.

"Too late now."

The last comment she heard with the tone of judgmental smugness that had played out in her head most of her life.

"No, it's NOT!"

That came out a bit more petulantly than she intended.

Enough of this! she thought, slightly embarrassed that she'd been not just talking, but arguing with herself out loud.

She decided that it might be time to make some dinner. Nothing like a little nourishment to take your mind off things. It did seem to have the intended effect. Fortunately, she still hadn't finished the book she'd brought with her for the plane ride as there wasn't much else to do and it was now too late to go outside. She was beginning to regret having made such a bare-bones move as the solitude closed in on her and without the distractions she'd usually had, she realized being alone wasn't as easy as she'd thought.

A fire would have been nice. This house was decidedly Southwestern style and she'd made sure it had included a kiva style fireplace. *That will give me something to do tomorrow*, she thought. *There must be some branches I can find to burn and, if not, I can call Joseph to see if he knows where I can get some firewood.* She'd found Joseph Ramos, her building contractor, to be more than willing to go the extra mile while she was having her house built and had offered to help her get settled once she moved in. She exhaled a sigh of relief and realized she'd been more anxious than she was aware. *Okay, Scarlett, you can worry about that tomorrow.* That was a mantra that she planned to change. *It's time to start living in today. This is supposed to be about living in the moment—not the past and not tomorrow. And for the moment, this has been a long day—time to call it a night.*

CHAPTER SIX

*S*he woke up early. *Still on east coast time, I guess. Give it another week.* She got the coffee started and sat down in the only comfortable chair. It felt strange to not have to be worrying about taking care of someone else and having the days stretch out before her without any real commitments. She'd begun working after school when she was 14 and except for a couple of years off after she'd had each of the girls, she'd been working all her life. Her plans to retire at 55 hadn't worked out, but she had been able to retire at 62. In addition to her own retirement funds, Tom had left her well-provided for and she'd been able to build this home free of debt and still keep her home in Maine. As much as she enjoyed warm weather and sunshine, she didn't think she'd be able to handle living here in the summer.

She hadn't had any dreams—that she remembered—the night before. *Two a day must be my limit,* she thought. She felt a bit of sadness that she hadn't had another one.

She got up to retrieve her laptop and settled back down. After a few frustrating moments of figuring out how to connect to the internet, she was able to check her email. Old habits die hard but she was hoping this would be one she'd wean herself off soon. That killed enough time to call Joseph at a more reasonable hour. Contractors usually start early but she didn't want to push it, especially when she was calling with a favor to ask.

"Joseph Ramos here. What can I do for you?"

"Joseph, it's Sharon Peterson. I hope I haven't caught you too early."

"Sharon, good to hear your voice. When are you coming back?"

"I'm here already. Got in the night before last."

"Is everything okay? Any problems with the house?"

"Not so far. I was actually hoping you might be able to give me a lead on a place to get some firewood. I realized last night that I didn't have any and had no idea where to look. I might go check around for some branches today but was hoping to have some delivered so I won't have to do that every day."

"Let me make a couple phone calls and see what I can come up with. What are you doing for lunch?"

"Nothing at all. I'm free as a bird. Why don't you meet me here at noon? I'll make us some lunch and you can let me know what you've found out."

"Sounds great. Look forward to seeing you again and welcome home!"

She smiled. "Thanks, that does sound great." It wasn't just lunch she was thinking about. "Welcome home" sounded great, too.

ood thing she'd gone shopping yesterday. It wouldn't take long to put a lunch together so she decided to take a look around the property to see if there were any branches she could use for the fire tonight as it was unlikely she'd be getting any wood delivered before then. She'd brought a small backpack as her carry-on for the plane so packed it with a couple bottles of water and an orange. Making sure she had her cell phone and keys, she headed out the door. The sun was already warm—at least for her. It would be several more months before daytime temperatures reached that high in Maine. *This is heaven!* All the years of complaining about the cold and snow faded as she headed out behind her house. *Keep your eyes open for snakes!* That thought made her extremely uneasy. She'd always been afraid of snakes but at least the ones in Maine didn't make rattling noises. *I'm not going to let that keep me a prisoner in my house. I've waited too long to get here and I'm going to enjoy it!* That silenced the voice—for now—but she kept a careful watch ahead and to either side as she walked. Sharon loved the smell of piñon pine and was hoping to find some nearby. *Does that even grow in this part of Arizona?* she wondered. Although she'd made several trips after she'd bought the property and while the house was being built, she hadn't really walked far beyond the footprint of the house and immediate area surrounding it. *So far, so good* she thought, glad that she hadn't encountered any wildlife. She crested a small hill and stopped, taking in the view. To many people she knew, this landscape would have seemed barren but to her it was beautiful. In the distance was a range of hills and here and there among the scrub grass were small cacti. She'd have to look those up to find out which variety they were, but they looked like they might be prickly pear. She'd been surprised by the landscape on her first visit to Arizona. Like many Easterners, she'd thought the desert would be completely flat and wasn't prepared for the mountains that stretched throughout the state. Although she preferred the red rock country of Sedona, it was too cold for her liking. If she was going to travel nearly two thousand miles to escape the winter, it had to be to an area where there wouldn't be any snow even if it did melt within a day or so of when it fell.

The parcel of land she'd bought had nearly 40 acres. She'd have to check to find out where exactly her boundaries were, but she felt secure that she wasn't straying onto someone else's land as she walked toward a small group of piñon pines confirming that they did, in fact, grow there. It suddenly occurred to her that she'd thought of almost everything—water, sunscreen, sunglasses, cell phone, keys—but she hadn't thought about how she was going to bring the branches back. *Guess I should have watched more episodes of Survivor Man.* Oh, well, she really didn't need a lot and could just take back whatever she could carry. She hadn't gone that far and she probably should get back anyway. *Note to self—get some rope to tie up bundles of branches.*

CHAPTER EIGHT

oseph showed up promptly at noon. Sharon guessed he was about her age, black hair graying at the temples, and still fit from years of construction work. He was a hands-on contractor who wasn't afraid to get his hands dirty even though he was the boss.

"Joseph, it's so good to see you again!" she said as she invited him in.

"Love what you've done with the place," he teased as he took in the meager furnishings.

"I'm taking minimalism to the next level," she smiled back at him.

"Ahhhh….think I'll stick to bachelor rustic."

She took on a slightly more serious tone. "I thought I'd start out fresh with completely new stuff but wanted to live in the house and get a feel for what I really want before rushing out to buy things on the spur of the moment just to get something in. I wasn't expecting company quite so soon…but I'm glad to see you," she added realizing that might have sounded uninviting.

"Welcome back, Sharon. I'm sorry about Tom."

"Thanks. It's getting better. *I'm* getting better. I guess they're right, it just takes time."

"A lot of it. There are still times when I forget Susan isn't here and it's been nearly five years."

"I'd forgotten. Then you do understand."

"I do. How are you liking the house?" he seemed anxious to shift the conversation to a new topic.

"So far so good." She'd been about to tell him about the strange dreams she'd been having but then changed her mind. She wasn't quite ready to share—they felt too intimate, but she couldn't explain why even to herself. "I've been sleeping better than I've slept in years. Maybe it's just the jet lag, but I'm going to give credit to the house. It's just beautiful, Joseph. Thank you so much for doing such a great job building it!"

"It was my pleasure—really. When you came to me with the plans, I thought you were a little crazy but I'm thinking about building one for myself."

Although it had a Southwestern influence, it was not your daddy's casa. This was a completely off-the-grid house. Sharon had seen a TV show years ago that featured them but living in New England wasn't your ideal spot for this style. This had been a dream house and proof that sometimes dreams do come true.

"I'll let you know in a month or two if I was as crazy as you thought. I hope you're hungry. It's nothing fancy—like I said, I wasn't planning to do any entertaining so soon so only picked up the basics."

"Any meal that I don't have to make myself is a good meal," he smiled.

"Go ahead and sit down. I'll be just a minute—everything's pretty much ready—I just need to set it out. Did you have any luck finding someone with firewood?"

"It took a few calls, but I finally found someone who could deliver some this week and wouldn't charge an arm and a leg." He reached into his shirt pocket and pulled out a scrap of paper with a name and phone number scribbled on it and handed it to her. "I told him it was for a friend, so he'd better do you right."

"Thanks, I really appreciate this." She smiled, eyes down, feeling suddenly shy. His comment about being a friend and feeling taken care of had hit a nerve she didn't realize was exposed. She'd been trying so hard to be independent since Tom died. This was a reminder that it wasn't such a bad thing to need someone to help out.

"So, what are you planning to do now that you're here?"

"Other than changing decorating styles, I hadn't given it much thought." This time she smiled and met his eyes.

"No offense, but I think that's a good idea. I never much liked minimalist."

Her smile in response let him know that she hadn't taken offense.

"I'm thinking about planting some fruit trees and a small garden. Do you know of any good nurseries and a gardener?" As soon as the words were out, she regretted having said them and blushed. "Oh, I'm so sorry. I don't mean to be so pushy. I've only been here a couple of days and I'm already wearing out my welcome asking you to do all this."

"I'm glad to help. Any time you need something, you let me know. If it's not a good time or I'm not up to it, I'll level with you. That a deal?"

"It's a deal. I feel better already."

"Good. You're a neighbor now and neighbors help each other when they can."

"Neighbors--that has a nice ring to it," she smiled.

"How about Saturday afternoon I pick you up and take you to a nursery I know of? I've worked with them on a few spec houses I've done and they'll give you a good deal if I'm with you."

"Let me check my schedule to make sure it's clear." She

turned around feigning checking an imaginary calendar. "It looks like I do have a window I can squeeze you in."

He smiled back at her. "Sounds like a plan." He glanced at his watch. "I'd better get on the move. I need to get back to the site and make sure the lumber has been delivered. Thanks for lunch, Sharon, it was delicious. Let me know if you have any problems with the firewood and I'll give you a call Saturday morning to let you know what time I'll pick you up that afternoon. If you need anything in the meantime, though, just give me a call. And I mean that—neighbors, right?"

"You got it. And *thank you.*"

She watched his truck as he headed back to town and then went back to clean up the remains of the lunch. She felt better— more connected. A sense of relief came over her that this was going to be okay and perhaps she hadn't lost her mind coming out here by herself where she knew no one. She reminded herself that wasn't exactly true—she knew Joseph and he'd made her feel welcome. Chances were, he wasn't the only one.

CHAPTER NINE

"*What is it, Running Deer?" She was looking at the hill ahead of them but didn't see anything out of the ordinary.*

"Up there, Shy Dove. To the left of the tree."

She finally saw what he'd been trying to show her—a small opening. Not big enough to call a cave opening but big enough that a large animal could enter. "That's what you were so excited about?" she asked incredulously.

"It's not the cave—it's what's in it that I wanted to show you."

"You want us to go inside there?! What if there's an animal living in there?"

"I've been inside and there's no animal. Come on, let me show you what I found. It's not hard to climb up."

She wasn't sure she wanted to do this, but she hated to disappoint him. He seemed so excited to share this with her. "You're sure there's no mountain lion or bear? There wouldn't be any way to get away if there is."

"I'm sure. Come on, you won't be sorry."

I think I'm sorry already, she thought to herself.

"Okay, but I hope you're right about there not being anything in there."

"I'll go in first and let you know when I've looked all around."

She gave him a look that said she still wasn't sure about this but said, "Okay, but I'm staying down there on that spot below the tree while you check just in case."

"Come on, then." And he started off in that direction. She could tell he wanted to run ahead but was restraining himself so that she could keep up. He was right that it was an easy climb and they soon reached the spot where she told him she would wait while he went on ahead to check for any animals that may have decided it was a good place to hide.

CHAPTER TEN

*S*haron woke up as the sunshine filtering through the solar tube bathed her room with soft morning light. She lay in her bed savoring the freedom of not having to jump up to start a work day but also not wanting to move until she was able to retrieve all the memories of her dream. *I should put a notebook by my bed so I can write these down as soon as I wake up.* She sensed again that these dreams were not just the usual random imaginings that most of her dreams were made of. And somehow she knew that there would be more. She rolled that over in her mind the way someone might roll an unfamiliar object through their fingers to experience every edge, every surface, cataloging it in their mental database.

Sharon remembered she had her notebook in the living room where she'd been making another of her beloved lists. Tom had always teased her about her list-making. The latest one was for plants and trees she wanted to look for when she met Joseph at the nursery. Wanting to start right then to write down the dreams while they were still clear in her mind, she hopped out of bed, anxious to get to her task. First, a quick detour to push the button to start the coffee that she'd already set up for brewing the night before—a habit of many years and while this coffeemaker did have an auto-start feature, she was still savoring not having to get up at any particular time. Retirement was something she'd looked forward to for a long time and that was one of the benefits that had been high on the list.

It took her a few minutes, but she was satisfied that she'd remembered everything and was brought back to the moment by the smell of the coffee carrying its siren song into her nose. She puzzled over the feelings she was having—a mixture of wonder at the clarity of the dreams and struggling with the acceptance that these had the texture of a memory not a dream. *Is this some past life I might have had?* She let that thought sit there while she checked for an emotional feedback. She wasn't surprised to get an intuitive yes response. That being the reason for her familiarity and sense of belonging to this area made sense. She'd suspected the possibility and the logical rational part of her, the one that always had the judgmental tone to it, informed her that she was just trying to make it all fit. *That's all it is, you know that. You're trying to make more of this than there is. It makes sense that you're living in Arizona and your imagination is making up dreams about Arizona. If you'd moved to Hawaii, you'd probably be having dreams of beaches and palm trees.* Did Hawaii even have palm trees? Sharon questioned herself. It was one of those moments like looking at a word that you think you've spelled correctly and you've never had a problem spelling before but this time it just doesn't look right.

Sharon shook her head. *Enough of this! Time to switch gears and get on with today.* Yesterday she'd thought about making that trip to Tubac to look for things to decorate her house and now she wanted to get on the road as soon as possible. She'd known the house was bare and had intentionally started out that way, but Joseph's visit had given her a nudge to not put off decorating any longer. After a quick bite to eat and a shower that helped shake off the remaining cobwebs of the night, she was on the road.

Shopping just for the sake of shopping had never been high on her list of things she liked to do but doing so with a purpose was different. Sharon thought about that as she drove. So much of her life had been lived with having to meet other people's expectations of what she should be doing. Was that really their expectations or hers? And, more importantly, was that how she wanted to continue living her life? This was a new start and she was on her own. The only one she had to answer to was herself and it was her choice to listen and follow the voice in her head or once and for all tell it to take a hike. As that thought registered in her consciousness, it was like a weight had been lifted and a childlike feeling of excitement came over her. It was as though she was finally able to do something she wasn't supposed to be doing but knew she wouldn't get caught or be in trouble for if she did.

She arrived in Tubac and nearly jumped out of the car in her exhilaration, ready to take on the day with an enthusiasm she couldn't remember having felt since before Tom's death. And maybe even much longer. This was going to be a great day! The sky was a cloudless blue and the sun's warmth felt wonderful on her bare arms. She gave a silent thank you for the blessings in her life that allowed her to be here now rather than in the cold, snowy winter she'd plodded through with increasing displeasure the past several years. Taking the list of items she wanted to look for out of her purse, she headed down the street toward the first of several stores she planned to visit today.

After checking out most of the ones on her list and several trips back to the car to store her purchases, she'd had as much shopping as she could take in one day and realized she was famished. Eating alone at a restaurant was something she'd avoided like the plague but that would be her only choice here as fast food wasn't an option. *Another growth opportunity*, she told herself. *Or you can take the easy way out and head to Green Valley.* She rationalized the latter choice by telling herself that it would be a good place to go to find more linens. The one set of sheets and two towels she already had would do but extras were something she'd already planned to buy. *I've had enough growth opportunities for one day.*

It was late by the time Sharon finally arrived back home and she still needed to call for the firewood. She'd meant to do it that morning before leaving home but had forgotten in her hurry to get on the road. Instead of reaching a voicemail message, the person Joseph had told her about answered and they soon had made the arrangements to have the wood delivered on Friday.

After bringing in all her treasures from the car, she realized she'd forgotten that she had no tools or way to hang any of the decorations she'd bought. It hadn't even occurred to her since she was used to having all of those supplies at her house in Maine. Unlike other times, though, Sharon was able to let this oversight go without the internal reprimands that would have usually been going through her head. There was a small hardware store in town and she'd go there tomorrow to get what she needed. *I'm liking it here more and more already.*

After dinner--a real dinner she'd cooked from scratch, she made a small fire with the meager bundle of wood she'd collected from the day before. Although collecting the wood had been a good idea, she hadn't learned the art of starting a fire by rubbing sticks together and since she didn't smoke, had not had a lighter or matches to start it with yesterday. Matches were one of the items she'd made sure to have on her list to pick up today. Once the fire was going and didn't look like it would go out, she picked up her iPhone and scrolled to the *Easy Listening* playlist she'd programmed in earlier, poured herself a glass of wine, and settled into her comfy chair to read the last few chapters of her book before heading to bed. It had been a good day. The book didn't have the appeal it did before she sat down but the wine, soft music, and the fire's hypnotic effect soon combined with the fatigue of shopping and driving and Sharon was sound asleep.

28

CHAPTER ELEVEN

Shy Dove watched as Running Deer first bent down to look into and then slipped through the cleft in the hill. It was a narrow opening, not much wider than his body. If there were any animals in there, she hoped he'd be able to get back out quickly. Within seconds, he reappeared and motioned to her to come along.

"It's all clear and there aren't any signs of any animals being inside."

"Are you sure? That didn't take very long for you to look."

"Shy Dove, just come on. I wouldn't tell you that if it wasn't okay. Do you really think I'd do anything to hurt you?"

He was beginning to sound irritated and she knew he was right. He'd always protected her even as toddlers.

She soon met him at the opening.

"Let me go in first so that you can see."

She hadn't noticed earlier that he had a torch lit when he'd come out of the cave as the sun had been bright in her eyes.

"I'd brought this earlier when I'd been exploring the cave," he answered her unspoken question after seeing the quizzical look on her face.

"Come on, it's over in the back corner."

He held out his other hand to her. Taking it in hers, they walked in. Although he had the torch, it took a few seconds for her eyes to adjust to the darkness after coming in from the sunlight. She looked around the cave, both to reassure herself that he'd been telling her the truth about the animals and out of curiosity. She'd been in caves before as they were not an uncommon phenomenon in the hills around their settlement. This one did not seem to be any different from the others so she could not understand what he had been so excited about.

"Look up—over here." He held the torch up so that she could better see what he was trying to show her.

Her eyes widened as she saw a small green mass on the ceiling. It looked like a clump of green bird's eggs hanging there.

"What is it, Running Deer?"

"It's some kind of rock. I had knocked a little of it off when I was here before. I left the pieces here." He picked them up and held them out to her. "Look at how different they are inside."

The pieces had a dull, solid green outer surface but inside they were banded with narrow stripes of brown and glittered in the light of the torch.

"They're beautiful, Running Deer." She smiled up at him.

"I knew you'd like them."

He seemed pleased that he had been able to make her happy. She noticed he was standing taller and his shoulders were pulled back which gave him the appearance of having even more height. She was also aware of feelings she hadn't had before and that she was seeing Running Deer in a way she never had. She suddenly realized how handsome he was becoming and she was grateful for the darkness of the cave. Perhaps he couldn't tell with only the light from the torch that her cheeks were burning or how she had been studying him.

Shy Dove had always loved rocks and had spent many hours

searching for unusual ones to add to her collection. She was touched that Running Deer had noticed and remembered.

"You were right, this was worth the trip." She opened the pouch she had tied to the sash around her waist and dropped one of the pieces inside. She held out the other to Running Deer. "Here, you take the other piece for your medicine bag. Maybe someday it will bring you good luck. You never know when you may need good luck," she smiled as she echoed his words.

CHAPTER TWELVE

*S*haron slowly looked around trying to get her bearings. The fire had burned out and the room was dark. The pain in her neck confirmed she was going to pay for having fallen asleep in the chair.

"Got to write this down," she mumbled aloud and went to retrieve the notebook she'd left by her bed. "So glad I put it in a place where it would be convenient." Although said sarcastically, she was able to smile about the irony. "May as well just do it here and with a little luck I'll be able to get back to sleep." She changed into pajamas and climbed into bed. After recording her dream in the notebook, she turned out the light and was relieved to feel sleep coming over her.

When she woke again, it was another sunny day but cooler than the previous ones. Still better than what she'd be experiencing back East. She thought about her dream as she prepared a light breakfast. She could picture the stone she'd dreamed of but couldn't remember its name. She had planned to stay home that day anyway so got out her laptop and did a search for minerals in Arizona. It didn't take long to find a site that confirmed that Arizona did have deposits of malachite—the green rock she'd seen in the dream. A little more research for images also showed a formation of malachite with the clumps that Shy Dove thought looked like bird's eggs. According to the definition on another site, the correct term for this was "botryoidal" or shaped like a bunch of grapes. Sharon reasoned that it wasn't likely Shy Dove would have had much experience with grapes, so thinking they looked like bird's eggs made a lot more sense.

An intuitive nudge sent her on a search for the metaphysical properties of stones. According to the site she found, malachite's metaphysical characteristics included the ability to balance and was especially helpful for balancing and clearing the heart chakra and is a very strong protective stone including children and protection from evil. It was purported to encourage true, pure love. Though she'd never lived her life by astrological readings, symbols, numerology or the like, she kept an open mind to the possibilities that the universe held more than just a scientific explanation for how things worked. The coincidence of all of this unnerved her and she sat for several minutes mulling it all over in her mind.

"Enough for now." It was a bit too much to take in and the need to come back fully to the present overtook her. She did bookmark the sites she'd been to before shutting down the computer, though. The hot water from her shower helped clear her mind and by the time she'd finished her morning hygiene and dressed, her earlier unease had passed. Today would be a good day to begin decorating with all of the items she'd purchased and to assess what still remained to make this truly feel like home.

The house consisted of two bedrooms, one on either side of the house, an open kitchen/living room area, a room dedicated for her crafts, a greenhouse along the front, and a garage on the side. There was also a separate casita for guests. One of the eco-features of the house was a gray water retrieval system which fed into large planters where she could grow vegetables and foliage plants. She also intended to grow the citrus and avocado trees in the planters and had an automatic watering system installed when the house was built so that they would be watered while she went back East in the summer. She'd done some research on-line for trees that could be grown inside including citrus and was surprised to find that could be done using dwarf or semi-dwarf varieties. She would check at the local nursery on Saturday to see if they had any but would order them later, if not. She wanted to check for vegetable seedlings, too, but if she had to start from seeds, this might not have been the most practical idea. They would be maturing about the time she had to return to Maine. "I could still do lettuce and herbs, and maybe some cherry tomatoes," she thought. "Time to think about that later. I need to get these things hung and make this place look nice."

She remembered that first she needed to buy the tools she'd need—a hammer, level, and cordless drill, and a kit with assorted hardware for hanging decorations and some rope if she wanted to collect any branches today for a fire that evening. After a quick trip to town to pick up her supplies, she was back and eager to get started. With tools ready, she began unpacking her treasures.

Sharon had never been one to be flamboyant in her decorating styles, preferring to play it safe. She'd loved the vibrant and earthy colors that were the hallmark of Southwestern decorating and had been looking forward to using them. It was about giving herself permission to go wild and it was as though that had breathed new life into her. She'd picked out a striped table runner with reds and orange as the primary colors that she now put on her kitchen table and topped with red ceramic candle holders and even red candles. She'd hesitated before buying them thinking it might be too much but in the end had decided to go for it. "If I decide I don't like it, I can always change it, you know," she'd told Ms. Judgmental. Ms. Judgmental had been silenced and Sharon had almost giggled as she thought of her pouting in a corner of her mind. "This is the new and improved Sharon you're dealing with."

She stepped back to inspect the tableau and decided she liked it—no, she didn't just like it. She liked it *a lot!* Encouraged by this success, she went on to her next bag of goodies. For the kitchen she'd bought deep blue dish towels and hung one on the stove's handle. Next out of the bag was a ceramic salt & pepper shaker set in a multi-colored floral pattern which she placed on the counter near the stove and a large bowl in a similar pattern which she planned to use for storing fruit. She filled it with the oranges she'd bought on Monday and again stepped back to survey the effect. "Not bad but still needs a little work," she thought. "I'm not sure what, but I'm going to live with this for a while." Ms. Judgmental seemed a little less petulant at that comment. "Maybe you haven't completely lost your senses," Sharon heard. "Don't get too comfortable with that thought. I'm not done yet," she responded. Ms. Judgmental retreated to her corner again.

Years ago, she'd seen small rustic wooden ladders in the shops and had thought how great they'd look for displaying towels in the bathroom and had made sure to pick one up. This would be a bit more involved of an installation so she'd need the drill. After unpacking it from the box, she set off with the rubber stoppers typically used for installing pegboards which would keep the ladder away from the wall so she could hang the towels. Fifteen minutes later—had to be a record for her for accomplishing what should be a simple task but usually ended up needing several more steps—the ladder was installed and she went back to the living room to find the towels she'd bought in Green Valley. Which color to put up first? She decided on the dark blue and then added the multi-colored soap dish to the countertop. "It appears you have a theme going here, Sharon." She realized she was talking to herself out loud again but shrugged it off. "Not as though you haven't done that most of your life. It doesn't mean anything so don't go trying to convince yourself that now that you're living alone in a place two thousand miles away from home where you don't have any real connections, that you've suddenly lost touch with reality." That statement was directed to Ms. Judgmental who pouted even more, if that was possible, and turned her back to face the corner.

Sharon had bought a wicker basket to corral all of her beauty products and picked them up from the counter and placed them inside the basket. She'd found a spiral wrought iron candle holder that would hold six votives which she installed over the spa tub and filled with the votives—white, but that was okay for now. She was looking forward to trying this out later that evening. After the obligatory survey, she gave a little nod of approval. A vase with flowers might be the only thing missing for now and she made a mental note to pick some up on Saturday when she went to the nursery. If they don't have cut flowers, maybe a flowering plant would do.

On to the living room. Sharon planned to go back to Tucson the following week to buy more furniture. It might mean roughing it longer if she wasn't able to have furniture delivered as soon as she'd like. She hadn't thought about that part of picking an area to live that was so far away from a major city.

"Do they even deliver this far away?" she wondered.

Perhaps she could do a little of both—pick out a few necessities from a buy it and go store and order the rest. She had the one chair, after all, and it wasn't as though she was planning to do any entertaining anytime soon that would necessitate having any other furniture immediately. The realization that she had days, weeks, and months ahead of her without any deadlines or having to go back to a schedule imposed by someone else hit her again. "I like this!" She smiled and felt a tingle of satisfaction. She'd had a chunky wooden mantle installed on the fireplace and now added candle holders—solid colors this time rather than the multi-colored design she'd picked for the kitchen and bathroom, but dark, earthy blues and rusts—and filled them with off-white candles. After rearranging them several times until they felt right, she stepped back to inspect the effect. She'd placed the candle tableau to one side. It looked terrific but she would need to find something to fill the other side to balance it. "I'll figure that out later."

Sharon had bought a small painting at a gallery in Tubac--a purchase that was uncharacteristic of her. She'd never been one to collect fine art but the painting of a mission church had spoken to her and had thought it would be perfect for the space above the mantle. She had forgotten that the curved line of the kiva fireplace would make that impossible and instead decided to prop it on the mantle leaning against the fireplace. The result was pleasing but the other corner now looked even more bare than before. She searched through the bags and found the wrought iron sculpture that had been an impulse purchase. At the time she bought it, she didn't have a place in mind to put it, but this is where it felt right. Sharon stood there taking it all in for a few minutes, hands on her hips, pleased that it had come together so nicely.

She looked around the rest of the room and realized that many of the other items she'd bought couldn't be put out until she bought more furniture. A bookcase or two and a coffee table might be all she'd need to help soften the bareness of the room and give her space to display them. The walls would need something but the inspiration for that would have to come another day. "There's plenty of time," she again reassured herself, "so don't worry about that now. Learn to live with it." *Learn to live with it.* She mulled those words over. What exactly was it that she needed to learn to live with? Not a simple answer. She'd mostly learned to live without having Tom in her life, but it occurred to her that maybe it wasn't an it. She'd spent the majority of her life avoiding looking in the mirror to see what she was about below the surface, focusing instead on everyone else's needs. Perhaps the time had come to face the mirror. Why did that have to feel so heavy? "What have you been avoiding all this time?" she asked. Ms Judgmental still wasn't talking and was no help. "Guess you're on your own, girl."

An audible growl from her stomach brought her back from her reflections and she realized it was nearly noon. Satisfied with the work she'd accomplished that morning, Sharon decided to call it a day with the decorating and put away the tools and returned the remaining bags of items to the spare bedroom before making herself some lunch.

After lunch she got the rope and cut off a length that she hoped would be sufficient to wrap up a bundle of firewood. It was probably longer than she'd need but better to be too long than too short. The day was still cool enough at this time of year even at mid-day and she was on a roll with getting things done so decided to do the firewood run now. Keeping a watchful eye out for snakes and other wildlife, she returned to the spot she'd been the other day and picked up the branches she hadn't been able to carry then. Having the rope made a lot easier job of it and she was soon back at her house. She was looking forward to having a stockpile of wood available so she wouldn't have to do this every day.

Her first thought was to take it easy and finish up the book she'd been reading last night before falling asleep under the influence of the wine and firelight, but that didn't catch her interest. Instead, she got out her laptop and started a new document to transcribe the notes she'd written down about her dreams. Reading them back as one continuous piece had an effect she wasn't expecting. It struck her that they were occurring as a sequential timeline, not just random imaginings. Her skin raised gooseflesh. There were obviously gaps, but the events in the dreams had been sequential. She thought about that for some time. She hadn't had any past life regression memories before but she felt certain that she was having them now through her dreams. *Is this what I've been feeling all these years when I sensed this was home?* she wondered. She got up and walked to the window to look out at the landscape trying to sense any feeling that would confirm this. Nothing. *You're getting a little weird.* Ms. Judgmental was back. That brought Sharon out of her pensive mood and back to the present. *Maybe you're right—for now, but I'm withholding final judgment,* she replied.

It had been enough to make her decide to leave this alone and move on to something else—but what? For the first time since she'd arrived, she was at a loss for what to do with herself. She'd had some of her craft supplies shipped to her but they hadn't arrived yet. Sharon had taken up decorating gourds several years earlier after seeing some in galleries in Tubac. Had anyone suggested decorating gourds before that, she would have thought of jack-o-lanterns, but these were not tacky craft projects and she'd gained a respect for the artisans who worked in that medium. She had only been self-taught but one of the gourd artists whose book she'd bought was located in Tucson and it occurred to her that she might have a workshop she could visit when she went to Tucson to shop for furniture. Which led her to the thought that she should be making a list of what furniture to order and/or buy when she went there next week. Making a list put her back in her comfort zone and away from the lingering feelings about the dreams she'd been having. *Now that's something I can handle.* She'd need some things for her craft room as well as the living room so that she could start working with the gourds as soon as her equipment arrived. After a couple of hours surfing the interwebs, she'd been able to make a preliminary list of items that she could look for and the address of the gourd crafter. She made herself some dinner and now felt up to reading the book she'd passed on earlier. At eight o'clock, she decided the bath by candlelight sounded fantastic. Bubble baths weren't her usual preference, but tonight, it seemed just the thing to do. She found matches to light the candles in her new candleholder she'd hung earlier that day and realized it would have been more practical to do this before having started filling the tub. *This may have been one of those times when it would have been a good idea to give me your opinion,* she said aloud to Ms. Judgmental, who apparently was still sulking in the corner. *Lesson learned,* she thought and took off her sandals and stepped into the water before it got too deep and lit the candles. Once the tub had filled, she undressed and sank into the warmth of the water and felt the bubbles tickle her chin. She let out a sigh of pleasure. It had been a long day but the warmth spread through her body and relaxed her. After the bath, she put on pajamas, started a fire, got a glass of wine and brought up her *Easy Listening* playlist. *Doesn't get much better than this,* she thought, *but tonight I'd better not fall asleep again in the chair. My neck would not appreciate that.* In spite of her best efforts to stay awake, the combination of bath, wine, music, and firelight were too much and within half an hour, Sharon was sound asleep.

CHAPTER THIRTEEN

Shy Dove woke early with the morning light just breaking. Her mother, Singing Song, expected her to stay at home today to weave a new blanket. Shy Dove was becoming quite good at weaving and enjoyed seeing the design come to life as she worked. She had an idea for a new design she wanted to try so was looking forward to the day's work. It looked like it would be a good day—the sun was appearing over the horizon and would soon warm up the air which had a slight chill. Her mother was already up and she could hear her outside greeting the day and giving thanks by singing her morning song. She waited until her mother was finished and then went outside.

"Good morning, Mother. I'm going to the stream to bathe and will be back to begin weaving."

"Your breakfast will be ready soon, so don't take long," her mother replied. She had already begun preparations.

"I won't," Shy Dove called over her shoulder.

At the stream two of her friends were already there. She waved to them as she approached the stream. "Sky Lark, Squash Blossom, good morning!"

The other girls waved back.

"The water is chilly this morning," Sky Lark called to her.

"That may be a good thing as Mother wants me back soon to work on a new blanket. What are you doing today?" Shy Dove asked them. She removed her clothing and tested the water with her toe before stepping in, shivering as she lowered her body into the cool water.

"Squash Blossom and I are going to look for cactus flowers," Sky Lark answered. "Do you think your mother would let you come with us before you begin weaving?"

Shy Dove knew her mother would not. The idea of going with her friends was tempting but she also wanted to work on the new design. "No, she is quite anxious for me to get back and I have an idea I want to try out, too."

The other girls looked disappointed but then began gossiping about the young boys of their tribe. At sixteen years of age they were nearing the time when they would be eligible to marry and were already thinking of whom they would like as their mate.

"I think Coyote Call is quite handsome," Squash Blossom was saying.

"He is very good looking," Sky Lark agreed. "But Running Deer is much more handsome and he can run faster than any of the other boys. He is a good hunter, too, and will be a good provider."

Shy Dove felt a twinge of jealousy at her friend's comments. She and Running Deer had been good friends for all of their life but she hadn't realized the feeling she had for him was more than friendship until the day he had shown her the green stones in the cave. She hadn't said anything to her friends as she was afraid they would tease her. Should she say something now or keep her feelings to herself?

Squash Blossom and Sky Lark had been discussing Running Deer's long legs and how manly he was becoming. They were giggling in the way young girls do as Shy Dove had been thinking about how she did not like their talking about him in that way.

"What's wrong, Shy Dove?" Squash Blossom asked as she noticed their friend was not laughing with them.

"Oh, nothing. I was just thinking about the weaving and that my mother told me not to be long. I should get back now before she gets angry." Shy Dove began squeezing the water from her hair and waded toward the edge of the stream. "Have fun looking for the cactus blossoms. I'll see you later." She retrieved her clothing, dressed and turned around to wave to them before heading back to her house.

Squash Blossom and Sky Lark looked at each other wondering what had bothered Shy Dove but did not give it much thought. They, too, finished their bath and went about their day.

Shy Dove returned to find her breakfast waiting but was not as hungry as when she'd gone to the stream. Her mother looked at the expression on her face and asked, "Why so quiet, Shy Dove? Did something happen at the stream?"

"No, Mother, everything is fine. I'm just thinking of the new design for my blanket." She smiled at her mother to reassure her that she was okay. "I saw Squash Blossom and Sky Lark there. They are going to look for cactus blossoms and asked if I could come with them but I told them I needed to work on the blanket."

Singing Song smiled back. "I'm glad you are thinking of your responsibilities. You are older now and need to be spending more of your time learning how to take care of your own home. Soon you will be old enough to marry. Your father and I have been discussing who might be the best choice for you."

Shy Dove looked up at her mother, distressed to hear that her parents were making the decision of with whom she should mate. She had always thought when the time came that that would be her choice to make. The timing of this discussion coming on the heels of her meeting with her friends this very morning caused an uneasiness that things were not quite right and that something bad may be happening. She tried to dismiss the feeling as just her imagination thinking the worst.

"Mother, why would you and Father be discussing this? Won't I be allowed to marry the boy I fall in love with?"

"Your father and I will make the decision. A young girl only thinks of love and not who the best person is to take care of her."

She knew not to argue with her mother and father but a part of her was trying to figure out how she would be able to convince them that Running Deer was the best person to take care of her. It occurred to her that she might also need to convince Running Deer of that. "Does he have the same feeling for me" she wondered "or does he only think of me as his friend?" She thought it was more than that. Even in the dim light of the cave, she had seen the look in his eyes when he had given her the green stone. It had made her stomach flutter and she'd realized then that her feelings for Running Deer had made the leap from friendship to the blossoming of love. They had not spoken of it, but she was aware that he was looking at her differently as she would catch him staring at her. And she was doing the same with him. She thought that they both had begun to entertain the idea that they would marry when the time was right but did he really feel the same or was that wishful thinking on her part? "No", she told herself, "he feels the same about me. I know it from the way he looks at me."

As she worked on the weaving, her mind wandered to how she should discuss this with Running Deer. Would he think she was being a silly young girl? Would it scare him that she would be bringing up such a serious topic? After all, she was only sixteen and he was but a year older, the time for them to marry was still some time away. But was it if her parents were already discussing who she would be mated with? She was making mistakes and needed to do the weaving over which was making her mother angry and frustrated with her.

"Shy Dove, what is wrong with you today? You should have

had much more done with this. Stop daydreaming and concentrate!"

She realized it would do no good to worry about her future and it was in her best interests to focus on the weaving instead but her excitement about the new design she'd woken with was no longer there.

"Yes, Mother, I'm sorry," She shook her head slightly as though to shake off the worry she was feeling and set her mind to the weaving.

CHAPTER FOURTEEN

*S*haron woke, once again with a crook in her neck from the awkward position in which she'd fallen asleep.

"I have *got* to stop doing this!" she muttered to herself.

She turned on the lamp by her chair and looked around for her notebook, anxious to write down the dream before she forgot any of the details. After reading back her notes, she felt satisfied that she had gotten it all. She sat for quite a while thinking about it before heading to bed.

The next morning was sunny and she woke to its glow in her bedroom and thankfully her neck had forgiven her for her earlier indiscretion. She yawned and stretched, in no hurry to get up. She once again savored the feeling of not having to rush to a job —her only commitment today was to wait for the arrival of her firewood order.

"I really am liking this," she became aware that she was hugging herself and the realization amused her. She bounded out of bed and into the bathroom to shower, eager to get on with her day.

She found herself with plenty of time and nothing to do and vowed to make sure she bought a book or two and craft supplies on her trip to Tucson. Although she was loving the freedom of not having a job, it was unsettling to be in a place where she had no distractions to keep her busy. That had never been a problem in Maine as she had accumulated scores of books and enough supplies for crafts over the years to always have something on hand to do. She hoped the supplies she'd shipped from Maine would arrive soon as she wasn't comfortable with just sitting around and not being useful. Her experience growing up was that it was not okay to just be---you had to be doing, and preferably something useful in order to be of worth. *Sounds like another growth opportunity* she thought to herself as she realized what was happening. She had the sensation that Ms. Judgmental had once again been thwarted and it surprised Sharon when she realized that there had even been a feeling of. . .*disappointment?.* . .no, it was more like fear from Ms. Judgmental when Sharon had made the pledge to not let past conditioning rule her new life.

This is really getting weird, Sharon muttered aloud. It was one thing to talk to yourself in your head---everybody does it, whether they admit it or not, but this was not your run of the mill head conversation. *This place is definitely having an effect on me and I'm not sure if I like it yet.* Her earlier excitement at making this a new life was wavering as she was stepping further and further away from her old comfort zone. *Don't give up yet.* The words had come to her unbidden and she felt better—lighter, as though a weight had been lifted. It would be okay. She just needed to take things a little slower. All the changes in her life were overwhelming her and things would sort themselves out as soon as she'd had a little more time to get used to the new routine.

She decided to check out her patio area, or more accurately, the place that would become a patio with some outdoor furniture and accessories. The need to get outside took on an urgency--as close to a feeling of claustrophobia as she'd ever remembered having in her life. Once outside, the feeling passed and she realized she'd need to add patio furniture to the growing list of things to shop for. She hadn't moved all this way to take advantage of the better weather just to stay inside but this wasn't a welcoming spot—yet. If she was lucky, the garden center might have something she could get. She looked around at the area, mentally decorating with planters and furniture. *I need to add this to my list,* she thought and headed back into the house and then smiled as she thought of how Tom would have been teasing her again about her lists and how she would have been defending herself. She also became aware that this was the first time in days that she'd really thought about Tom. It had been quite a while since she'd had a day, much less three or four, without thinking of him. For a moment she felt guilty but then accepted that this was okay. It was normal. It meant she was healing and the grieving process had done its work.

"I'll always love you, Tom, you know that," she said aloud, something she'd continued doing even after he died. It made her wonder if it was just her who thought it was still necessary to talk out loud to departed loved ones, as though there was some unwritten rule that they could hear you but only if you spoke out loud and they couldn't read your thoughts. *Because?*

"It would be rude, of course. An invasion of privacy." Ms. Judgmental informed her.

"Works for me," Sharon thought and went inside for her notebook.

Before long she had sketched out her ideas for the patio and added the items she'd need to her list. She realized having the gardens inside and out would also give her something to occupy her time and she was glad that she'd be going to the nursery the next day. Shortly afterward she heard a truck approaching and went out to show the driver where to unload the firewood. She hadn't ordered a lot so it didn't take long to stack most of it outside and another small stack in the space in the fireplace that had been built just for that purpose. It pleased her to see how this touch added a feeling of coziness to the room.

She was startled out of her reverie to hear her cell phone ringing. It was her daughter, Jessica, calling to say hello.

"Hi, Mom, how are you doing out there?"

"Other than falling asleep in front of the fireplace which has turned out to be literally a pain in the neck, not too bad. I've started getting the place decorated and it's beginning to feel more like home."

"Sounds nice. Are you going with the Southwestern theme?" Jessica asked.

"I am. You know how I've always been a little afraid of color?"

They both chuckled as this was an understatement. Sharon was known for her neutral colors decorating schemes and had been teased about it by her daughters who weren't afraid to experiment.

"You won't believe what I've done here but somehow it just feels right so I'm not afraid to get out of my comfort zone."

"You'll have to send me pictures or it's not real," Jessica teased.

"I'll email some to you tomorrow."

It was good to hear a friendly voice and they spent the next half hour catching up.

Later that night she made her first real fire. Although the branches had been enough to satisfy the itch, there was no comparison to the ambience of the firewood's dancing flames and Sharon ended the day with what was now becoming her new routine: firelight, glass of wine, and soft music.

CHAPTER FIFTEEN

*S*hy Dove continued to work on her weaving for the next couple of hours and as she shifted her focus to the loom, her worries about her future fell away as the magic of the material taking shape before her eyes drew her in. The weaving calmed her as all the outside distractions were blurred. It was as though a part of her became woven into the cloth and was as close to a birthing as she would have experience of in her young life. Her blanket was coming to life before her eyes and it was she who was creating it. Her friends didn't understand why she chose to do this instead of spending time playing with them. They thought it was because her mother had made her do it, but the truth was she was growing tired of some of the childish games they still enjoyed.

"Shy Dove!"

She startled as she realized that her mother was calling her name.

"It's time to eat now," Singing Song was telling her.

She looked around as though she'd just woken from a dream, surprised that several hours had passed, and her stomach growled as the aroma of the food her mother had cooked reached her nose.

Her father, Black Bear, and older brother, Little Bear, were already eating their meal and she followed her mother to join them. They smiled at her and her brother teased her.

"Shy Dove, how can you weave while you are sleeping with your eyes open?"

"I wasn't sleeping!" she retorted. She didn't know how to explain to him the feeling that she had when she was weaving. It felt too intimate and she doubted he would understand. And, more importantly, she didn't want to have him make fun of her. What she felt was too sacred to be diminished by his teasing.

Her mother glanced at her, noticing the look on Shy Dove's face and recognized what was happening. She felt a similar connection when she wove and she was known not only in their community for the beautiful blankets and quality of the cloth she made, but traders sought out her work as it fetched a high price for them in other villages.

"Leave your sister alone, Little Bear," she rebuked him. "She has been working hard all morning. Did you not see how well she is learning to weave?"

"Shy Dove has inherited your gift, Singing Song," Black Bear nodded approvingly at his daughter.

Shy Dove was her father's delight and had had a special bond with him but his words of praise filled her with pride. She could tell that he meant what he said which made them all the more special to her, validating her feelings that she was good at this. And combined with her mother's praise, she felt a glow throughout her body that she had not had before. It was a shift in her concept of who she was and another nudge that she was leaving childhood and becoming a woman. She sat taller as the feelings permeated her being and her awareness of everything around her sharpened. She felt the warmth of the sun on her skin, the color of the sky *looked bluer and the few clouds in the sky were fatter, she tasted all the nuances of her food and the seasonings her mother had used. It was a strange sensation to be aware of all these ordinary things as though she was experiencing them for the first time. It wasn't just her blanket that had come alive—Shy Dove felt it, too.*

52

CHAPTER SIXTEEN

When Sharon woke, she couldn't believe that she had managed to sleep the entire night in the chair. Her neck was not about to forgive her this time and she painfully turned her head from side to side to try to work it out. Not too bad to the right but the left side barely budged--this was one of those stiff necks that meant turning your body instead of your head. She groaned and admonished herself for not having gone to bed when she first felt tired.

"No wine tonight, kiddo," she promised herself.

For a moment, the pain of the stiff neck had made her forget that she'd been dreaming but it came knocking at her memory's door as though to say, *I'm out here waiting--let me in!* As it sifted through to her consciousness, the sensation that this was more important than ordinary dreams again overtook her. She found her notebook and wrote down the dream in spite of her desire to hop in the shower and let the hot water try to undo the night's damage.

"Okay, *now* the shower," she said after she was finished.

The warmth of the water did not loosen up her muscles as

much as she'd hoped and she accepted that this was probably going to be with her all day. She was about to make herself breakfast when the phone rang.

"Good morning, Sharon. I didn't wake you, did I?" Joseph responded to her hello.

"Good morning, Joseph. No, I've been up awhile. I was just going to make myself some breakfast."

"I won't keep you long. Just wanted to see if we're still on for today?"

"Absolutely! I've been looking forward to this. I'm hoping a little gardening will help keep me occupied. I thought it might take at least a little longer before I got tired of doing nothing," she replied.

"I have my crew working until noon but how about I pick you up about 12:30 and take you out to lunch before heading to the nursery? I was thinking we could go to Dos Pollos—you remember that one I took you to last time you were here?"

"That would be great! The food was fantastic there."

"Sounds like a plan, then. I'll see you at 12:30."

"Thanks, Joseph. I really appreciate your doing this for me."

"My pleasure, Sharon."

She realized she'd been staring out the window unaware of her surroundings. "No need to get all dreamy. This is just lunch and a trip to a nursery," she (or was that Ms. Judgmental?) told herself. That got her moving and any thoughts about her feelings were stuffed away.

She began checking the driveway at 12:20. "Nervous or just bored?" she asked herself. "A little of both," she replied. In spite of her admonition to herself that this was no big deal, she'd noticed she had spent more time than usual picking out clothing, finally deciding on a pair of khaki capris and a tee shirt in a shade of turquoise blue that complemented her eyes. She'd even paid more attention to her jewelry and rather than putting on the usual watch and silver hoops, she picked out a pair of dangly silver earrings with a totem pole design and accessorized further with a silver bracelet and necklace inlaid with turquoise.

As promised, she could see Joseph's truck rolling up the driveway at 12:30, throwing up clouds of dust as it made its way forward. She grabbed her purse, checking first to make sure her list was there and went outside to meet him.

"Right on time!" she called to him as he got out of his truck and walked to the passenger side to open the door for her.

"Don't want to keep a lady waiting," he smiled.

The warmth of his smile made her realize that she'd been missing human interaction more than she'd been aware. She smiled back at him and walked over to the truck.

"I really appreciate your help, Joseph. That patio is sadly in need of some comfort and style. And I'm hoping the plants will give me something to do with my time. I'm loving being retired but still haven't quite gotten used to having so much time on my hands."

"I'll have to take your word on that one. Doesn't look like I'm going to be able to experience that first-hand for a while," he smiled again at her.

"Don't wait too long, if you can. Life doesn't always give us the chance to take advantage of it," she almost regretted having spoken the words as it put a somber mood on what had started out as a happy occasion. Joseph didn't seem to have let them bother him, though.

"Susan told me that all the time. Guess I'm not very good at taking that advice. I'm one of those people who gets antsy when I slow down. You hungry?"

She was grateful he'd changed the subject.

"Absolutely famished," she answered. "I've been looking forward to going back to Dos Pollos ever since you mentioned it."

"You okay?" he asked with concern, his forehead wrinkling and his eyebrows scrunching up.

At first she was confused as she felt fine and didn't think anything was amiss and then realized she was moving her body instead of her head.

"Made the mistake of falling asleep in the chair last night. The fire and wine were a little too effective," she blushed in embarrassment. "I tried working it out in the shower, but this may be one of those all-day pains in the neck." She thought again about sharing the dreams she'd been having but something held her back.

"Those are the worst," he answered. "When are you planning on getting some more furniture?"

"I think I'll head up to Tucson on Monday and see if I can find something that won't cost a fortune to have delivered. I didn't think about that when I moved out here."

"The trade-off for being out here is worth it."

"I couldn't agree with you more," she replied.

They chatted about the weather, what she had in mind for plants at the nursery, and small talk about how she liked being here so far. It wasn't long before they reached Wilmont and pulled into the only available parking space at Dos Pollos. It appeared this was a hot spot for dining in the town as the other four spaces were already taken. The building was painted in the dark shade of blue that was so prevalent in Southwest style, bright yellow trim around the windows, and a cherry red door with two white chickens painted in the middle, confirming that this was, indeed, Dos Pollos. The windows hung with striped curtains of red, blue, and yellow complemented the exterior décor and there were large terra cotta pots filled with orange and red gazanias arranged on either side of the entry. The window boxes were filled with gazanias as well. The place had a cheer-ful, welcoming aura about it that announced that this would be a place where you'd come back out feeling well-fed physically and emotionally.

It was as Sharon remembered it inside. Lining each of the side walls was a row of booths with red cushioned banquettes and in the center aisle were rectangular wooden tables with four chairs, each one set with salt & pepper shakers, and plastic squeeze bottles of what she assumed was hot sauce. At the far end were doors leading to the kitchen on one side and on the other the bathroom doors were hidden behind multi-colored beaded curtains. The walls were a muted yellow plaster that gave the interior a sunny appearance and were decorated with South-western details—paintings with desert scenes, ropes of peppers here and there, but tastefully, rather than overdone. The Mexican music was playing but at a level that still allowed conversation to be carried on without having to strain to be heard.

They found a booth near the window still unoccupied and several people greeted Joseph with waves and hellos as well as curious looks about his company. He waved back and exchanged hellos.

"I suspect I'll be getting a few phone calls later," he spoke quietly but not so quietly as to not be heard. It had the intended result of having the curious go back to their eating instead of checking them out.

"I've lived in a small town most of my life, so I understand," she replied, letting him know that she wasn't flustered by the attention. "Hopefully, I'll get to know people soon so that I won't just be that crazy lady from back East with that weird house up on the Silver Spring Road."

The waitress arrived with glasses of water, a bowl of what were obviously freshly made chips with a side of salsa, and menus.

"Mary, this is Sharon Peterson. She's just moved out here from Maine. I built her house up on the Silver Spring Road."

"Nice to meet you, Sharon," Mary replied. "I hope you like it here. Must be quite a change from what you're used to."

"You can say that again," Sharon replied. "But definitely a good change as far as I'm concerned. I'm not missing shoveling snow and freezing to death at all."

"Well, glad to have you here and hope to see you around," Mary smiled at her. "If there's anything I can do to help you feel welcome, just let me know."

"Thanks, I may just take you up on that. I'm hoping to get to know folks here and be a part of the community, not just a snowbird," Sharon smiled back.

"I'll let you two have a few minutes to decide what you'd like and be back to take your order."

"What do you recommend?" Sharon asked Joseph.

"Embarrassed to say I eat here quite a bit as it's easier than cooking for one, but there isn't anything bad on the menu."

Sharon looked over the menu one more time, finally deciding on the enchilada combination plate. Still a safe choice, but not the same one she'd made the last time they'd eaten here when she'd had chili rellenos. *Baby steps, Sharon, don't be too hard on yourself,* she reminded herself before letting Ms. Judgmental come back on the scene to tell her she was falling into a rut already.

"Looks like you've made a decision." It was a question more than a statement she realized as she looked up at Joseph.

"The enchilada combination plate has my name on it today," she answered him.

Joseph caught Mary's attention and once their order was placed turned back to Sharon. It surprised her at how smoothly their conversation flowed. While it was true that they had had the opportunity to get to know each other during the house construction, making the transition from a business to personal relationship wasn't a guarantee. Sharon learned that Joseph also had two children, a boy—man, really as at 35 he'd earned the right not to be called a boy—named Peter who was working with Joseph and daughter, Melinda, who was a nurse, married, and had two children of her own. It hadn't been easy for Joseph after Susan had died as his children were close to their mother, but they'd all pulled together to keep the family strong. His features had softened as he talked about his children and grandchildren and it was obvious how much he loved and was proud of them.

After finishing their meal and saying good-byes to Mary with a promise to return again soon, they headed to the nursery.

"I'm really excited about getting the plants. I'm going to need something to keep me working off calories if I eat like that very often," she joked.

"How big a garden are you planning? Should I have brought the dump truck instead of the pickup?" Joseph teased back.

"*Darn!* Wish I'd thought of that earlier!"

He shot her a look just to make sure she was kidding.

On a more serious note, she asked, "Are you sure you're okay with getting patio furniture if they have something I like? I know you'd only signed on for plants when you first made the offer to take me to the nursery."

"Of course. And there's no need to apologize. Like I told you before, I'll be right up front with you if you ask for more than I'm willing to do. That's always been my philosophy both with the business and in my personal life. Keeps things from getting complicated when you know what you can expect."

"You're so right." She thought back to how she'd spent most of her life doing things she'd sometimes rather not have done just because she'd been thinking of the other person's feelings instead of her own. Although Joseph's viewpoint sounded like a better way of doing things, she wasn't sure how easily it was one she could adopt.

They arrived at the nursery which was located about two miles past the outskirts of the town's business district. Sharon was surprised at its size considering that Wilmont was not near a major metropolitan area.

"Joseph, I'm impressed!" she exclaimed.

He smiled at her. "I thought you'd be surprised. We're lucky to have this here but Wilmont has been having a building boom the past few years and folks moving in are more concerned about the landscaping than they used to be years ago. Frank has been able to do a pretty good business and has expanded the nursery to about double what it was when he started out."

Sharon retrieved the list she had in her purse and they got out to begin searching for the items she'd written down. It was a bit much to take in at first, but she soon got down to business. Tom may have teased her about the lists but at times like this, it helped to have a plan to keep focused. It didn't take long to fill up several flatbed carts that were there for customers to carry their purchases while making their selections. It had taken one cart just for the bags of potting soil and amendments she'd need as she'd decided to do container gardening on the outside as well rather than trying to disturb the existing soil around her house for the few vegetables she planned to grow. Another cart was filled with the vegetable and flower seedlings. The gazanias at Dos Pollos had inspired her and although not on the original list, they'd been added.

"I thought I was just kidding, but the dump truck might not have been a bad idea!" Joseph looked amused rather than annoyed, so Sharon's initial reaction of anxiety quickly disappeared.

"And we haven't even gotten to the furniture section yet," she replied. "I wouldn't mind waiting here while you went back to get it."

She was enjoying the light-hearted banter. It felt comfortable and was the kind of teasing old friends would have with each other.

"I think for your wallet's sake, I better stay here with just the pickup."

"That is probably a good idea. Nurseries have always been a weakness for me. I want one of everything and buy more than I should. Once I get it all home and have to plant it, I realize that but then it's too late."

"Susan had the same problem," Joseph said chuckling.

"Let's call it good for now with the plants and check out the fruit trees and furniture. I can always add more seedlings later if I don't have enough. I'll be able to fit those in the SUV, no problem," Sharon decided.

They found the section with the trees and selected a lemon, orange and avocado tree, and returned them to where she had her other purchases in what was beginning to look like its own display. They found the area with the patio furniture and Sharon was pleased to find two comfortable chairs, a table with an umbrella to provide some shade and two more chairs to sit at the table. She knew she was going to need some large pots for the patio but resisted the urge to get those as it was obvious that the pickup was going to be full once the furniture items were added. Now that she knew where the nursery was, she would be able to come back later for any other items she wanted. Even though he'd not seriously complained, she didn't want to push it and the old feelings of stepping too far over an invisible line kept her in check.

"I think that's it," she told him.

"You sure?"

"For now," she answered and quickly added. "I can get anything else I need later. This is going to keep me busy the rest of the weekend."

"I think you're right," he agreed. "Let's see if I can find Frank and introduce you so that when you come back, he'll be sure to treat you right." He looked around and spotted a man about his age in the section where they'd found trees. "Why don't you wait here and I'll bring him back over?"

"Sounds good. I'll just check through my list to make sure I didn't forget anything while I'm waiting."

He shook his head and chuckled but walked away without commenting. Sharon had the feeling that he was enjoying himself and the teasing was just that, not annoyance disguised as teasing as had often been the case with Tom.

Frank looked up as Joseph called his name. Sharon couldn't hear their conversation but could tell that Joseph was talking about her as Frank looked over to where she was standing. He nodded his head and tipped his hat slightly at her. That gesture brought a smile to Sharon's face and she waved in reply. She had a feeling she was going to like him already. He was of average height, about the same as Joseph, and was dressed in jeans and a short-sleeved shirt revealing tanned arms which made the graying hair on his forearms stand out in contrast. His hair was mostly hidden under the straw hat he'd saluted her with, but she guessed it was black or dark brown salted with patches of gray from what she could see of it. His face was tanned and wrinkled--for men those were known as character lines. Apparently, women weren't supposed to have character since they spent so much time and money making sure they didn't allow their faces to develop those traces of a person's life.

Frank smiled broadly as he surveyed the carts filled with plants. Sharon had a fleeting mental image of herself as a nineteenth century western pioneer circled by Conestoga wagons. And just as quickly she realized that in her own way she was a pioneer setting out for a life unknown and in total contrast to the life she'd known back East. Instead of fear, she felt excitement at the prospect of what was to come.

They shook hands as Frank introduced himself. "Looks like you're already one of my favorite customers even without Joseph's recommendation."

"I may have been a little overzealous," she blushed as she looked at the carts. "But I'll probably be back again . . . several times." She blushed even more.

"Now I *know* you're one of my favorites. Anything I can do to help you out, you just let me know. I hear you're from back East so gardening out here is going to be a lot different for you."

"Did Joseph tell you about my house?"

"No, he just gave me the brief introduction – said he'd built your house and that you just moved out here from Maine this week."

"Frank, I thought the woman was a bit crazy but her money was good so I did what she asked," he grinned at Sharon as he said this.

She raised an eyebrow and cocked her head in his direction, but smiled as she replied, "Ahhh . . . and now the truth comes out."

"This house has a system that recycles all the gray water into these huge planters in a greenhouse area at the front of the house. And there's a water cistern to collect rainwater with a purifier so you can use that even for drinking water. Have to say that even though I thought it was crazy, it earned me a lot of respect for Sharon to be mindful of how important water is for us living here." This time his comments were in a serious tone and made her feel proud of what she'd done and that she'd been accepted as one of them rather than just another snowbird. That feeling was validated as Frank gave her an approving look as Joseph described what she'd done.

"So are all these plants going inside?" he asked.

"Most of them will. I do have a patio area where I want to put some potted plants but the planters Joseph was telling you about are also on a timer for an automatic watering system. Being lazy about watering has always been my downfall with gardening and even though I'm retired now, I'm not confident

I'd do any better. The fewer things I have to water myself, the better they have a chance of actually doing well."

"She even had me bring in all the potting soil to fill the planters up before the house was done."

"I'd like to say that I was planning ahead but the truth is I didn't want to have to clean it up after the house was done if I spilled dirt all over everything. And if I'm really going to be honest, it had a lot to do with being afraid of snakes."

They all laughed at her confession.

"Planting this shouldn't be as bad as I thought then," Frank said. "If you'd be willing, I'd love to see how you've got this all set up."

"It would be my pleasure." The words were out before she even had time to think about whether that would be a good idea. That Joseph liked him enough to introduce them was enough for her that she wouldn't need to worry about inviting a relative stranger into her home. "I'm sure I'll be back next week once I get this planted and see if there's anything I forgot, although I can't imagine that I did." She shook her head as she surveyed her treasures once again. "Why don't we set up a time when I come back? Will you be here every day?"

"I'm here seven days a week but you're more likely to catch me in the morning or later in the afternoon. You caught me by chance today. I'd usually be taking a midday break."

"Well, I'm glad we did. It was my pleasure meeting you."

"Nope, the pleasure's all mine and I'm not just saying that because of the business." She knew his smile was genuine as it reflected in his eyes.

Joseph and Sharon loaded up the plants and furniture in his truck with no room to spare and headed back to her house and reversed the process once they arrived. He helped her set up the patio furniture and brought the potting soil and amendments out to the patio as well.

"Would you like me to stay to help you get this planted?"

She almost answered yes, not because she wanted the help but out of habit of not saying no. After a second's hesitation she answered, "Thanks, I really do appreciate the offer but I think I'm going to take my time setting the plants out and making sure I get them just where I want them so that may take a while and I've already taken more of your time today than I should have."

"I had a good time. No, I really mean that," he said as he saw the skeptical look on her face. "It's been a while since I've done much more than work, go home, and then back to work again. It felt good to spend time with someone who wasn't wearing a tool belt."

"I left mine back East," she teased but felt younger than she had in years. *Amazing what a little flirting can do for your ego,* she thought.

"You know, I believe you," he smiled back. He finished the glass of water Sharon had given him and set it down on the counter. "I'll give you a call tomorrow and see if you've changed your mind."

"It's a deal. Thanks again, Joseph, I really had a good time, too."

After he left, she walked around the greenhouse inspecting the plants and tried to visualize where she'd put them but became overwhelmed. *I need to just step back from this for a bit and come back to it.* That was all the permission she needed and she noticed the relief that flowed through her body. It was now late afternoon but too early to begin making supper and she realized she was tired enough to take a nap. *Just a little power nap* she told herself *and then maybe I'll have the energy to figure out this mess I've made for myself. Maybe I'll even get a little done tonight after supper.* She noted that she was still making deals with herself in order to not feel guilty about not doing something. Retirement was harder than she thought it would be. She'd always imagined that once she was retired, it would be okay to take things slower. *I guess it's going to take more time to get used to than I thought.*

"Now for my next big decision," she said out loud, "Do I take a nap in the living room or in the bedroom?" She'd forgotten about her sore neck until that moment. "The bedroom!" she said without any further hesitation. "Right after I put on more *Sore No More*." That done, she laid down on her bed and as she was thinking about the day, slipped into a deeper sleep than she'd imagined possible.

CHAPTER SEVENTEEN

Shy Dove didn't remember feeling awkward around Running Deer before, and it irritated her that she was feeling this way now. Why was she feeling shy around this boy she'd known all her life, who had been as much of a friend and playmate as her female friends?

"Shy Dove, did you hear me?" Running Deer was looking at her with a puzzled expression.

"No, my mind was somewhere else. What did you say?" she tried to concentrate on his words this time instead of thinking about how jealous she felt when remembering what her friends had been saying about Running Deer that morning.

"I said I'm going to be going on a hunt tomorrow," his chest puffed out as he said this with a tone of pride. "My father says that I am old enough now to be doing a man's chores. So I won't be able to take you back to the cave."

They had made several trips back to the cave where they'd discovered the green rocks. It was their secret place and they enjoyed getting out of the heat of the day and gossiping about the other members of their village.

"I'm happy for you, Running Deer," She was genuinely

pleased as she knew how important this made him feel and he stood even taller as he could see she meant what she'd said.

He hesitated, also overcome with shyness he'd never felt around Shy Dove, but then blurted out "I want to show you that I can be a good provider, Shy Dove. I can . . ." He stopped in mid-sentence, not sure if he wanted to say aloud what he was thinking. "I want to be the one to provide for you when you are old enough to be my wife."

His face reddened and she realized she was holding her breath as he spoke. She wasn't sure what to say but knew she must speak soon or Running Deer would think she did not care for him.

"I would be honored to be your wife, Running Deer," she managed to get out before he fled.

He let out his breath with a look of happiness and relief on his face.

"I will always take care of you. You have been my friend all my life and there is no other girl I would want to be with."

"And I feel the same about you, Running Deer." She thought for a moment and then went on. "This morning while we were washing, Sky Lark and Squash Blossom were talking about you and I felt angry with them because I wanted to be the one you were with. It was then that I realized I no longer think of you as just a friend. I'm so glad you feel the same." She smiled up at his handsome face and they held each other in a quick embrace and then walked hand in hand back to the village.

"Will you ask my father for permission to marry me?"

"I would like to wait until after the hunt so that I can prove to him that I will be able to take care of you. He only sees me as a boy who has been your playmate."

"How long must we wait before we can marry?" She was becoming excited at the thought of being his wife and having their own place to live. Thoughts of cooking his meals and weaving blankets and clothing for them also filled her mind and

her excitement grew so that she was almost skipping rather than walking with him.

"You are not quite old enough yet so we must wait until you reach that age, but I want to ask now so that I can earn your father's respect by proving myself worthy to him. I also do not want your parents to promise you to someone else."

She stopped in her tracks as she remembered her conversation with her mother. She'd been so excited to learn that Running Deer had feelings for her that she'd completely forgotten that her mother had talked to her about finding her a mate.

"They couldn't do that, could they?" she asked but knew they could.

"You are young, Shy Dove, but not so young that they would not be thinking about your future. I overheard Turtle Dove and Leaping Frog talking with your parents about it being time to make arrangements for your marriage. I knew I could not wait any longer to go to your father before they made plans with someone else. I've been thinking about this for a little while but was afraid to say anything to you."

She looked up at him in surprise. "Why would you be afraid, Running Deer?"

"I was afraid you only thought of me as your friend and that you might not want me to be your mate."

"There is no one else I would want. I know now I've never imagined spending my life with anyone else but you." She smiled up at him and he knew the truth of her words.

CHAPTER EIGHTEEN

*S*haron woke and was surprised that she'd not been asleep that long but felt energized and with a sense of happiness that was connected with her dream. She reached for the notebook on her nightstand, but decided instead to put this onto her laptop. Her digital journal of her dreams was intriguing her and she tried to process her feelings as she wrote down this latest installment. Never before in her life had she had dreams like these that were telling a story. She realized this was something quite out of the ordinary, perhaps even for those who had no difficulty remembering their dreams as she usually did.

The next day she woke with a purpose. She'd spent the night before arranging and rearranging the best layout for the plants with the exception of the trees. Taking Frank up on his offer for gardening advice, at least for those, sounded like a good idea. She was anxious to get started so that she could move on to the patio area so she could spend more time outside. It occurred to her that she was defeating the purpose of being in a warmer climate if she was spending most of her time inside. The next couple of hours were spent in the meditative state that always overcame Sharon when she was connected with the earth – literally as well as figuratively. Though many might find this to be work, she found it to be calming and peaceful and along with any sore muscles, there was a sense of accomplishment from doing a job that had purpose. The inside finished, she moved on to the patio. Joseph had helped her set up the furniture the day before but upon further inspection, it still didn't feel right. It took a few tries, but she settled on a vignette with the two chairs facing the mountain view and the table off to the right where she could still see the mountains but created a separate area. Once the umbrella was inserted and the chairs in place, she sat down to survey her work.

"What's missing?" She realized it was time for another list and smiled. "Don't go anywhere, I'll be right back once I get myself a drink and paper and pencil."

"You're losing it; you do know that, don't you?"

She startled as she heard Ms. Judgmental's voice again for the first time in a few days. "Am not. I'm just connecting with my new surroundings." The response sounded petulant, even to her, but she decided to grab the phone along with the drink and paper and pencil. She hadn't spoken with her daughters for a couple of days and this would be a good time to do that. It was good to hear their voices again and catch up on their lives.

She sat for several minutes after their conversations and reflected on her life and how she wanted to spend the rest of it. Being alone wasn't such a bad thing, was it? It felt comfortable – mostly. But what was she missing by keeping to herself so much? Would she turn into some hermit and be thought of as "that weird old lady out on Silver Spring Road"? What if something happened to her and there was no one to notice she hadn't been seen for days? The thoughts created a strange turmoil in her subconscious, like an itch you can't seem to scratch in just the right place to make it stop. It was as though they were stirring up old memories and feelings but there was nothing in her lifetime that would have caused them.

Sharon brought herself out of her reverie with a need to shake the unease that had come over her. She had an urge to get up and walk around, to physically move her body and her emotions. Her water had warmed so she took it into the kitchen to replace it and this seemed to have the intended effect.

Putting those thoughts on the back burner, she went back into the patio area to make her list of what she'd need to create a place where she could enjoy the outdoors. A side table to put between the two chairs, pots for the flowers, maybe even a chaise or ottomans for the chairs along with seat cushions and that should finish it up nicely. She remembered that the nursery was open seven days a week so even though it was Sunday a trip there to pick up what she could find on her list might be just what she needed to completely shake the somber mood that had overcome her earlier. She might even be able to catch Frank for advice about the trees. If nothing else, getting the pots so she could put out the flowers would be worth the trip. She intended to leave the land surrounding her home as natural as possible with potted plants to add some color to brighten up the area. Being one of those easterners who tried to convert the natural beauty of the desert into a cottage garden wasn't on her agenda.

The phone rang, making her jump but she smiled as she saw Joseph's name on the caller ID screen.

"Hello, Joseph."

"Hello, Sharon. How are you doing with the plants? Is there anything I can help you with or have you already taken care of it?"

"Except for the trees, I'm in pretty good shape. I was thinking of going back to the nursery in just a little bit to get some pots for the patio flowers, though," she admitted.

"Would you like some company?"

She hesitated briefly, but then thought of her earlier concern about becoming too solitary. "Are you sure? I feel guilty about dragging you on my errands."

"Remember what I told you before? If it wasn't something I wanted to do, I'd let you know and besides, I offered so that's not exactly being dragged into doing it."

She could feel the warmth in his voice so didn't feel as though she'd been rebuked.

"Ok, then I'd love to have your company. When would be good for you?"

"How about now?"

"That's perfect. I'll see you in, what . . . about fifteen minutes?"

"Shouldn't take me much longer than that. See you then."

As she disconnected from the call, she realized she was looking forward to having the company. Another sign which validated that it might be a good idea to establish some human connections here. There was something that needed to be changed in her life – no, that didn't resonate; it wasn't something which needed to be changed, but something which needed to be healed. *An interesting concept*, she thought, but it felt right. *There's some karmic stuff going on here.* That also resonated within her. The dreams, the feelings, her being here at this time in her life all felt connected in a way that were leading to what she called "the karmic 2 x 4 upside the head." It was an expression she used when she was on the verge of making life changes that should have been obvious but had taken a while to sink in. *Fasten your seatbelt, girl, you may be in for a bumpy ride.* She smiled at this thought but instead of dread, she felt a tingle of excitement at what might lie ahead. She gathered her list and purse and took one more look around to see if there was anything she'd missed. Joseph arrived shortly after and she met him in the driveway.

"You're looking pleased with yourself. Gardening must be good for you," he smiled as he was walking around the front of his truck to open her door, a gesture which touched her.

"This doesn't offend you, does it? I'm a little old-fashioned this way," he asked.

"Not at all," she responded. "I'm not that hard-core. It still surprises me when men open car doors, but I figure it's courtesy not because you think I'm incapable. That is what it is, right?" She pretended to give him a disapproving look of appraisal with one eyebrow raised.

"Yes, ma'am. Wouldn't even suggest you were anything but capable. You proved that to me long ago." His smile and tone of respect touched her.

"Okay, then, as long as we have that out of the way. And I would have mentioned it when you did it yesterday if I'd been offended."

"So, should I have brought the dump truck today?" he teased.

"Darn, I wish I'd thought of that when you called!"

She could tell from his expression that he wasn't sure if she was teasing.

She laughed. "Just kidding," she assured him.

"After yesterday, I wasn't so sure."

"I might like to have a chaise if I can find one I like but mostly I just need some pots or planters for the patio flowers," she paused, "and maybe just a few more flowers. And some cushions for the chairs. And some cactus . . . cacti, I guess is more accurate. Who can have just one?"

"I'll take your word on that one. I figure all I need to do is look around and I can see all I want for free."

"Spoken like a man. You mentioned that Susan gardened?"

"She did. I'd tried to take care of the garden at first but Melinda took over after her mother died. My skills are in building, not gardening, though, and some of it has suffered. Susan had some beautiful roses that could use a greener thumb. Why don't you come over for dinner this week and I'll give you the tour. Maybe you could give me some tips."

"I'd really like that. I hadn't thought about having roses

because I wanted to keep it more of a xeriscape but those would really be lovely," she responded a bit wistfully.

"Uh, oh, I think I've just added more to your list," he nodded in her direction at the paper she had in her hand.

"I do believe you have, sir," she answered and reached for her purse to get her pen.

"How about Wednesday night, say around 6-ish?" he asked.

"That would be great! I just realized I have no idea where you live, though."

"I'm over on Sidewinder Road. I'll draw you a map when we get back to your place."

"Sounds like a plan." She had a GPS system in her new SUV but didn't feel the need to bring that up.

The rest of the trip to the nursery was spent in easy conversation. It occurred to Sharon that the transition from professional relationship to friendship had happened like slipping into a pair of comfortable shoes that you rediscovered hidden in the back of your closet.

She saw Frank as they pulled into the parking lot of the nursery. He had seen them, too, and smiled as he walked toward Joseph's truck.

"I didn't think I'd see you back so soon. Do you already have everything planted?"

"Mostly," Sharon replied. "I do have some questions about the fruit trees but I'm here to pick up a few more things I forgot yesterday. I know, hard to believe I could have forgotten anything with all I bought, isn't it?" she appeared a bit embarrassed.

"I may have to give you a bigger discount for bringing me such a good customer, Joseph," Frank teased.

Joseph chuckled. "Just doing my part to make a new neighbor feel welcome. I'll go grab a cart while you ask Frank about the trees."

By the time he returned with the cart, Sharon had the answers to her questions and a book on gardening in the Southwest from the nursery's book section to refer to when she got home.

"Oh, thanks, Joseph. I'm all set on the trees thanks to Frank." She smiled at Frank. "I'll need to check out the furniture and get a few pots for the patio plants but it shouldn't take that long."

True to her word, thirty minutes later they were back on the road with a much lighter load in the pickup than the previous day. Once they arrived back at Sharon's home, they unloaded the truck and with Joseph's help, the chaise was added to the patio furniture.

"Why don't you take a break and I'll get us some water. Tell me if the chairs feel right."

He raised an eyebrow but kept his thoughts to himself and instead picked out one of the chairs she'd arranged facing the mountains. Sharon returned a few minutes later with the glasses of water and some salsa and chips.

"Sorry, I need to do some more shopping. The cupboard is a little bare and I don't have much in the way of supplies for entertaining yet. So, what's the verdict on the chairs?"

"Thanks, no need to apologize," he said as he rose to take the tray from Sharon and put it on the table with the umbrella.

"*Darn!!*" she exclaimed.

"What's wrong?" he hesitated as though he'd done something wrong.

"I knew there was something else I wanted to get! I wanted to add a table in between those two chairs for drinks and whatever else."

"Well, not that you needed one, but now you have an excuse to go back again," he grinned at her.

She looked a little sheepish. "You're probably right about that."

"No worries. This will give me another perspective to check out your decorating skills. I really like the chairs over there. They're pretty comfortable and the view of the mountains is great. I don't do much sitting around enjoying the scenery. It made me realize I should do that more often."

They spent the next couple of hours enjoying the afternoon sun and getting to know each other more. He seemed reluctant to leave and when dinner time came, he invited her to go to Dos Pollos with him. The thought of spending another night eating alone convinced her to say yes. When they returned, she felt as awkward as a teenager on a first date trying to decide whether to invite him in but he either sensed her hesitation or, more likely, was truthful in letting her know he needed to call it a night as it was an early morning wake up for him.

"I've really enjoyed the day, Joseph. Thanks so much for everything."

"It's been my pleasure, ma'am." And with that he turned and headed back to his truck, waving to her before driving off.

It was an ordinary gesture but still, a warmth overcame her upon seeing it. It had been a long time since she'd had these feelings. She and Tom had settled into a comfort zone in their last years together and although they had loved each other deeply, the passion and spark they'd had when they first met had long passed. Later as she drifted off to sleep, she smiled remembering what a wonderful day it had been.

CHAPTER NINETEEN

It was the day of Running Deer's first hunt. Shy Dove was trying not to show how nervous she was as she wished him luck. She could tell that Running Deer was also trying not to show his nervousness. They both knew that he had to prove that he was a man, capable of being with the other men on the hunt, but even more important was that he could prove that he would be able to provide for a wife and family. They had not been able to spend much time together since they had shared their feelings for each other and Shy Dove worried that her parents would agree to an arrangement to marry her to another but so far there had not been any more visits from Turtle Dove or Leaping Frog. She hoped that was a good sign that no mate had been found for her and that there was still a chance for her and Running Deer.

The other men were gathering and the final preparations were being made. The night before the shaman, Gray Feather, had performed the ceremony to bring good luck for the hunt. Running Deer had looked proud to be among those chosen and would steal glances in Shy Dove's direction when he thought it would not be obvious. Her eyes had met his and she had smiled encouragingly to let him know how proud she was of him and sharing their secret. Soon all was ready and the small group of men, Running Deer and Coyote Call, who had also been chosen among the young men for his first hunt, were on their way. It should not be a dangerous trip but still Shy Dove felt anxious. What if Running Deer was not able to make his first kill? What if something did go wrong and he was hurt?

"Don't think like that, Shy Dove," she told herself. "It will all go well and soon you will be able to let everyone know that you and Running Deer will be wed." Her thoughts went to the day that they would be together as mates, having babies, and at first she didn't hear her mother calling to her.

"What is wrong with you, Shy Dove?! Stop your daydreaming and help me. We need to tend the garden and I need to speak with you."

Shy Dove became anxious as she heard the serious tone in her mother's voice.

"I have been speaking with Turtle Dove."

Shy Dove held her breath, afraid of what was coming next.

"It is time for your Maiden Blossoming Ceremony." This was the coming of age ceremony for all young girls.

Shy Dove let out her breath in relief. It was not too late. She'd forgotten about the Maiden Blossoming Ceremony with all that had been happening. She became excited as this would mean that she would be considered old enough to marry and that she and Running Deer would not have to wait, and if he was successful with the hunt…

"Shy Dove! What is wrong with you today?!"

She realized she had not answered her mother as her thoughts had been on the possibilities that awaited her.

"I'm sorry, Mother. I was thinking about the Maiden Blossoming Ceremony," she smiled up at her mother. "I'd forgotten about this and didn't realize my time was now."

"The ceremony will be held at the summer gathering and

there is much we need to do to prepare you. You will begin lessons with Turtle Dove today once we are done with weeding the garden."

"Will Squash Blossom and Sky Lark be part of the ceremony, too?"

"Yes, you will all be preparing together."

Shy Dove knew about the physical preparation that would be required to endure the four days and nights of dancing, running, grinding corn, and prayers that were part of the Maiden Blossoming Ceremony but there were other, more secret ceremonies that were carried on in private and now she would be included. Her excitement took her mind off Running Deer's hunt and she hurried through the weeding so that she could begin her lessons with Turtle Dove and her friends.

CHAPTER TWENTY

*S*haron woke with a sense of purpose. She didn't know if some of Shy Dove's excitement had carried through her dream or it was the anticipation of finally making her house feel like a real home instead of a hotel suite. With list in hand, she headed off toward Tucson after a quick breakfast. She'd printed off map directions to the places she wanted to check out more as a security blanket than necessity as she planned to use her car's GPS feature. Her trips over the years had helped with making her feel more like a native than a tourist but an innate sense of direction wasn't something she'd been born with. She'd been known to get lost even with a GPS, something Tom had teased her about on more than one occasion.

It took her a couple of stops before finding everything she wanted and to make arrangements for delivery and by then it was nearing lunch. She headed away from the mall toward the down-town area to check out some of the galleries first. She hated eating alone at restaurants and had never been comfortable doing so even with the single person's prop of a book or newspaper, so decided to put off eating until she was done and just pull through a fast food place on her way back home. A clerk approached her as she was admiring a decorated gourd. This was not a hobbyist's version, but a work of art.

"That's done by a local artist, Barbara Gideon," the clerk informed her.

"It's stunning," Sharon commented. "I've taught myself to do some of the basics, but I've always wanted to learn how to do these from an expert."

"Must be your lucky day," the clerk smiled, "Barbara is going to be teaching a workshop beginning next Monday evening and there's one slot left. Would you like to sign up?"

Sharon hesitated a moment, considering all the pros and cons and whether she would want to travel the distance.

"What the heck," she responded, reminding herself that this move was about making changes in her life and not staying in the same rut.

After getting the details for the class and paying the fee, she left the shop with her receipt feeling a bit bewildered about what she'd just done. This wasn't something the Sharon Peterson who'd left Maine not that long ago would have done.

By now her stomach was sending urgent SOS signals that lunch was long overdue and she felt ready to head back to Wilmont, after first stopping for take out.

The next week passed quickly with getting her furniture delivered and in place and a dinner with Joseph that had turned out much better than she had expected. They were developing an easy friendship and discovering they had a lot in common. She was settling into a new routine and retirement was, after a slow start, becoming all she'd hoped for.

Sharon felt both excitement and a bit of anxiety about the gourd class as she drove back to Tucson on the appointed day. She'd purchased the supplies that had been listed on the receipt —not many as it was mentioned that some would be supplied as part of the fee and had decided to put off purchasing those on a list of others that would be optional just in case this wasn't something she would want to continue. She worried about whether she'd be accepted but reminded herself that this was not high school and was supposed to be fun. If she met somebody there she liked, cool beans, but it wasn't the main purpose for her taking the class.

When she arrived, there were six others there. There was a nice cross-section; two were younger women probably in their thirties, an older man who looked like he might be trying the retiree's version of a pick-up class—she made a mental note to make sure she had two or three others sitting in between her and him when they sat down—and the others were closer to her age. One woman in particular caught her attention. The instructor had set up a table with an assortment of gourds, presumably what they would be using for tonight's class. The woman was picking each one up and studying it from all angles as though she may have already had an idea in mind for what she wanted or perhaps to check for imperfections. There was nothing remarkable about her appearance but for some reason Sharon felt drawn to her and decided to bite the bullet and strike up a conversation.

"Is there anything special we should be looking for?" she asked the woman.

She looked up from her scrutiny of a gourd with a long, curved neck and met Sharon's eyes.

"No idea," she answered somewhat conspiratorially, "but I wanted to stay busy so Don Juan over there didn't try to put the moves on." She tilted her head slightly in his direction and winked at Sharon.

Sharon suppressed the urge to look over and risk having him realize they were talking about him. She smiled and turned her back away from him and began inspecting the gourds as well.

"I had the same feeling when I saw him. How much do you want to bet we'll be asked for our sign before the night is over?"

"I'm not letting him near enough to find out!" she answered with an attitude that said she meant business. "Those are the ones that always want to latch onto me and tell me their life stories. I swear I'm some kind of dirty old man magnet. Promise me you'll sit next to me and save me if Don Juan tries to make a move."

"Only if you do the same for me," she smiled. "My name's Sharon Peterson by the way."

"I'm Donna Mackenzie."

"Have you ever done this before—gourds, that is?"

"I did a little on my own but I've never taken a class. Just moved here a few months ago from Washington state and thought it might be a good way to meet some people in the area. I'm a little too old to be a barfly."

"Me, too. Well, sort of. This is my first winter as a snowbird here from Maine but signing up for the class was more of an impulse than an intention. I'm glad I did, though. It's nice to meet someone else near my age."

"Can I have everyone's attention, please. We're ready to start the class now, so please find a seat and we'll get started."

"Remember your promise," Donna whispered as they made their way to the table.

"You, too," Sharon smiled back.

The class went well with no advances from Don Juan. After the class, Donna asked if Sharon would like to grab a cup of coffee. She almost said no as it was a long drive back but realized she could sleep in if she wanted to as there was no alarm or job putting her on a schedule.

"You know, I'm almost insulted," Donna confided. "That's a big *almost*. I must be losing my touch with the old guy magnet."

"Maybe I was putting out the back off vibes and kept him away from both of us."

"Whatever it was, I'm glad you'll be around."

They found a coffee shop within walking distance of the class and spent the next hour getting to know each other a little better. Donna had recently divorced her husband of 30 years. She also had two children, but both young men, about the same ages as Sharon's daughters. She'd also had an affinity to the Southwest and decided to start a new life there. They exchanged phone numbers and promised to get in touch before the week was over.

The ride home was long but the caffeine helped keep her awake and in spite of her fear that it would also keep her from getting to sleep, a hot bath and cup of chamomile tea did the trick.

CHAPTER TWENTY-ONE

*S*hy Dove finished the weeding in record time.

"I'm done, Mother. May I go to Turtle Dove now?"

Singing Song looked over the garden to inspect Shy Dove's work and found it satisfactory. "Yes, you may go now."

Shy Dove kissed her mother's cheek and hurried off to Turtle Dove's home where she found Sky Lark and Squash Blossom waiting. They both looked as eager as she felt but also apprehensive. Turtle Dove was known for her impatience and temper and other girls who had been through the Maiden Blossoming Ceremony had often left her house in tears.

"Turtle Dove told us to wait outside until you arrived," Sky Lark explained why they were still waiting.

"I'm not late, am I?" Shy Dove's brows wrinkled and her face expressed the concern that was reflected in the sudden knot in her stomach. "Mother wanted me to weed the garden and told me I had to finish before I came."

"I don't think so," Squash Blossom responded. She looked toward Turtle Dove's house and whispered, "Turtle Dove seemed to be in a good mood today."

The other girls let out their breath at this bit of news, relieved that they might be spared Turtle Dove's temper—at least for the moment.

Turtle Dove moved aside the covering at her doorway and told them to all come inside. Her house was small, as were all the houses in the village, and built of stone and mud adobe which served as mortar. She had laid out mats for the girls to sit on and told them to each take a seat. Each mat also had a bowl and grinding stone.

"The Maiden Blossoming Ceremony will require tests of strength and courage from each of you. It is not all feasting and celebration. As you know, your families must provide the food and gifts for all of those who attend, and part of your initiation will require that you grind enough flour to make the corn cakes. Each day you will bring corn and leave your grinding bowls I have provided here to store the flour which you will make as I teach you the prayers you will need to recite. You must listen carefully. Maiden Blossoming requires strength and discipline. You must prove that you are worthy in your spirit, not just because your bodies are changing now and passing from child-hood to womanhood. It is you who are chosen to carry on the people. It requires courage, strength, and stamina to be a woman. In addition to our lessons here, you must begin to train your bodies for the dancing and running that is part of the ritual. You will need to begin running every day. Start slowly so that you do not strain your muscles unnecessarily but do not slack. You must push yourself to do more as you find that the running becomes easy."

The girls all sat still, not daring to move in case they might upset Turtle Dove. She reached for a bowl beside her and emptied a handful of corn into each of the bowls on their mats.

"Begin grinding and I will tell you the story of Maiden Blossoming." The girls began grinding their corn trying not to make much noise so that Turtle Dove could be heard.

"In the early days of our people, the first young maiden was

chosen to be the Mother of us all, but the Great Spirit first tested her to make sure she was ready. The maiden must prove that she could do all that was expected so that her mate and children would not go hungry and would be cared for. Her legs would need to be strong to carry her children on her back, to bring water from the stream, to tend to the crops in the field, and so the Great Spirit told her that she must run every day to build strong muscles. When the Great Spirit was satisfied that she could do those tasks, she was then told that she must grind corn from early in the morning until late at night. She must grind it into a fine powder to make the corn cakes that would feed her family. At first her arms were too weak to grind more than a handful of flour but as the days went on, she was finally able to produce enough of a very fine flour that satisfied the Great Spirit that her family would not starve. And finally, the Great Spirit told her that now that she could provide for their physical needs, she must also provide for her family's spiritual needs and to do so in a way that would bring joy to herself as well as them. Maiden Blossoming thought and prayed as to what she could do. She thought about what it would be like to have a family of her own and she could see in her mind's eye the children that she would have and a mate to help her. A song of joy and thanks filled her mind, and she began to sing and as the music of her song came forth, she began to dance. The Great Spirit was pleased and knew that she was ready. From that time forward, every young girl of our tribe has been asked to repeat this training which we now call the Maiden Blossoming Ceremony before they can be proven to be ready to become wives and mothers."

By the time she finished, they had made a respectable start on grinding the corn.

"That will be enough for today. Perhaps tomorrow you can do better with the grinding. Stack your mats and bowls on the shelf in the corner. Be here after your breakfasts are done."

"Thank you, Turtle Dove," they spoke in unison and put

away their utensils and mats and left before she could make any further demands or complaints.

The day was nearly over and the hunting party had not yet returned. Shy Dove began to worry that something had gone wrong but told herself that all would be well, all would be well; a mantra or perhaps more of a protective spell to calm her worries that was not quite working. The shouts from the other side of the village caught her attention and she knew that they were back.

CHAPTER TWENTY-TWO

*S*haron couldn't believe it was now the third week since she'd arrived. How had she ever settled for those two-week trips? She knew she was not at all ready to return to Maine and felt an inner peace with her new life. It had found a rhythm with the daily chores of moving in and making her house a home and her nightly dreams. She marveled at how the story was unfolding to her and often pulled up the document on her laptop in which she'd been recording the dreams. They'd taken on a magical vibration for her and she still had not told anyone else about them. These were not ordinary dreams and she wanted to savor and hoard them for herself. It felt that somehow the spell would be broken if she shared them. It wasn't that she was embarrassed by the dreams but they held a mystery for her that she wanted to solve on her own and she knew that somehow sharing them would diminish them, make them less--or worse, they would stop. They were hers and she didn't want the spell broken by someone who would dismiss them as just dreams.

She was researching information online about gourds—books, supplies, and other sites for ideas—when she was startled by the sound of her phone ringing. The caller ID was a local number she didn't recognize but she answered anyway.

"Hello?"

"Sharon? It's Joseph."

"Oh, hello, Joseph. I almost didn't answer--I didn't recognize the number."

"I'm calling from the office but it's not on the main line so maybe it doesn't show up with the company name," he offered as explanation.

"Maybe, that's it. How are you?"

"Doing fine but was checking in to see how you are doing. I hadn't heard from you since we had dinner and was beginning to worry. I thought I might have to come by and check to see if you'd been bitten by a rattler," he teased.

She laughed and felt a warm glow at the idea that he'd been thinking of her and was transported back once again to her younger years.

"No, no snakes have dared cross my path yet, but I've made that a little harder to do by being inside more than out the past week. You'll have to stop by and see all the changes I've made. There's actually furniture and accessories now. And the plants are all doing great!"

"Is that an invitation?"

She was taken aback at her boldness when she didn't hesitate in responding, "How about dinner tonight? What time do you finish up work?" She tried not to let any of her anxiety creep into her voice. *Did she even have anything to offer to eat?* she wondered to herself.

"I wouldn't want to insult a lady by turning down a meal. How about 6:30? That'll give me time to go home and clean up before coming by."

"Sounds great. I'll see you then."

She hung up the phone and shut off the computer. Although she was a good cook and liked to cook for other people, she hadn't been as diligent the past week about her promise to herself to eat healthy meals. Her pantry reflected that and she didn't think heating up a frozen dinner was the way she wanted to treat a guest especially when she'd offered a meal. A trip to the grocery store was in order—right after she figured out what she would make.

This is ridiculous, she thought to herself. *Again you're acting like a teenager on her first date. This is just a friendly dinner— no need trying to make it into anything more.* Still, she noticed her anxiety level was up a notch. Ms. Judgmental was in the corner waiting to pounce.

"Don't even go there," Sharon warned.

Deciding to keep it simple, she fell back on an old tried-and-true chicken recipe that she and Tom had enjoyed. A quick trip to the grocery and cleaning of the house and she was good to go. By the time Joseph arrived, she'd calmed her nerves and was back to adult status. Repeating the mantra *this is a friendly dinner*, emphasis on friend throughout the day had worked.

"Well, what do you think?" she extended her arm and slowly waved it toward the living room thinking that she must look a little like one of those game show assistants displaying that must-have prize to the contestants.

"Very nice. I like what you've done with the place—and I mean that! You've got good taste, Sharon."

"Thanks! Would you like something to drink—beer, wine, soda?"

"Soda?" he teased. "That's pop around here. You'll be pegged for a tourist if you keep saying that."

"Ooh, thanks for the tip," she smiled to let him know she wasn't offended. "So, what will it be—beer, wine, *pop*?"

"Beer sounds good. Is there anything I can do to help?"

"Nope, have a look around and I'll be right there. I've got some chips and salsa. I thought we could sit out on the patio and enjoy the sunset while the chicken is grilling. I'll meet you out there in just a sec."

She gathered together the chips, salsa, glasses and beer on a tray along with the chicken she'd been marinating and headed out to the patio to meet him.

"This really is looking good, Sharon. I'm impressed."

"Thanks! It's coming together," she smiled. "Have a seat." She set the tray down on the patio table and handed him a glass and bottle of beer.

"Wow, fancy!" he smiled up as he noticed the glass had a thin frosting of ice from having been chilled in the freezer.

"Too East coast?" she asked.

"I don't know about that, but it's definitely more uptown than I'd get at my other friends' houses," he grinned. "Thanks, I appreciate all the extra work you've gone to. I hope I haven't put you out any." His sincerity made her feel less uncomfortable that she'd committed some faux pas with the glass.

"Not at all. I'm happy to have the company and it's a lot more fun to cook for two than one. I still haven't quite gotten used to that."

"It takes a while. Heck, I still haven't gotten used to it."

"Well, let me get the grill fired up and the chicken started." She sensed they both felt a bit awkward about going on with the current line of conversation.

"So, tell me what you've been up to the past week," he changed the subject confirming her suspicions. "Other than creating a layout for *Better Homes & Gardens*," he teased.

She chuckled. "I always referred to it as *Better Homes Than Yours,* but you may be right. This one is getting close to being eligible for one of their spreads. You deserve some of the credit with the fantastic job you did with building the bones." She raised her glass in salute. "And the setting here doesn't hurt either." She looked around at the beauty of the desert landscape, taking it all in and unconsciously sighing as she did.

"You picked a perfect spot," he agreed. "Soooo, tell me about your week," he reminded her.

"Ohhh, right," she came back from her reverie. "Well, most of the week I put the house together, but I also signed up for a class on decorating gourds. I took my first one on Monday. One of the other ladies and I hit it off and had coffee after the class. I think we might become good friends. We seemed to have a lot in common and I really like her sense of humor."

"No, kidding," he smiled. "You know, Susan did that, too. I kept her tools because I thought I might be able to use them, but they're really not meant for the kind of work I do. If you think you could use them, you're welcome to have them."

"That would be fantastic! Are you sure?"

"Absolutely! They're just taking up space and if you could use them, we'd both be happy. I'll get them together and drop them by later this week, if that's okay."

"Thanks, I really appreciate that," she smiled back at him.

She finished grilling the chicken and brought out the rest of the dinner from the kitchen so they could eat on the patio. The conversation was light and easy and the night passed quickly.

"You know, I may have to have you come back and build a fireplace out here," she shivered as the night air cooled once the sun went down.

"Just give me the word when you're ready," he smiled. "In the meantime, though, why don't we take this all back inside and try out that new furniture? I'll get a fire going in there if you like now that you've got wood."

"Sounds like a plan," she smiled back at him.

They gathered up the dishes and he carried the tray back inside and put it in the kitchen.

"Can I help you clean up?" he asked.

"No, no, I'll do this if you start the fire."

"I think I got the better end of this deal."

Kitchen cleaned and fire going, they sat down on the new

couch, both quiet but comfortable in their own thoughts gazing into the cozy glow of the fire's flames. The next hour passed in easy conversation and then Joseph checked his watch.

"I'd better be heading out or I'm not going to want to get up tomorrow morning and I've got a busy day. Thanks for the dinner and the company, Sharon."

"My pleasure."

"I'll drop those tools off in the next couple of days. Should I give a call first to make sure you're home?"

"Chances are I'll be here no matter when, but I don't want to put you out. Just come on by and if I'm not here, you can put them on the porch. I don't think anyone would bother them—it's not like I have a lot of traffic by here." She smiled thinking about the remoteness of the location of her house.

"Good point," he agreed. "Well, maybe I'll see you later this weekend, then."

"I hope so," she smiled and stepped out on the porch behind him as he headed toward his truck. She waved as he backed around and drove down the driveway. As he did, he extended his hand out the window and waved back.

That was nice she thought to herself. The glow of the evening stayed with her as she headed to bed.

CHAPTER TWENTY-THREE

During the night Shy Dove had come up with a plan to spend more time with Running Deer that she thought would not arouse suspicion and was anxious to see if it would work. She arose early and approached her mother as soon as she was done with her morning ritual of greeting the day.

"Mother, Turtle Dove told us that we must start training our bodies so that we will be able to run during the Maiden Blossoming Ceremony," she began.

"Yes, that is true. The ceremony will require much endurance from you during the four days," her mother replied.

"I was thinking that perhaps Running Deer could help me. He is known for his ability to run long distances and he would be a very good teacher. Even though we are good friends, I know he would make me work hard."

She spoke with her head down as she helped her mother prepare their breakfasts hoping that her face would not reveal her eagerness at having it be Running Deer who would train her. Singing Song continued preparing the breakfast meal and did not respond. Shy Dove's heart beat in her chest and she realized she was holding her breath. "Had she been too eager?" she worried.

At last her mother replied, "Yes, I think that would be a good idea. Running Deer is a good boy and you are right, he would be a good teacher for you."

"Then may I ask him if he can start teaching me today?" Shy Dove asked, hoping with all her heart that the answer would be yes.

"You must first go to your class with Turtle Dove but then you can go. Make sure that Running Deer asks his parents for their permission also."

"Of course, Mother, thank you!" Shy Dove replied and kissed her mother on her cheek.

She hurried through her breakfast so that she could try to find Running Deer before she had to go to her training with Turtle Dove and found him at the river. They hadn't had a chance to speak with each other since his hunting trip. She knew they had been successful but was anxious to hear the details.

"Running Deer, I'm so glad I found you! Tell me all about your hunting trip but first I need to ask for a favor from you," she smiled at him.

He looked up and smiled back as he saw her approach.

"Good morning, Shy Dove, I'm glad to see you this morning. The trip was a good one and I hear you have begun training for the Maiden Blossoming Ceremony."

"Yes, that's what I've come to ask you. Turtle Dove has told us that we must begin running so that we will be able to keep up with the running and dancing for the ceremony. I've asked my mother and she has agreed it will be okay as long as it is okay with your parents, too, that you can train me for that. We will be able to be together more often without it raising any suspicions." It came out all in a rush and her face was beaming with excitement as she wanted him to see how clever she was to have come up with this idea.

"That was a very good idea, Shy Dove," he replied. "Are you sure you want me to do that? You know I will not be easy on you

just because we are friends," he replied, his tone serious but his eyes twinkling.

"I know, but I don't want you to be," she answered. "I need to be strong to finish the ceremony and prove that I am not a child anymore—for both of us."

"Just remember that when you are asking me to stop because you are tired and think you cannot go on," he continued to tease. "Meet me this afternoon and we'll begin. Perhaps we can run out to the cave as a practice."

She perked up at that suggestion. It had been a few weeks since they'd last been there and she realized she'd missed not seeing it.

Just then Squash Blossom and Sky Lark walked in their direction on their way to Turtle Dove's house. Realizing it was later than she'd thought, she told Running Deer that she would see him later and he could tell her about the hunt then. They agreed upon where to meet and she ran toward her friends to join them.

"Oh, I almost forgot, my mother told me you must ask your parents for their permission, too," she called back.

"Good morning!" she greeted them.

"Good morning, Shy Dove," Sky Lark answered. "What were you and Running Deer talking about?"

"My mother told me I could ask him if he would help me train for the running we will have to do," she explained.

"Oh," Squash Blossom said, "He will be a very good teacher. He is the best runner in our village."

"Do you think he would help us, too?" Sky Lark asked.

This was not something Shy Dove had thought of and didn't know how to answer. She didn't want them to come along. She wanted to have time alone with Running Deer but how could she say no without arousing suspicion as to why she did not want them to come along?

"You will have to ask him," she answered, hoping that they

would not. She also did not mention that they had already made plans to run together later that day.

They arrived at Turtle Dove's house soon after and found her waiting for them at her door. She appeared impatient for them to begin and they followed her inside after exchanging greetings. As the day before, the mats were set out and their bowls and grinding tools were waiting. They sat down and Turtle Dove nodded in the direction of their bowls to let them know that they should begin grinding more of their corn. The lesson seemed to go on forever for Shy Dove and it was all she could do to concentrate as she worried about how she would be able to meet Running Deer without having Sky Lark and Squash Blossom see them and ask to come along. Perhaps she could say that she needed to go home first to do chores for her mother and then sneak away. That seemed like the best plan. Luck was with her, though, as the other girls' mothers were waiting for them when their lessons were done so she did not have to make up a lie. She hurried to the place where she had agreed to meet Running Deer and found him there waiting.

"Did you ask permission?" she asked.

"Yes, and they have said it will be okay. They say it is an honor to be chosen to help," he replied.

"Sky Lark and Squash Blossom want you to help them, too. I didn't know what to tell them but I don't want them to come along!"

Running Deer frowned as he thought about how to resolve their problem. "Perhaps I can tell them I cannot train so many people all at once. Don't worry, Shy Dove, I'll think of something. I don't want them along either. I'd much rather be spending my time with you."

Their problem put away for the moment, they started running at a slow trot to warm up their muscles. The trail to the cave was about a mile from the village so their first run would not be a hard one, or so Shy Dove thought. Running Deer had other plans, though, and much sooner than she'd expected he picked up the pace and her breathing became more difficult.

"Come on, Shy Dove, run faster," he called back to her as he began to outdistance her.

"I'm...trying...but..I can't...breathe," her words came out in short gasps.

Running Deer smiled and trotted in place as she caught up to him, then sprinted away laughing as he did.

She began to get angry that he was teasing her like this and, in spite of her fatigue, she began to run faster to prove that he would not get the best of her. He disappeared around a corner at a section of the trail where an outcrop of rocks obstructed her view. As she reached the rocks and turned the corner, suddenly someone grabbed her. She started to scream in surprise until she realized it was only Running Deer. He began to laugh at her and she punched his shoulder in anger and relief. He held out his water bag and offered her a drink. She drank a big swallow but he took her hand and would not allow her to drink more.

"Not too much all at once," he warned. "It can make you have cramps if you drink it too fast."

"I need to just walk for a bit," she said as her breathing began to resume its normal rhythm. "I know I told you I didn't want you to go easy, but I didn't want you to kill me on the first day!" She tried to appear angrier than she really was but he knew her too well.

"We can walk for a while but we'll have to go faster on the way back," he warned.

They weren't far from the cave and she was looking forward to getting out of the hot sun. Even though it was still winter, the days could be hot once the sun rose high in the sky. As they walked, Running Deer told her about the hunt and how he was the first to spot the mule deer. The elders had let him track it and take the kill. His chest puffed up as he retold the story and again Shy Dove saw not just the young boy she'd always known, but the man he was becoming. She couldn't imagine being with any other man and worried about how they would be able to convince their parents that they should be allowed to marry instead of being forced to marry outside the tribe as was their custom. How could she possibly be happy with anyone else?

CHAPTER TWENTY-FOUR

True to his promise, Joseph brought the tools by on Saturday morning on his way to a job site so did not have time to stay. Sharon's disappointment didn't last long as she felt that she'd been given new toys. She was anxious to try them out but the gourds she'd ordered from an internet site hadn't arrived, so she would have to wait for Monday's class. That reminded her that she hadn't heard from Donna during the week. In the past she would have waited for an invitation rather than extending one, but she reminded herself that Arizona was about making a new start, a new life. She found her cell phone and brought up her contact list where she'd stored the number. Hesitating just a moment, she went through the prompts and hit the Send button. In spite of her resolve, the butterflies in her stomach had been put on alert and she was about to hang up as the third ring sounded in her ear.

"Hello," she heard Donna's voice and brought the phone back up to her ear.

"Hi, Donna. This is Sharon Peterson from the gourd class."

"Oh, hi, Sharon, I'm glad you called. I've been meaning to call all week but you know how it goes," Donna's reply sounded genuine and Sharon relaxed as she breathed a silent sigh of relief.

"I do. I've been meaning to call you, too, but have spent the week trying to get my place in order with furniture deliveries and settling in. Before I knew it, it was the weekend! I don't know how I ever got anything done before I retired as it seems like I'm even busier now," Sharon realized that was an overused cliché as soon as the words left her lips. *Just keep going,* she tried to encourage herself. "I was wondering if you might like to meet for dinner before class on Monday?"

"That's a great idea, Sharon," Donna replied. "There's a restaurant not too far from the class that has good food and isn't bad on the pocketbook. And that way I don't keep you out too late. It must have been a long day for you last week."

"I'm not much of a night owl," Sharon admitted. "At least I get to sleep in now but meeting earlier than later would be great."

They agreed on a time and Donna gave her instructions for how to find the restaurant. Sharon hung up feeling proud of her initiative. She'd had moments of doubt, sometimes bordering on panic about moving even for a season on her own. This was feeling more and more like a good move on her part. That geographic cure might be right on target after all.

She realized it had been over a week since she'd spoken with her daughter, Amanda. Mandy to her family and friends had been on a trip to Italy and Sharon was anxious to hear how it had gone. While Jessica was more introverted like Sharon, Mandy was the type who had no problem going to concerts or on trips even if it meant going by herself. She had taken after Tom even though he was not her biological father.

Mandy picked up on the second ring.

"Hi, Mom. It's so good to hear from you. I've got so much to tell you!"

Sharon laughed. "That's why I'm calling. I wanted to give

you a little time to get your feet back under you after you got back but I've been dying to hear about your trip."

"It was amazing! You really need to come with me next time."

"Next time?! You just got back! It must have been wonderful if you're already thinking about another trip."

"It was. I have a bunch of pictures to go through and I'll put them up in a Shared Album for you and Jess to look at. The food was incredible and even though I had gelato every single day, I didn't gain any weight because of all the walking. My shoes may need to get replaced, though, because I'm pretty sure I've worn out the soles."

Sharon laughed. "That's a diet plan I could live with!"

"So enough about me. What have you been up to?"

"Well, I've had a lot of fun decorating the house, I signed up for a class on decorating gourds and met a really nice lady around my age there who I'm going to have dinner with before our next class, and Joseph Ramos. . . .you know, the builder of the house. . . .has been really helpful with putting me in touch with someone for firewood and a garden supply center."

Sharon didn't also mention they'd had dinner and lunch a few times but Mandy had always been very close with Tom and she thought it might be too soon for her to hear about Sharon's friendship with Joseph, even though that's all it was.

"That's great, Mom. You sound happy. I admit I was a little worried about you going out there by yourself."

"No need to worry, love, I'm doing just fine."

They chatted a few minutes more and Mandy promised once again to send Sharon pictures of her trip before ending the call.

* * *

SHARON AND DONNA arrived at the restaurant at almost the same time and greeted each other like old friends. The food was as good as Donna had promised and the conversation flowed, in part due to Donna's ability to keep Sharon talking. She had a naturally inquisitive mind and unabashed curiosity which at first took Sharon aback as it was such a contrast to her upbringing of not prying into other people's affairs. Donna's warmth and sincerity came through, though, so before long Sharon was telling her things that she would never have shared until much later in a friendship. She knew the dinner invitation had been a good move on her part and before dinner was over, she'd invited Donna to visit her during the week so they could get to know each other better.

"We'd better get going," Sharon looked at her watch and noticed the time.

"Oh, my goodness, I didn't realize how late it was!" Donna exclaimed. "I've been having just the best time. I'm so glad you called," she smiled.

"Me, too," Sharon smiled back. "I'm excited to get past the cleaning part of the lesson. I sure hope we can do something a little more interesting tonight."

"I know exactly what you mean. And if Mr. Baggy Pants makes any moves in our direction, we're sitting at a different table, right?"

"Mr. Baggy Pants?" Sharon laughed.

"I decided that's what I'd call him instead of Don Juan. Didn't you notice those horrible pants he had on?"

"Oh, most definitely! I think he's got his eye on that other gal, though. I never thought I'd be glad to be older, but in this case, I'm counting my blessings," Sharon rolled her eyes.

The class passed without incident from Mr. Baggy Pants and they agreed to meet at Sharon's house on Wednesday. Feeling like she'd turned another page in this new chapter in her life, Sharon drove back to her house excited about the upcoming visit with Donna.

CHAPTER TWENTY-FIVE

By the time Running Deer finished his story of the hunt, they had reached the entrance to the cave. He went in ahead of Shy Dove to check for animals as had become their custom whenever they went to the cave.

"It's all clear, Shy Dove," he called back to her.

She started inside and had only walked a short distance before stopping to look around in confusion. She blinked to make sure her eyes had adjusted to the light in the cave and realized her mouth was open.

"Running Deer, has someone been here?" she whispered as though afraid that whoever had been there might still be in the cave.

"I did all this, Shy Dove. For you," he looked at her with pride in his eyes. "Do you like it?"

Shy Dove looked at him with wonder in her eyes and then back at the cave taking in all of the changes that had been made since her last visit. The cave floor had been cleaned of all the rocks and debris that had cluttered it. There were fresh mats set out for them to sit on. He had fashioned a shelf in the back where there were bowls stored in case they wanted to eat a meal and he had placed some of the rocks they had found there as well.

"You did all this for us?" she asked in wonder.

"For you," he answered. "I hope you like it."

"Thank you, Running Deer. It's wonderful," she smiled up at him.

He seemed suddenly shy and walked toward the back to set down his water pouch.

"We don't have much time to rest. We don't want to cause any suspicion that we're spending too much time together," he warned.

"You're right," she agreed and sat on one of the mats and took another look around at all the improvements Running Deer had made. The cave felt even more like their special hideaway.

"You're sure no one knows about this place?" she asked.

"No one has ever mentioned it and I've never seen any signs of someone else being in here. I think the trees hide the entrance so well that no one even suspects that it is here," he replied. "It will be perfect for us to be able to see each other."

They spent only a short time while Shy Dove stretched her legs and rubbed them to ease her muscles for the run back to the village. She turned to look one more time and left with reluctance but knew they would be able to come back again the next day.

The next months of training passed quickly and Running Deer was true to his word of making her work. They did not return to the cave every day, though, as they realized someone might follow them or notice that they always ran in the same direction. As the time drew near for the Maiden Blossoming Ceremony, Shy Dove had grown stronger and could now keep pace with Running Deer for longer and longer distances. Her parents had not mentioned any more about having chosen a mate for her and she hoped there might still be a chance that Running Deer would be able to convince them that he would be accept-

able. It was not common but sometimes exceptions had been made—perhaps they would be one.

The preparations for the girls had been hard and they had had to make gifts for all of the guests that were expected to attend in addition to training physically and spiritually for the upcoming ceremony. It was customary that the families of the girls who were part of the ceremony had to provide food and gifts for all of the guests and because of this the ceremony would be held once a year so that not just one family would have to bear the expense. As the time drew near, Turtle Dove's reputation for a short temper became more apparent.

"You must work harder. We do not have much time left to prepare," she chided them, but they knew not to argue as that would only make her work them even more.

Finally, the time had come and guests from nearby villages were arriving to share in the festivities. Among them was the family of Eagle Feather, an important trader. His son Broken Wing was the same age as Running Deer and it was rumored that he would be among those chosen this year to mate with a girl from their tribe. Shy Dove had never liked Broken Wing. She had seen him tormenting animals and he had often picked fights with other children but was allowed to get away with it because his father was important and no one wanted to have to bargain more for the goods they traded with him. Shy Dove saw him arrive with his family strutting in self-importance as though he knew that no one would deny his standing and that everyone should acknowledge his presence.

"What a nasty person," she said to Squash Blossom and Sky Lark.

They nodded in agreement. They all had been the brunt of his childish temper over the years and it was only because their parents had insisted they play with him when he visited that they would have anything to do with him.

"I hope I am not chosen to be his mate," Sky Lark whispered

so as not to be overheard by anyone who might tell him to try to earn his favor.

Both Squash Blossom and Shy Dove agreed that they hoped they were not chosen as well. There were still a few older girls in the village who would be among those eligible so they might be lucky.

When Shy Dove arrived back at her house after her training with Running Deer, she was surprised to find Turtle Dove and Eagle Feather speaking with her parents. Her body tensed with dread as she wondered why they might be there.

"Please do not let them be talking about marriage," *she whispered.*

"Shy Dove, you're finally home," her mother called to her. "Please come here and welcome Eagle Feather."

Her dread increased but she did as her mother had asked.

"Welcome to our home, Eagle Feather. You honor us with your presence," she said respectfully.

"You have grown much in the last year since the last Maiden Blossoming Ceremony," he remarked. "Turtle Dove tells me that you are well-prepared and have been her best student."

"Thank you," she answered and looked both to Eagle Feather and Turtle Dove to acknowledge her compliment..

"Your mother tells me that you have become an expert weaver as well," he continued.

Shy Dove felt herself relax a bit. Perhaps that was it—he was only interested in her weaving. He was a trader, after all. It would be natural that he would want to examine her weaving to trade with other villages.

"Thank you very much. Has Mother shown you the blankets I have woven?" she asked hoping that this would be the real reason for this visit.

"She has. Your skill will be of much value to my family. You will bring Broken Wing much success as he begins to trade with

me. A wife who can bring a skill to her husband is worth having," he smiled at Turtle Dove and her mother.

"A wife?" Shy Dove asked, looking to her mother.

"Your father and I have made the arrangements with Turtle Dove and Eagle Feather. You have been promised to Broken Wing and the wedding will be next year following the next Maiden Blossoming Ceremony. In the spring Broken Wing will come to live in the village," her mother told her.

Shy Dove kept her tears from coming only through sheer will and was able to keep her emotions from showing as she looked to her mother and then to Turtle Dove and Eagle Feather. She didn't know how to respond so only nodded acknowledgement. The rest of the conversation was a blur as her mind raced and denial of what was happening was the only thing she could feel. This was not possible. To not be able to have the chance to convince her parents that she and Running Deer should be married was hard enough but worse to be promised to Broken Wing. How could she possibly survive this? At long last they all said their good-byes and she was able to ask her mother if she could leave to tell her friends the news.

"Yes, you may tell them now. The announcement will be made at the end of the Maiden Blossoming Ceremony but it is already known that the arrangements have been set. I hope you realize what an honor it is to be chosen. You will be very well provided for as the wife of a trader," her mother told her but Shy Dove was not able to share her mother's feelings of being fortunate.

She left their home and headed out of the village. She needed to get away, to release the emotions inside her and to try to think about how she could possibly change her parents' minds, but knew that was hopeless. How could she break the news to Running Deer? Suddenly she realized he might already know. Her mother had told her that the announcement would not be made until after the Maiden Blossoming Ceremony but the arrangements had been set. Perhaps the news was already being circulated in the village. She must find him to tell him she did not want this to happen. Perhaps they could come up with a plan. She turned to head back to the village and saw him coming after her. From the expression on his face, she knew that he had heard the news.

"Running Deer, what will we do?" she asked.

"I don't know, Shy Dove. Is the news true? Have your parents already made the arrangements?" he asked. She knew from the tone of his voice that he was also hoping that this was just a bad dream.

"Yes, Eagle Feather and Turtle Dove were at my house when I returned and they have told me that I have been promised to Broken Wing but the wedding will not take place until next year. Maybe I can tell them that I do not want to be married to him. That I want to be married to you. Maybe we still have time," she rushed the words out. In her heart she knew that would not be possible, but they must keep the hope alive. She was not ready to accept her situation. "Maybe if we can get them to see that you and I should be married, they will not make the announcement."

Running Deer thought for a moment, but she knew he was not convinced that would work.

"Let me think about it, Shy Dove. Don't say anything to your parents yet. Let me talk to my parents and tell them how I feel about you. Maybe they can talk to your parents and convince them that we should be promised instead."

She agreed to let him try and walked home feeling a little better but the dread she'd felt earlier continued like a bad omen waiting to materialize. All of the plans she and Running Deer had made these past months while she trained for the Maiden Blossoming Ceremony had come to nothing. They had waited too long but they had never expected for her to be promised this year.

CHAPTER TWENTY-SIX

The days were getting warmer now and it was a bright sunny day so Sharon decided that it might be nice to have lunch on the patio. She wanted to make things as pleasurable as possible for Donna's visit. She'd added more pots and plants and the patio was coming together. Donna arrived and Sharon gave her the tour explaining the eco features of the house.

"Wow! This is really something, Sharon," Donna looked around in approval and Sharon knew she was sincere in her praise.

"Thanks," she smiled. "Joseph did a wonderful job. I have to say it was the first time I've built a house that I could say that by the end of the project. He takes a lot of pride in his work and it shows."

"The planting area is just amazing," Donna exclaimed. "I wouldn't have imagined ever doing something like that inside a house."

The plants she and Joseph had bought were beginning to fill in the planting beds and added a cozy touch to the house. Hearing Donna's compliments set off Ms. Judgmental.

"Still needing someone else to give you approval, I see," Sharon heard in her head.

Feeling taken down a peg, Sharon responded, *"I'll get back to you on that later."* To Donna she said, "Let's get something to drink and I'll show you the patio."

They spent the day chatting like childhood buddies catching up on their lives rather than women who'd only met each other two weeks ago. *There it is again,* Sharon thought, *that feeling of familiarity. There's something about this place that has me thinking I've been here before and the people I'm meeting have been here, too.*

Sharon replayed the visit with Donna in her mind as she slipped into bed that night feeling the sense of contentment that came with it as sleep overtook her.

CHAPTER TWENTY-SEVEN

The day had finally arrived for the beginning of the Maiden Blossoming Ceremony. The girls participating gathered at Turtle Dove's house, each looking nervous and pale in spite of their excitement. Shy Dove was feeling like her world was upside down. She had been looking forward to this day for months but hearing the news that she was to be promised to Broken Wing had stolen her joy. Sky Lark kept glancing over at her and she realized that she would have to pretend to be excited or the other girls would begin to ask questions about what was wrong. Shy Dove didn't want to have to tell them about her parents' plans before the announcement was made at the end of the four days that the Maiden Blossoming Ceremony would take. She still held out hope that Running Deer could come up with a plan to convince her parents that he would be suitable instead and she wouldn't have to go through with the marriage to Broken Wing.

Turtle Dove looked each of them over narrowing her eyes to catch any sign that they were not ready, either in body or mind. Shy Dove stuffed her feelings deep inside her so as not to arouse any suspicion that she was anxious about anything other than the ceremony.

"You have all studied and worked hard to reach this day," Turtle Dove spoke to each of them. "You must now prove to the community that you are worthy to take your place as women. There will be tests of your strength but you will be helped through it. Remember that you are a woman and it is we who really are the strength of the tribe. The men may be the ones to hunt and provide for us but it is the women who are the true courage. Without women to carry on, to bear the children and to raise them, the tribe would die just as surely as they would without food or water. You must each seek Maiden Blossoming's ways in your heart, mind, and body. Are you ready?"

"Yes, Turtle Dove," they answered in unison.

"We will see," she answered in typical Turtle Dove fashion.

They followed Turtle Dove to the village's center and stood behind her as she addressed the families and guests gathered there.

"The next four days are perhaps the most important day of these girls' lives. Maiden Blossoming will test their mental and physical strength to see if they are worthy to carry on as women in our community or if they fail, to wait another year to try again. They have trained many hours for this challenge."

Everyone listened respectfully and the anticipation was building.

Turtle Dove began the song that would signal the girls that at its conclusion they would begin the first of many hours of tests of endurance and was joined by Canyon's Echo playing the haunting melody on his flute. As the final notes of the song hung in the air, they all began to run. They were accompanied by young men of the village who beat on drums or shook rattles and yelled to scare away any evil spirits that might try to keep the girls from completing their run. In the afternoon, they would grind corn and would be judged at the end of the ceremonies by Turtle Dove as to how much they had ground and how fine the finished product was. In the evening, there would be singing sacred songs they had learned for the ceremony and dancing until late in the night.

Shy Dove was exhausted in spite of all the training that Running Deer had put her through over the past months but she was glad for the physical distraction. It meant she did not have to think about her situation and the coming announcement. Running Deer had not come up with a plan by the time that she had to begin the Maiden Blossoming Ceremony and she was fearful that it would be too late, but she couldn't give up hope. The girls were only allowed short breaks and only their sponsor could be with them then so there was no way that she could speak with him before the final ceremonies and feast.

The days passed in a blur of running and dancing day and night with only short breaks in between. By the fourth day, Shy Dove was not sure she could make it through the day, but she thought of how disappointed Running Deer would be and how he would think he had failed her in their training. It was that thought that kept her going even while her dread of the announcement grew stronger. Finally, the announcement was made that the Ceremony was done and the girls were brought before the gathering. They had all passed their initiation and were now welcomed as women.

Shy Dove joined her family who were looking on with pride. A feast had been set out and the gifts that the girls had made were passed out to each of the members attending. Shy Dove had woven a small cloth bag which she had adorned with shells and feathers. Eagle Feather was examining the tightness of the weave and appeared to be impressed.

"Your parents have spoken true. Your skill at weaving is very impressive for a girl your age. Tell me again, how many blankets have you woven as well?"

"I have woven only three," she replied.

"Shy Dove has only just begun weaving a short time ago and she has been very busy weaving the gifts for the Maiden Blossoming Ceremony," Singing Song interjected as though she feared that Eagle Feather would be disappointed and call off the wedding announcement.

Eagle Feather turned to Broken Wing and handed him the bag Shy Dove had made for him to inspect. "You will be rewarded greatly with a wife who can make goods for you to trade of this quality."

Broken Wing looked at the bag for no more than a couple of seconds and handed it back to his father as though it was of no interest. "Better that she can provide me with sons and a good meal," he answered with disdain.

Shy Dove was angered both with his dismissal of her work and his lack of respect for his father. Even though she did not want to be any part of their family, she knew it was wrong to disrespect any elder.

Eagle Feather gave Broken Wing a hard look but said nothing to him in response. Rather, he turned to Singing Song and Black Bear and said, "My son has much to learn about trading. He will be spending the next months with me on my trading missions. We will return to your village in the spring of next year before the wedding ceremonies."

Shy Dove knew then that Running Deer had not been able to speak with her parents yet or, worse, that they had rejected his request.

Eagle Feather and Broken Wing said their good-byes and returned to the feast.

"Mother, may I speak with you, please?" Shy Dove asked.

"What is it, Shy Dove?" Singing Song asked.

"Must I be promised to Broken Wing? He is a terrible person. I have hated him since we were young. He tortures animals and picks fights with the other children. Please, please, I do not want to be married to him," Shy Dove was crying now

and nearing hysteria as she begged her mother to change her mind.

"Shy Dove, get control of yourself," her mother responded. "You are just tired from the Maiden Blossoming Ceremony. You know this is best for you. Your father and I have discussed this over many months and this is what will be best for your future."

"But I do not love him," Shy Dove wailed inconsolably.

"I would not expect you to love him but that is not what is important," Singing Song answered.

"But I love Running Deer. How can I be married to Broken Wing when I love someone else?" Shy Dove knew as soon as the words were out that it had been a mistake. Her exhaustion had let her guard down, but the words could not be taken back.

"You're just a child, Shy Dove. These are the words of a child," her mother answered, dismissing her feelings.

"I am not a child, Mother! I have just completed the Maiden Blossoming Ceremony and I am now a woman, not a child," she answered defiantly.

Singing Song began to respond but stopped, thinking twice about the words she was about to say and acknowledging that Shy Dove was right.

"You are right, Shy Dove, but in matters of marriage, your father and I make the decisions. You know that it is against the laws of the tribe to allow you to marry Running Deer," she spoke as though that was all that needed to be said to end the conversation.

"But exceptions have been made, Mother. Autumn's Song and Brave Fox are married and they are both from our tribe. And Running Deer loves me, too. You know he would be a good husband for me. He is already one of the best hunters," she pleaded with her mother.

"It's too late, Shy Dove. The arrangements have already been made and we cannot risk Eagle Feather's anger. He is a powerful man and your father needs him to trade the knives he

makes. It would be an embarrassment and insult to back out now."

Shy Dove was too tired to continue to argue but could not accept defeat. She needed to get away to think so that her mind was more clear but her absence at the ceremonies would be noticed so she let her mother take her hand and lead her back all the while feeling that her future, no their *future, hers and Running Deer's, was doomed.*

CHAPTER TWENTY-EIGHT

*I*n spite of the bright sunshine when she awoke, Sharon's mood was down as if Shy Dove's distress had consumed her as well. She moped about her house wandering from room to room trying to find something that would draw her attention, but nothing worked.

Enough of this she chided herself. It occurred to her that a mini geographic relocation would do the trick so grabbed her purse and left with no particular location in mind. She headed toward Interstate 10 and drove on replaying her dream in her mind. On a logical level she knew that trying to find a resolution for Shy Dove's dilemma didn't make sense but still she played scenarios over and over in her mind. Without realizing how much time had passed, she found herself nearing Phoenix. The idea of just driving on toward Sedona crossed her mind and she dismissed it as crazy. Sharon Peterson was not the sort of person who would just pack up unprepared and take off.

Not the Sharon Peterson who left Maine a month ago, maybe, she thought.

"You can't be doing this," Ms. Judgmental admonished.

"Why not?" Sharon asked.

"Because you don't have any clothes. You didn't tell anyone you were going. You don't have reservations. You…"

"So what?" Sharon interrupted. *"They have stores in Sedona where you can buy clothes. They have plenty of motels to choose from. Surely there will be at least one that will have a room available. I have my cell phone and there's no one who is expecting me to be anywhere right now and if they need me, they can call me on my cell."*

Ms. Judgmental had no response.

Feeling smug with her arguments that had left Ms. Judgmental silent for once, Sharon drove on, her excitement at this adventure growing as she headed north. Sedona had always drawn her. The beauty of the red rocks was magical. New Age claims about mystical energy from vortexes (their word but it had stuck) aside, it truly did resonate with her soul and there was something about the area that calmed her. This was part of the reason she'd moved to Arizona for the winter. She realized that she'd spent more time at her home than she'd intended and had this not happened, she might have spent the entire winter there. She was reclaiming more of the person she knew had always been inside her but that she had put aside while trying to please others. She now had the freedom both of time and connections to do the things she'd thought about but hadn't.

"All the time wasted," she thought to herself. *"No, not wasted,"* she corrected herself. *"I was just waiting for the right time. And that time is now so embrace it without regrets about what could have been. Be with what is now."* She sighed and noticed her shoulders relaxing like a weight had been lifted. She'd finally given herself the permission she'd been waiting for to do this and not taken on any guilt.

She stopped at a motel she'd stayed at before in Oak Creek just outside Sedona and when the clerk asked how long she'd be staying, realized she had no idea. That hadn't even occurred to her on the way there. She thought of what she might like to do and calculated in her head the time she'd need and to be sure she got back by Monday for her gourd class.

"How about 3 nights?" she asked. "And if I need more, I can just let you know?"

"That would be fine," the clerk answered.

The paperwork filled out and room keycard in hand, she realized there was no need to check in yet as there was nothing to take to the room. She headed back out secure in the knowledge that she at least had a place to sleep for the next few nights. As she drove toward Sedona, the scenery filled her with wonder. No matter how many times she'd visited, it always took her breath away. The red rock formations filled the vistas on either side of the highway and a smile crossed her face as they brought back memories from previous trips to the area.

First thing on her list was to buy some clothes for the next few days. She'd worn jeans and sneakers so could make do with those and add a few basics. The motel was near Bell Rock so would be a nice place for a hike which meant a backpack for water and a few snacks. Nothing that would be a problem to find in an area that catered to hikers along with the usual tourist souvenir shoppers. Shopping bags in hand, her mind turned to food as her grumbling stomach reminded her she'd not had anything to eat since breakfast. The thought of eating alone stopped her for a moment but she reminded herself that this was a trip about being okay with herself and not worrying about what others would think for a change. She settled on the food court and chose a table toward the back so that she could people watch while she ate.

Fed, new clothes and hiking supplies purchased, she headed back to the motel. On her previous trips there, she'd only had a rental car, but she now had an SUV that would navigate some of the roads she hadn't been able to travel before. Still feeling a sense of adventure, she decided seeing the sunset from Schnebly would be the perfect end to the day. And it was. She still wasn't brave enough to go all the way to the top but found a scenic lookout that had an ample parking area where she could look out at the mountains and still feel secure about driving back down in the dark.

Back in her motel room, tired from the drive but feeling satisfied with herself, she reflected on all that had brought her to this place as she drifted off to sleep.

CHAPTER TWENTY-NINE

he feast was being enjoyed by everyone around her, but Shy Dove had to force herself to eat. The girls had eaten only small meals during the Maiden Blossoming Ceremony, just enough to keep their energy up so her lack of appetite didn't attract much attention but still she found her mother glancing at her from time to time. She wondered if Singing Song was afraid she might say something before the announcement and cause a scene. Shy Dove had not been able to speak with Running Deer and scanned the groups around them to see if she could catch his eye and make some excuse to leave. Perhaps he'd come up with a plan but hadn't been able to tell her yet. Her heart hoped that would be the case but her mind told her not to expect that and be disappointed. At last she saw where his family was sitting and saw him looking at her. His head shook slightly and her heart fell but did that mean he had failed or that he didn't want anyone to notice them looking at each other? She looked away for a moment and then looked back hoping no one was aware that she was looking at him. Their eyes met again and he looked over his shoulder toward the edge of the village and then back at her. She nodded slightly to let him know she understood.

"Mother, I need to leave for a few moments. I will be back before the announcement is made."

Singing Song looked at her face and Shy Dove knew she was trying to decide if she should tell her she could not go. Shy Dove felt her heart hammering in her chest but kept her expression calm not letting on that anything was wrong.

"Just be back soon. We don't want to cause any embarrassment if you are not here when the announcement is made."

"Of course, Mother," Shy Dove answered and fought her desire to run toward Running Deer. She spoke with some of her friends as she moved toward the village edge just in case Singing Song might be watching her leave hoping that would allay any suspicions she might have about Shy Dove's motives.

When she reached the last of the houses, she looked around but could not see Running Deer anywhere. It had grown dark by this time but the moon still provided enough light to see without too much difficulty.

"Shy Dove!"

She recognized Running Deer's voice and whispered back, "Where are you, Running Deer?"

"Over here behind the piñon," he whispered back.

She glanced around to see if anyone else was around and satisfied they were alone, she headed toward his direction.

"Did you come up with a plan?" she asked, already knowing the answer.

"I tried to talk to my parents to see if they would intercede but they told me I could not be married to you. They had already heard that the arrangements have been made and would not agree to even try. They told me I must accept that you will be married to Broken Wing and to follow the rules," he told her. His pain was apparent on his face and Shy Dove could not be angry

with him. He had tried his best but their fate was not in their hands.

"I don't know what to do, Running Deer. I tried to talk to my mother and told her I did not want to be married to Broken Wing but she wouldn't listen either. She is afraid that Eagle Feather would be angry and would not trade my father's knives if they back out."

"She is right, Shy Dove," Running Deer replied. His voice reflected his dejected spirit. "When will the wedding take place?" he asked.

"Not until next summer," Shy Dove told him. "Eagle Feather will be taking Broken Wing on his trading missions to teach him how to become a trader. They will return next spring and he will stay here until the wedding," she explained.

Running Deer's face showed some hope. "That is good news, Shy Dove. We may have time to change their minds...or something may happen on their trips and he might decide to marry someone else. We can't give up yet, Shy Dove," he told her and she caught some of his excitement.

"You may be right, Running Deer. We still have almost a year. A lot can happen," she smiled at him. "I need to get back now before my mother gets suspicious. I love you, Running Deer. No matter what happens, please do not ever doubt that."

"I love you, too, Shy Dove, and I always will."

Shy Dove hurried back to the feast feeling somewhat better. She knew she would have to go through with the announcement of her engagement to Broken Wing but she did not feel as hopeless as she had. A year is a long time she told herself hoping that would keep her spirits up. She had to get through this without bringing shame to her family. She had to put her needs aside for the moment and do what they wanted for her but there was a piece of her soul that would never surrender. The Maiden Blossoming Ceremony had changed her in many ways and knowing when to give up for the needs of others was a part of that, but she recognized that even becoming a woman would not kill the desire to be her own person. It just taught her how to hide it when it served her purposes.

"It is time for the announcement," Singing Song told her.

Turtle Dove had entered the circle where the dancing and drumming had been going on. The drumming stopped and all eyes were on Turtle Dove. She was standing tall, basking in the importance of her position.

"The Maiden Blossoming Ceremony has been completed once again and we now have three more women in our tribe. Their days as children are now over and they can carry on our traditions. They will become wives and mothers. The time has come to announce who among them will be married in the next year," she paused to let the suspense of who would be named bring even more attention to herself. It was working as all eyes were on her and the quiet was palpable. No one wanted to miss a word.

Shy Dove held her head up and forced herself not to look in Running Deer's direction. His words I will always love you echoed in her head. They still had a year, she reminded herself for the hundredth time. I can do this. I must do this but not give up hope.

Turtle Dove turned slowly to scan the crowd. Shy Dove began to become impatient to get it over and found herself wanting to scream at Turtle Dove to just make the announcement. Finally she began to speak again. "A marriage has been arranged with the families of Eagle Feather and Singing Song and Black Bear."

Shy Dove could feel many eyes upon her and was grateful for the darkness. With only the firelight and moonlight, they could not tell if she gave away any indication of her disappointment. She kept her eyes on Turtle Dove and her face remained as expressionless as possible.

"Shy Dove and Broken Wing, join me in the circle," Turtle Dove commanded.

Her head held high, Shy Dove walked toward Turtle Dove ignoring Broken Wing as he approached from her right. She did not want to even look in his direction, afraid that if she did so she would not be able to fight back her tears. She did not want to see his arrogant face and to think of having to spend the rest of her life with someone she detested. She stood to the right of Turtle Dove and, to her relief, Broken Wing stood on Turtle Dove's left.

"During the next months Broken Wing will be traveling with Eagle Feather to learn to be a trader. He will join our people in the spring and after the Maiden Blossoming Ceremony next year, their wedding will take place," Turtle Dove announced.

The crowd cheered and clapped. Shy Dove stared straight ahead not wanting to make eye contact with anyone. Her urge to cry was still too strong. She heard the cheering and clapping only faintly as her heart had put a distance between her body and her emotions. She moved back to where her parents were sitting feeling numb. Sky Lark and Squash Blossom were running up to congratulate her and she smiled back at them pretending to be happy but not sure how long she could keep this up. Her attention was drawn like a magnet to Broken Wing who was staring at her with a smug smile on his face. She looked away as soon as their eyes met, feeling soiled. There was no way she could go through with this marriage. Just seeing him look at her in that way brought up such strong feelings of repulsion she knew she could not live the rest of her life with such a man. She and Running Deer had to find a way to end the arrangement or, she realized, they would have no other alternative than to leave the village on their own. And that would mean they could never come back. Her heart sunk at that thought but if that was their only choice, then so it must be.

CHAPTER THIRTY

*S*haron woke the next morning feeling disoriented at first and then remembered she was in Sedona. Once again Ms. Judgmental appeared asking her what was she thinking just running off like that?

"I'm thinking it's time I started really living my life," she answered out loud. "But first, I need a cup of coffee!"

The motel had a breakfast room near the pool and Sharon debated whether to head there first instead of making coffee in the room, her dislike of eating alone temporarily taking over once again.

"Just put on your big girl pants and go downstairs," she chided herself. Or was that Ms. Judgmental? Either way, she quickly brushed her teeth, washed her face, threw on her jeans, bra, and a sweatshirt, ran her fingers through her hair calling it good and headed down to the breakfast room deciding on the way that she could take her food and coffee back to her room if she got too uncomfortable. It was early and there were only a few people, some at tables set up throughout the room and a young woman, probably in her thirties, and a man about Sharon's age filling plates at the buffet area. Sharon glanced at them briefly thinking they were a couple and collected a tray and utensils, and checked out the fruit choices while they finished. She poured coffee and decided to splurge with waffles. As she was reading the directions for the waffle maker, she realized the man was standing beside her.

"Oh, I'm sorry. Am I in your way?" she apologized and started to move. "I always forget how to use these things from one time to the next," she smiled as she explained.

"You're fine," he caught her arm before she had time to leave. "I'm in no hurry," he smiled back at her and she realized just how handsome he was. His hair was silver and his eyes a blue the color of cornflowers. His face was tanned in spite of it being February but it had the look of someone who had acquired the tan from being outdoors rather than the electric beach—the term Sharon used for tanning booths. There were lines around his eyes but on him they looked good and his expression was warm. She couldn't help but smile back.

"You're sure?" she asked. "I might need to take a minute to figure this out."

"I'm sure. It's no problem. Just spray a little of that on the griddle first," he nodded toward a can of cooking spray on the counter near the waffle supplies. "That's where most people go wrong and have to dig the waffle out when it's done. Then just make sure to turn it when the buzzer goes off," he smiled again.

"You're right about that," she replied. "I can't tell you how many times I've hit myself in the forehead *after* I've poured in the batter. You'd think after the first couple of times, I'd remember," she smiled.

"You're not alone," he replied in a way that made her feel less like she was incompetent. "My name's Hal Jackson," he said and balanced his tray to extend his right hand.

"Sharon Peterson," she replied and shook his hand. "Nice to meet you, Hal Jackson."

"What brings you here?" he asked.

She hesitated for a few seconds trying to think of how to respond to that.

"Sorry, didn't mean to be too personal," he apologized.

"Oh, no need to apologize," she smiled. "I was trying to answer that question myself and wasn't sure just what the answer was."

"Sounds mysterious," he replied.

She made herself busy with preparing the griddle as she tried to organize her thoughts and chuckled out loud. "Nothing that exciting," she smiled. "It was a spur of the moment thing. I woke up not knowing what to do and ended up driving up here. How about you?" she asked as much to deflect the attention from herself as to stall for an answer.

"Sounds a little like my explanation," he answered. "Was getting bored and decided this would be a good cure for cabin fever. Thought I'd do a little day hiking and take in the scenery."

"So, do you live in Arizona or is this a vacation?" she asked.

"I'm retired now and live in Tucson in the winter. How about you?"

"Same here," she answered. "This is my first winter and I'm absolutely loving it. I don't miss the snow at all!"

"You lucked out this morning, then. There was snow yesterday morning but it melted early."

The buzzer on the waffle maker went off interrupting their conversation and Sharon opened it to find a perfectly done waffle.

"Now for the true test," she joked. "Does it come out in one piece or do we have to go for the jackhammer?" They both watched as she proceeded to remove the waffle, all in one piece.

"Would you look at that?" she remarked. "Amazing what a difference the cooking spray makes!"

"Do you mind if I join you when mine's done?" he asked.

"Not at all. I hate eating by myself and I'd love to have the company," she replied.

They picked out a table and she headed there. He joined her just as she was ready for her second cup of coffee.

"Did you have any plans for today?" Hal asked as she returned to the table.

"I was going to hike the trail that circles Bell Rock but didn't have any plans beyond that," she answered. "In all the times I've been to Sedona I've never hiked there. I wasn't sure how long it would take so didn't get any further than that for an agenda."

"Would you mind some company? I didn't have anything in particular in mind and that sounds like a great way to spend some time. It's been quite a while since I hiked up there but I could help show you the way," he offered.

Sharon's hesitation must have been more apparent than she realized as Hal added with a smile on his face, "I promise I'm not a serial killer."

"That's what they all say," Sharon replied but with a smile to let him know she caught his joke. "I hope I didn't offend you. I was just thinking about how different this is from the life I left in Maine just a month ago."

"I imagine it must be," Hal answered. "Why don't you tell me all about it on the hike? We can stop at the convenience store across the street and get some snacks. Maybe a sandwich for lunch once we get to the top. Do you need a backpack?"

"No, I'm all set. I bought one yesterday when I got here," she said. After just a few seconds, she decided why not. Even at this time of year, there would be others around and she had a cell phone. *Do they have 911?* The thought went out almost as quickly as it had entered. "Sure, that sounds like a plan. Why don't I meet you in the lobby in half an hour?"

He gave her a smile that would have rivaled George Clooney's. *Oh, boy, this could be dangerous,* she thought.

"Half an hour it is," he said.

Sharon took a quick shower and dressed in the clothes she'd bought yesterday, layering as the day would warm up and remembering she had a fleece jacket in her car in case she needed it this morning. She could put it in the backpack if she didn't. Before leaving the room, she gave herself an appraising look in the bathroom mirror. *Why didn't you buy some makeup?* Ms. Judgmental chastised. *Because I wasn't expecting to need any!* she answered but for once thinking maybe Ms. Judgmental had a point. *Nothing I can do about it now.* She gave one last run of her fingers through her hair calling it good and headed for the parking lot to retrieve her fleece before meeting Hal in the lobby.

The day was looking to be spectacular. The air had a slight chill but the sun would soon take care of that. Hal was already in the lobby and after a brief discussion about whether to take a car, they decided to walk the short distance to the convenience store and then on to Bell Rock. After picking out the essentials of plenty of water, snacks, and a sandwich that would be safe to not have to refrigerate, they headed toward the trailhead.

The red rock scenery of Sedona cast its spell over them both and they remarked at its beauty as they made their way up Bell Rock, stopping here and there for Sharon to capture a scenic vista with her cell phone camera. She promised to send Hal an email if any came out good, thinking to herself how easily she'd trusted this stranger. Something about his manner assured her that she could. The day was warming up as she'd expected and they picked a spot to rest and have some water before continuing on.

"It's magical here," Sharon commented. "I always feel completely at peace—like I've shed pounds of worry whenever I come to visit."

"I know just what you mean," Hal responded. "That's a great way to put it."

His smile took her breath away and she wondered why in the world someone as gorgeous as he was would have picked her.

Probably just didn't have any other options, she thought to herself but wondered if that was true as his smile seemed so unself-conscious and genuine, as though he really did enjoy being with her.

They sat together in silence, enjoying the rest and view, and as soon as they'd both finished their water, continued on their way. The trail didn't take long to hike and Sharon was enjoying being out in the fresh air and getting exercise. She reminded herself that she'd been spending far too much time inside her house. This was just what the doctor had ordered and the melancholy mood she'd been in when she'd left Wilmont was far behind her. Once they approached the apex of Bell Rock, one look at the slick rock that she would need to scale in order to get to the top was all she needed to decide that was far enough for her.

"Oh, boy, there's no way I'm going up there," she exclaimed.

"It's not that bad and you seem like you're in good shape. You haven't had any trouble keeping up so far," he encouraged.

"Nope, it's not that. It's my fear of heights…or more accurately, my fear of *falling off* from heights," she smiled. "If you'd like to go on ahead, maybe I can wait for you here. How long do you think it might take?"

"To be honest, I really don't mind staying here and keeping you company. It's been a while since I've done any hiking and going the rest of the way would have felt like a mistake tomorrow. How about we have our lunch and then head back?"

"You sure? I don't want you to miss out on getting to the top on my account."

"Sharon, no need to apologize. Honest, and I've worked up an appetite. Lunch sounds like a much better plan right now."

They finished their sandwiches and headed back to the motel taking a lot less time on the way back as there was no need to make frequent photo op stops. They spent the rest of the day checking out the shops in downtown Sedona—something Tom would never have enjoyed but Hal didn't seem to mind. After dinner they returned to the motel and headed to their separate rooms after making plans to meet the next day and take a drive through Oak Creek Canyon. The day had been wonderful—one of the best Sharon had had in a very long time—and she fell into a deep sleep anticipating the day to come.

CHAPTER THIRTY-ONE

*S*hy Dove was not able to speak with Running Deer for the remainder of the time of the celebration and dared not take any chance of making contact in case that would put him in danger now that her mother knew her feelings for him. They exchanged quick glances but her expression let him know that it was not safe to do more. Finally, the feasting and exchanging of gifts was done and Broken Wing left with Eagle Feather. She had managed to avoid any more than polite interactions, just enough not to be disrespectful or to cause embarrassment to her parents. Her mother continued to watch her and Shy Dove knew she must at least pretend to be accepting of her fate.

Now that Eagle Feather had commented on her weaving, her parents encouraged her to spend more of her time weaving blankets so that when he and Broken Wing returned, there would be many for them to impress him with what a good arrangement they had made for her marriage to Broken Wing. Shy Dove obliged but her heart was not in it. She continued to improve her skills but the spark of creativity was no longer there and that only added to her sadness. Just when she thought she could not bear it anymore, she remembered the idea that had come to her at the Maiden Blossoming Ceremony of how to avoid the marriage. Her exhaustion and emotions at the time had buried it in her subconscious until now. She and Running Deer would have to leave the village and travel far away. It would mean she would never be able to see her family again but the thought of being married to Broken Wing outweighed that. And perhaps they would forgive her and let them return to the village after a while. She and Running Deer would have to store supplies at their cave and wait for the right time to leave but that would give them time to convince her parents that she had come to accept their arrangement and that she was no longer thinking of Running Deer as more than her childhood friend. The thought gave her hope and at last she was able to shed the melancholy that had overtaken her for the past week.

"I'm glad to see you looking more like yourself, Shy Dove," her mother commented.

"I'm sorry I acted like such a spoiled child, Mother. I've had time to think about this and you and Father are right. This is what is best for my future," she smiled hoping that her mother would believe her lie.

Her mother looked at her as if trying to sense whether Shy Dove was telling the truth and seemed relieved. Her tone must have been convincing and Shy Dove's shoulders and stomach relaxed at seeing no doubt in her mother's expression.

"When I'm done with this next section, would it be okay if I take a run? I know I don't need to now that the ceremony is over but I'm missing not having the exercise and my legs are cramping at having to be sitting for so long."

Her mother smiled at her. "I never thought I'd hear you asking to take a run after all the complaining you did about it before the Maiden Blossoming Ceremony!"

Shy Dove smiled back and her face reddened. "I know. I'm sorry I was such a complainer. You really do know what's best for me."

"Yes, you may take a run but don't be gone long. I will need help later."

"Thank you, Mother. I promise I'll be back in plenty of time to help you."

Shy Dove hurried through her weaving, trying not to make mistakes in her rush to be done so that she could find Running Deer and share her plans. They still had not had time to do more than say hello when they saw each other in the village and she had missed his company. Luck was with her and she found him alone at his home. Making sure there was no one to watch them, she approached and asked if he would be able to run with her to their cave. She thought of it now that way…as their cave.

"Are you sure that would be okay?" Running Deer asked. "Now that you are promised to Broken Wing?"

"We have always been friends, Running Deer. It would seem strange for us not to spend any time together and we can just make sure that no one is watching us when we get close to the cave. If they are, we can just return and go another day."

He seemed reluctant at first but then agreed that should not arouse any suspicions especially if they appeared to only be getting exercise. As they ran, Shy Dove told him about Broken Wing's lack of interest in her other than as a commodity that would bring him sons and a skill to trade. Running Deer was silent but she could tell how upset he was. When she shared with him her idea for leaving the village, she thought he would try to talk her out of it but instead he seemed as eager as she to at least try. They spent the remainder of the run discussing the details of what would need to be done to prepare. As they neared the place where they would need to turn off the trail to head to their cave, they met Squash Blossom who was returning with a basket of prickly pear cactus and had to cancel their plan to go there for that day but were both filled with a new sense of hope that all was not lost for their future.

CHAPTER THIRTY-TWO

*S*haron awoke the next morning feeling her muscles complaining but not as loudly as she'd expected given her lack of exercise over the past month. Still, she was glad that her plans with Hal didn't involve another hike. She glanced at the clock on the nightstand and sat upright seeing that she'd slept until 7:30 and would now have to hurry to be ready in time. She showered and dressed and once again wished she'd thought to bring or buy makeup.

If he can be okay with me looking au naturel, then that's a good sign, she thought . She gave herself another appraising look in the mirror and decided what she saw wasn't that bad.

"You're making progress, Sharon," she said aloud. "I don't think you would have been this laid back in Maine. Arizona is good for you."

She still managed to be ready in time to meet Hal in the breakfast room where they had a quick meal and took some fruit for the road. The day was another of those with a glorious deep blue sky and white puffy clouds contrasting against the red rock. The air was crisp and dry but the sun would soon raise the temperatures to be warm enough for a light jacket or even tee shirt weather. It was a perfect day and the ride through the Oak Creek Canyon would be spectacular. As they drove, Hal answered her questions about how he came to live in Tucson. Like her, he was a transplant but he had divorced several years before from a marriage that had gone on longer than it should and there were no children involved. He had worked for many years as a graphic designer and now free-lanced on the side just to keep his finger on the pulse but with no full-time ties and being able to work wherever he might be as long as he had an internet connection, had made the move to Tucson for the winter months. He'd also had an affinity to the area from early in his travels there and they found they had been to many of the same places over the years. The connections continued with their draw to Native American archaeological sites. Sharon found herself liking him even more as they shared so much in common and wondered about the coincidence of her having decided to come to Sedona on the spur of the moment. Was this fate drawing her here?

"Should we stop in Flagstaff or go on to the Grand Canyon?" Hal asked as they reached the intersection of Interstate 40. "We got a pretty early start, so we'd have time to do at least a drive-by," he smiled.

"I hadn't even considered that option, but I'm up for it if you are," she returned his smile. "I don't have to be back in Tucson until tomorrow night so I'm in no hurry today."

"Why not, then? It doesn't look like there are any storms in the forecast so we should be okay and 180 is a nice drive. We wouldn't be back until late this evening—you sure?"

"It's a perfect day for a road trip—go for it!" she smiled, reveling in the spontaneity of the decision.

The weather held for them and the drive was postcard perfect. Sharon had traveled this route before but never this time of year so it was as if seeing it for the first time. They arrived at Grand Canyon Village in early afternoon, famished as there was not much more than scenery along the way and their breakfasts had long worn off; even the fruit they'd thought to bring along hadn't assuaged their hunger. After a quick lunch, they continued on to the Grand Canyon and this truly was like a first time visit for Sharon as her trips here had always been later in the spring.

Hal put his arm around her as they stood at the lookout and a gust of wind whipped past them. Sharon shivered but not sure if it was the wind or his touch that was the source.

"You look cold. I wasn't thinking about the fact that we hadn't brought winter jackets when I suggested this," he apologized.

"It's not that bad—the sun is warm but that gust of wind went right through the fleece. I'm really glad you suggested it. The Canyon is always amazing but I'd never thought to come here at this time of year and probably wouldn't have if you hadn't brought it up. I'm glad I've gotten to see it even if it does mean seeing snow again. Something I swore I wouldn't miss when I left Maine!" Sharon assured him.

She found she didn't mind that he kept his arm around her and was almost sorry when he suggested they return to the car and drive on to the next scenic lookout. They didn't spend nearly as much time at each lookout as they might have later in the year but it was still a trip that Sharon knew she would always remember even if she didn't have the pictures she'd taken with her iPhone. They returned to the motel late that evening tired but satisfied with a day well-spent.

"Thanks so much for today," she said as they waited in the lobby for the elevator. "It was perfect!"

"It was my pleasure," he responded. "What time are you heading back tomorrow?"

"I think check-out time is 11 but I'll probably stick around a little bit in Sedona. I don't have to be back in Tucson until 6 but don't want to drive home and then have to turn around to go back."

"Makes sense. You could drop by my place if you want. I don't know if you've got your heart set on staying here or if it's just to kill time, but you're more than welcome to wait until it's time to go to your class there instead."

Sharon considered that option. She really didn't have anything in particular she wanted to do here but was this going too fast for her? Hal was charming and hadn't shown any signs that she couldn't trust him but still she hesitated.

"No pressure," he interjected. "Just thought that might be a more relaxing way to kill your time."

"Sorry, I didn't mean to make you uncomfortable. I wouldn't want to intrude, though, and I feel like you've already taken so much of your time with me. I wouldn't want to overextend my welcome."

"I wouldn't offer if I didn't want to spend more time with you. It would be very easy to just say, it's been great and never see you again, but that's not what I want. I hope you don't either."

The elevator arrived giving Sharon a moment to process Hal's offer before responding. She realized she didn't want this to end here. It had been a long time since she'd been with someone else. Her mind went to Joseph but their relationship was one of friendship and neighbors; this was something else. And wasn't this move also about getting out of her comfort zone? To take some risks? *Just don't let this be one of those Lifetime movies that ends up with the woman being taken advantage of or, worse, killed,* she thought.

"Well, as long as you're sure I wouldn't be a nuisance, I'll take you up on your offer."

He smiled back at her and once again her heart skipped a beat as she looked into those gorgeous blue eyes. It was a relief to step into the elevator to break the spell and regain control of her hormones. *Slow it down, Sharon!* Ms. Judgmental cautioned. This time, she was taking that advice!

Hal followed her to her room to write out directions to his house. She was relieved she'd picked up this morning before leaving so no embarrassing personal effects were out in the open.

"Maybe I'll see you at the breakfast room tomorrow but I may head home early to pick up a few things at the grocery store before you get there. I'll make us dinner before you have to go to your class."

"Are you sure this isn't putting you out?"

He cupped her face in his hands and kissed her lightly on her lips.

"I assure you, you are not putting me out," he smiled. "I'll see you tomorrow and be sure to call me if you have any trouble finding the house."

She shut the door behind him and touched her fingers to her lips, still feeling his touch. It was just a light kiss but had stirred emotions she'd stored away long ago.

She slept like a baby again that night and woke feeling refreshed and excited with the anticipation of seeing Hal that evening. She debated whether to go to the breakfast room to see if she could catch him one last time before he left but decided it would be better not to.

No need to act like a teenager with a crush, she thought to herself.

Isn't that exactly what you're acting like? Ms. Judgmental scolded.

Maybe, but I still know when to put on the brakes, she responded.

We'll see! Ms. Judgmental replied in a knowing tone that implied that Sharon would prove her right.

Get a life! Sharon growled. I'm *trying to in case you haven't noticed.*

Just be careful about it, you know that's the only reason I'm telling you this.

Sharon realized the conversation was beginning to be a little weird and it was time for the voice in her head to take a rest. She pulled back the covers and headed for the bathroom to shower. The aroma of the coffee that she'd started earlier drew her out of the shower and she sipped it as she packed up the few things she'd brought with her and accumulated during her stay, planning as she did how she would kill the time before heading back to Tucson. She was not going to prove Ms. Judgmental right and head out the first opportunity she had to leave. Maybe one more time through Sedona village wouldn't be a bad thing. This might be the last time she'd have a chance to get this way before heading back to Maine in April. Her stomach growled and she realized that even if she didn't go to the breakfast room, she was going to need some nourishment soon. That settled the matter and she gathered her things and headed to the lobby to check out with the intent of finding a restaurant in Sedona to have some breakfast. She wished she'd thought to bring her iPad with her to have something to read while she ate but realized she could always do the old-fashioned way by finding a newspaper—probably in the lobby. She was a little disappointed she didn't run into Hal and noticed his car was already gone from the parking lot. Her disappointment was only temporary as she reminded herself that she would be seeing him later.

Now, go enjoy yourself in the moment! she thought to herself and realized what a New Age sentiment that was but smiled as she thought how apropos it was given Sedona's reputation as a New Age mecca.

Her breakfast alone in a restaurant wasn't nearly as torturous as she'd feared and with a happy stomach, she made one last visit to some of her favorite haunts in the downtown area and considered whether she should kill a little more time by going through Tiaquepaque Arts & Shopping Village on her way back through before returning to Tucson. She calculated backward from the time she estimated would be okay to arrive at Hal's and realized she wouldn't need to delay as much time as she thought given the time it would take to drive there.

She arrived at his house at 3:30 with no problem and her stomach did a flip when he opened the door and smiled at her.

You are going to have to pull yourself together, girl! If this keeps up you're going to find yourself head over heels—slow your roll! She wasn't quite sure if it was her internal voice or Ms. Judgmental's but either way, the advice was good.

"Come on in. Did you have any problem finding me?"

Hal stood aside, his hand still on the doorknob and waved her in with his left. He closed the door behind her and before she had a chance to answer, pulled her to him and gave her a big hug.

She felt her cheeks redden and her pulse quicken as she hugged him back.

"Your directions were perfect!" she answered as they broke the embrace. I did put the address into the GPS as a backup but really didn't need it."

She looked around to take in his house. It was obvious a man lived here but not in a bad way. His furniture and accessories were decidedly minimalist but not with the starkness that often accompanies that style. He had managed to do minimalism in a way that still felt welcoming.

"You have a beautiful house."

"Thanks! I'm pretty happy with it. This was the first one I attempted to do on my own and it suits me."

"It does indeed," Sharon smiled at him.

"How was your trip? Can I get you something to drink— beer? Coffee? Water? Something else?

She smiled again and responded, "The trip was long but uneventful, which was a good thing, and some water, or if you have tea, that would be great."

"How about a glass of water while I get water boiling for the tea?" he smiled back at her.

"Perfect!"

"Coming right up. Have a seat and make yourself comfortable."

The kitchen opened up to the great room area and there was an island that divided the area where Sharon took a seat so they were able to talk while he got the tea prepared.

"I decided to keep it simple and bought a couple of rib eyes to grill. I know you don't have much time before you have to get to your class but it's only about a 15-minute drive from here so we should be okay."

"Love rib eye—it's my favorite cut of steak! You must be psychic," she teased.

"I knew we had a lot in common, but that's my favorite, too. I have to confess that had a little bit to do with it," he said apologetically.

She laughed and assured him he had no need to apologize.

"I don't think there are any women who would complain no matter what was being cooked. It's just nice to have someone else do it," she said.

"Here, let me take those for you and let's go out on the patio so you can keep me company."

"Is there something else I can do to help?" she asked.

"Not a thing. I've got everything pretty much under control. The salad is chilling in the fridge and the potatoes are already in the oven. Hope you like baked the old-fashioned way. Nuked are okay in a pinch, but there's nothing like an oven baked when you're having steak."

"Couldn't agree more. Thank you for everything. I hope you haven't gone to too much trouble on my account."

"No trouble at all. Besides this is my chance to impress you with my culinary skills without having too much to worry about on my account—unless I burn the steaks. How do you like yours cooked, by the way?"

"Medium-rare is my first choice but as long as it isn't well-done or dripping blood rare, I'm not that fussy."

"Once again, madam, we are on the same page," he smiled and in spite of her determination not to let it happen, the butterflies in her stomach did that flip that was becoming all too familiar.

The dinner was perfect and the time flew by much too quickly. She thought about ditching her class but reason returned.

"Thank you for everything, Hal. It was wonderful! I hope I can reciprocate. Do you have time later this week to come to my place?"

"I would have been very disappointed if you hadn't asked and as it so happens, my schedule is wide open. What's good for you?"

Her first impulse was to say *How about tomorrow?* but she restrained herself and suggested Saturday instead more out of a throwback to the dating tradition of a Friday or Saturday night than anything else. His expression reflected a hint of disappointment.

"I was hoping for sooner, but Saturday it is."

She was not sure whether to suggest a change or stick to Saturday but in the end decided it might be a good idea to slow it down. She didn't want to wear out the welcome or burn out the feelings by getting on each other's nerves.

She gave him directions to her house and thanked him once again for the dinner. She hesitated but in the end decided to take a risk by giving him a quick kiss and started to head out the door.

"Not so fast!" he protested and drew her back in, holding her in an embrace and kissing her deeply, leaving her weak in the knees and feeling like a schoolgirl for the millionth time since they'd met.

She opened her eyes and met his seeing a crinkle at the edges as though he was pleased with her response, not in a way that felt like he was taking advantage of her feelings but rather that he was reassured.

"I'd better run or I'll be late. I'll see you Saturday. You've got my number if something comes up and you need to get in touch before then."

"Nothing's going to keep me away," he answered. "I'll probably be giving you a call before then, but it won't be to cancel. Have a good time at your class."

She turned and headed to her car and looked back before getting in to see him still standing in the doorway. He smiled again as they waved goodbye.

She arrived at her class with no time to spare, still feeling a little flustered by all that had happened over the past few days.

"Hey, stranger," Donna greeted her. "Whoa, what's happened to you?" her tone was concerned as well as curious.

"You're not going to believe it. *I* don't believe it!" she answered. "I'll give you a call tomorrow to give you all the details but I think I need a little time to process it all."

"Is everything okay?" she asked.

"Oh, it's nothing bad," Sharon reassured her. "In fact, it couldn't be better. Or, at least, I don't think it could. I'm just still trying to take it all in. I took an unplanned trip to Sedona and met someone there." She realized she was blushing.

"Oooohhh, yes, I am going to expect a full report!" Donna smiled mischievously.

The instructor was beginning the lesson for which Sharon was grateful as it took the pressure off having to say more and gave her something else to focus on than her feelings.

When the class ended Sharon promised one more time to call Donna the next day and tell her about her trip and headed home. She felt a tangible difference as she opened her front door and walked in, not quite a stranger in her own home but the vibe was not the same. It felt emptier somehow and it was not a feeling Sharon liked. She'd just started her new life and had been determined to do it on her own—*finally*—and in less than two months already there was someone else in her life. Or at least it appeared to be heading in that direction.

Not again! She said out loud as though to declare that not just to herself but to the Universe.

It doesn't have to be that way.

The response startled her as it was not Ms. Judgmental this time who was speaking in her head.

Shaking off the initial reaction that maybe she was spending too much time alone and beginning to hear voices, the epiphany of what it meant sunk in. Being with someone else didn't mean she *had* to give away herself—this could be a real opportunity to have a relationship on her terms. The unease she'd first felt upon arriving home disappeared and she felt a new determination not to let the past dictate her future. Exhausted, but at ease and now anticipating the challenge of having someone in her life again but in a different way, she headed to bed.

CHAPTER THIRTY-THREE

It had been three days since Shy Dove and Running Deer had been able to meet again after their failed attempt to go to their cave. Shy Dove's mother was beginning to watch her less but she still avoided making any unnecessary contact with him fearing that she would be forbidden to see him. She had been using the time to formulate a plan for how they would be able to get away and wanted to get his ideas, too. At last, they had found an excuse to meet that didn't arouse suspicions and had met no one along the way that would necessitate their turning back to the village.

"I've missed you, Shy Dove," Running Deer held her when they were at last alone and she returned his embrace, cherishing the feeling of his body and wishing again that he was the one who had been chosen for her instead of Broken Wing.

"I've missed you, too, Running Deer," she answered. "It has been torture to not be able to be with you and to think that I might have to marry Broken Wing. I would rather die than be his wife."

"I won't let that happen, Shy Dove. I have a plan if you are willing."

He then set out nearly the identical plan that she had been thinking of—to hide supplies in the cave that they would need to start a life on their own and when the time was right, to slip out under cover of darkness so they would have time to be far away before it was discovered that they were gone. She grew more excited as he told her his plan, thinking that perhaps this would *work if they had both had the same idea about how to make it happen. His expression told her he had expected her to object but hoped she would be convinced that it could succeed.*

"Running Deer, that is just as I had planned it. It has to work!"

His relief was obvious and he, too, became more excited as they spent the next hour working out how they would prepare for the trip, where they might go, and how long it would be before they could leave. They would each make separate trips to the cave to bring supplies so that it would not cause too much suspicion if they were spending a lot of time together and would use different routes in case someone was watching them always heading in the same direction.

"We'd better go back now or my mother will worry," Shy Dove reluctantly told him.

"Yes, I know but I'm okay now that we know we can one day be together. Are you sure you still want to do this? You know that we can never return if we leave?"

"I have already thought of that and, yes, I would give that all up to be with you. I will never submit myself to Broken Wing and if it means I must leave my family, then that is how it will be. I begged my mother not to promise me to him but she would not listen. There is no other way."

"I love you, Shy Dove, and I will never make you regret this decision. I will always take care of you."

"I love you, too, Running Deer."

CHAPTER THIRTY-FOUR

Sharon woke feeling disoriented for a brief moment and wondered if she'd also dreamed that she'd been in Sedona. As she came more fully awake, the reality of the past few days sank in and she smiled and stretched thinking that life was good.

After breakfast and a shower, she called Donna to fill her in on the details as she'd promised.

"Are you sure you can trust this guy?" Donna asked with concern in her voice.

"I know, I know. It all happened really fast and I should be careful—he could be a serial killer, a rapist, or an opportunist preying on gullible widows," Sharon replied. "Believe me, that's all gone through my head already, but there's something about him that makes me trust him."

"How many gullible widows have said that after their bank accounts have been cleaned out?" Donna reminded her.

"You sure do know how to bring a girl down." Sharon's doubts surfaced once again hearing Donna repeat the same things Ms. Judgmental had already told her.

"I'm sorry, I don't mean to bring you down, but I don't want you to get hurt either. Forget I'm such a Debbie Downer and see how it goes—just take it slow, okay?"

"I promise," Sharon replied. They talked for a few minutes more about their class and made plans to meet later in the week for lunch before hanging up.

Sharon knew that Donna was doing what any friend would do but the glow she'd felt when she first awoke had been dimmed. She needed to pick up a few groceries and was about to head out the door with keys in hand, when her phone rang.

"Hello?"

"Hi, Sharon. It's a gorgeous day—what do you say you meet me in Tucson for lunch and I'll take you for a tour of the Botanical Gardens when we're done. You haven't been yet have you?"

Sharon's pulse skipped a beat as she heard Hal's voice on the other end of the line.

"Hi, Hal. No, I haven't been yet since I came back—it's been a couple of years since I've visited, now that I think of it. Aren't you tired of keeping me company, though?"

"On the contrary. I woke up this morning and you were the first thing on my mind."

Sharon could see Hal's smile as she heard his voice and all of Donna's warnings and her promises flew out the window.

"I was just about to head out to pick up a few groceries—the pantry is getting bare, but I shouldn't be long. What time would you like me to meet you? Should we meet at the Botanical Gardens or did you want to do lunch first?"

"Why don't you meet me at my place at say 11:30 and we can go in my car from there? Would that give you time to do your shopping and drive back? I don't want to rush you and I don't have anything else on my schedule for today so I'm wide open."

Sharon quickly calculated the time it would take to do the shopping, get back and put on a little makeup, change out of the work clothes she was dressed in and drive back to Hal's place.

"11:30 would work fine. I'll give you a call if I'm running late," she answered.

"Sounds like a plan. Can't wait to see you," Hal's voice sounded sincere.

"Me, too." The words came out before she had time to stop them and she hung up wishing she hadn't come across as being so eager.

Her shopping done and the groceries put away, clothes changed and just enough makeup to enhance without looking made up, Sharon gave herself an approving glance in the mirror and headed out the door. She arrived at Hal's with a few minutes to spare and sat in the car not wanting to ring his doorbell until the appointed time but he must have heard her car pull in as he opened the door and waved, smiling that dangerous smile that she feared was going to be the end of any resolve to take things slowly. She smiled back and gathered her purse and keys.

"Are you ready to go now or did you want me to come in first?" she asked.

"I'm ready. Just give me a sec' to lock up and I'll be right out," he answered.

Sharon was relieved not to have to go inside and felt more at ease that there was nothing amiss in the invitation's true intent.

"See," she said to herself as much for her benefit as Ms. Judgmental's. *"Just like I told you—just a lunch date and a trip to the Botanical Gardens. No need to worry it's anything more than that. Get a grip on yourself."*

Hal appeared just then and locked the door behind him before Ms. Judgmental had a chance to reply.

"Gorgeous day, isn't it?" he asked without waiting for a response before asking, "Do you have any place in particular you'd like to go for lunch?"

"Not a clue—I'm completely at your disposal," she answered.

"There's a new restaurant I've been wanting to check out

that's not that far from the Gardens so I thought we'd go there if you didn't have any preferences. Hop in, it's unlocked" he gestured toward his car.

"This was a great idea," Sharon told him after they'd finished their lunch. "Thanks!"

"My pleasure. The food was great and the company even better."

"How is it you're still single? That's a lot of charm going to waste!" Sharon teased him trying to deflect the attention away from herself.

"Haven't had anyone I wanted to spend that much time with. Until now," Hal replied.

His eyes and mouth were smiling but Sharon knew his tone was serious and instead of deflecting the attention, she now felt even more the center of it.

"Would you look at the time?" she feigned concern as she glanced at her watch. "We should probably head over to the Gardens, shouldn't we?"

Hal's expression turned serious. "I'm sorry, Sharon. I didn't mean to make you feel uncomfortable. I meant what I said, though. It's been a long time since I've had someone whose company I've enjoyed as much as yours. It's a sincere compliment but if I'm putting too much pressure on you, just let me know, okay? I don't want to scare you off."

Sharon looked down at her empty plate, trying to gather her thoughts. She looked up to see him watching her and smiled to lighten the mood.

"It's been a very long time since I've been in the dating game, Hal, and I'm very much out of practice. I'm feeling a bit out of my element with the social graces. I don't want to come across as some love-struck schoolgirl with her first serious crush but I'm a little confused and scared at how easy it is to be with you. I don't want to come across too strong and scare you off either," she confessed hoping that honesty would be the best approach.

"I hear you. We'll take it slow, okay?" He reached out and put his hand over hers. "I meant it when I said I don't want to do anything to make you uncomfortable."

"It's a deal," she smiled back at him. "Now, we have places to go and plants to see."

The rest of the afternoon went well and the distraction of talking about the various exhibits helped. Hal was familiar with many of the species and shared Sharon's love of gardening. They arrived back at his place close to dinnertime.

"I don't want to send you back home hungry but don't want you to think I'm pushing it by asking you to stay for dinner. I'd really like you to stay but tell me what you'd like."

Sharon considered the offer.

"I'd love to stay for dinner…and then head back early if you don't mind an eat and run. I really do need to spend some time at home after being away and night driving isn't high on my list anymore."

"No need to make any excuses. I understand completely."

True to his word, Hal made them dinner and made no complaints when Sharon told him she needed to leave shortly after they'd finished but did take her in his arms and kiss her good-bye. It was a light kiss but told her all she needed to know about how he was feeling. Sharon was grateful the ride home was more than just a few minutes away as it gave her time to compose herself and ensured that she wouldn't change her mind and stay just a little longer.

CHAPTER THIRTY-FIVE

*S*hy Dove spent the next months improving her weaving skills as well as learning how to card and spin wool and make yarn from cotton. Her mother taught her how to dye the fibers using plants near the village which gave her an excuse to make trips to the cave claiming that she was spending the time looking for just the right plants. She was able to produce a number of blankets for Eagle Feather and Broken Wing's return but had also managed to set up a loom at the cave where she took yarns a little at a time so as not to arouse any suspicions about the missing supplies. She and Running Deer would need blankets to take with them. They had decided that they would stay through the winter to give them enough time to put together all they would need to live on their own and leave in the late spring before the wedding. It would mean that Broken Wing would be back in the village but there was no other way to safely leave before then. They would need to wait until after the crops were harvested to take corn and squash seeds to start their own crops, not knowing what might be available to them. They had only decided to head north. Running Deer had been scouting *that direction for short trips and listened to others in the village who had been farther north and south than he had had time to go. Running Deer thought it would be the less likely direction to be followed once it was discovered they were both missing.*

As Shy Dove had been improving her weaving, Running Deer had become an accomplished hunter and had been able to kill enough meat and dry it to get them started on their journey. He knew from talking with elders that they would find good hunting along the way but he didn't want to take any chances. It wasn't just himself he had to think about--there was Shy Dove, too, and providing for her was his primary focus. He knew she trusted him completely but even though she hadn't told him so, he sensed she was afraid of leaving the security of the village and her family. He didn't want to disappoint her or put her in any harm. He wished they could leave right away but knew she was right that they had to make preparations if they were going to head north. He had never seen it, but he'd heard stories from others about the snow and cold weather that was in the northern areas during the winter months. Shy Dove would have to make warmer clothing for them without attracting attention, so he had skinned a deer and had found a secluded spot to tan the hide. He wasn't sure if it would be enough for clothing for both of them, though, and was contemplating the necessity of killing another. Having the extra meat dried would be a good idea, too, but that presented another problem of how much the two of them could carry especially since they would have to leave without being detected. He wondered if he could find and train a dog between now and then that could help them pack their belongings. He was so deep in thought he almost didn't hear the approach of someone outside the cave. He was in the rear of the cave where he and Shy Dove had made a partial wall to hide their belongings by haphazardly stacking rocks to make it look as though it was just natural rubble inside the cave. As he was deciding whether to come out to meet whoever was there or hide until they left, he heard Shy Dove call his name.

"Running Deer, it's me. I saw you heading this way but waited to catch up so no one would see us together."

He exhaled in relief, not having realized he had been holding his breath.

"You scared me, Shy Dove! I thought someone had found the cave," he said as he came out from behind the wall.

She smiled at him and his worry melted.

"I'm sorry. Maybe we should agree on a sign like a whistle that we can do when we come to the cave so we know it's one of us and not frighten each other."

"That's a good idea. I was also thinking I should try to kill another deer so we would have more hide for you to make winter clothing."

She frowned as she thought about this. "Wouldn't we have time to do that after we leave and we get to wherever we decide is a good spot to stay? That way we wouldn't have to worry about taking so much with us."

He realized she was right.

"I'm just so worried that I won't be able to provide for you and want to make sure you have everything you'll need. You are right, though, we can do that along the way. We will be leaving in the spring and should have plenty of time before it snows to get another hide. You're sure you'll have enough time to make an outfit if we need it?"

"I'm sure. I'm getting very good at my sewing," she beamed with pride. "And Mother says my weaving skills are improving, too. She thinks Eagle Feather will be very pleased." Her expression quickly changed from pride to disdain.

"Don't worry, Shy Dove, we'll be gone long before you have to worry about marrying Broken Wing," he assured her.

"We have to, Running Deer," she said as her eyes filled with tears. "I can't bear the thought of being married to him."

He took her in his arms to comfort her as she softly wept, but her tears did not last long as the security of being in his arms calmed her.

CHAPTER THIRTY-SIX

*S*haron lay in bed the next morning thinking of her dream and how her life was changing. It was as though the momentum of each was changing. What a strange existence she was having now, so unlike her life in Maine. She realized how naturally she'd fallen into the routine of her life here, again musing at how much like home it felt—that she *belonged* here. She got out of bed and added this latest one to her dream journal. Something else she'd rarely done before as it hadn't been often that she would remember more than a fragment of any dreams she might have had. *Why* these *and why* now? she thought to herself. The phone ringing took her out of her reverie before she had time to give that more thought, much less answer.

"Tell me you weren't throwing my advice to the wind yesterday! I tried calling all afternoon and your phone kept going to voicemail. I was beginning to think I might have to report you missing!" she heard Donna's voice on the other end of the line exclaim.

Sharon wasn't sure whether to be annoyed or touched by the concern.

"I'm fine—honest!" she said. "And good morning to you by

the way," she added, hoping she had kept her tone light. "I went to Tucson to have lunch with Hal and we went to the Botanical Gardens so had turned my phone off."

"I'm sorry," Donna must have realized how she had come across. "I was just worried about you and afraid my teasing really was something to be concerned about. And then my imagination went wild when I couldn't get through."

"Why don't you come to my house and I'll tell you all about it?" she offered. "Maybe I can assure you I'm not going to be an episode on *Dateline* after they find my mutilated body by the side of a deserted road."

"Not funny about the mutilated body but I'd love to come see you."

Sharon looked around to make sure the house was company ready and was glad she'd done a little shopping the day before so that she would have food on hand when Donna arrived.

* * *

"I KNOW I told you this the last time I was here, but your house is simply gorgeous, Sharon," Donna exclaimed. "I love the way you've decorated it and the layout of the house has a really nice feeling to it."

"Thanks!" Sharon replied. "Having a good builder makes all the difference, too. Joseph really listened to what Tom and I wanted and has a pride in his work that shows. I wish Tom had lived long enough to see how it turned out."

She realized it was the first time she'd thought much about Tom in a while and felt a twinge of guilt.

"I'm sorry he couldn't be here, too. I'm sure he would have been as pleased with it as you are. But it seems like the Universe had other plans for you," she winked. "And now I want all the juicy details so that by the time I leave here I won't be embarrassing myself again acting like a mother hen!"

Donna's smile assured Sharon that she could relax on that account and would no longer have to feel like she was breaking curfew when she was with Hal.

"Let's get that pitcher of lemonade and sit out on the patio and I'll tell you the latest update but there's really not much to say beyond what I've already told you."

After they settled in under the shade of the patio umbrella, Sharon filled Donna in on her time with Hal the day before.

"And he's a perfect gentleman," she finished. "He's made it very clear he wants to give me space to be comfortable and not rush things."

Donna had sat quietly as Sharon told her about their date.

"It sounds wonderful, Sharon," she smiled reassuringly. "I hope things work out for you. It sounds like you're due for some gentlemanly attention after all you've been through with Tom's illness and I hope you're not feeling guilty that you're having a good time if that's what's on your mind. But as your new best friend forever, I hope I get to meet him soon. I promise I'll be good. Cross my heart," she said adding the hand gesture.

Sharon had to laugh at the serious expression on Donna's face.

"Then why do I feel like I'm a teenager again having my parents meet my first date?"

"Because that's what friends are for!" Donna laughed with her.

They spent the rest of the afternoon chatting about their gourd projects and discovered there were other crafts they both enjoyed doing. They were both amazed when Donna looked at her watch and discovered it was three o'clock.

"Oh, my goodness, where did the day go?! Here let me help you clean up the lunch dishes and then I need to head home."

They finished clearing up the dishes and putting food away and Sharon walked Donna out to the car in the warm afternoon sun.

"I'm not sure I'm ever going to get over how wonderful this is not to have to be living with cold and snow!"

"I know exactly what you mean, Sharon. I don't miss it in the least!" she agreed. "Thank you so much for inviting me to visit. Next time you'll have to come to see me. And I'm not kidding about getting to meet Hal but now it's because you've convinced me he truly is Prince Charming and I gave up on believing in him a *loooong* time ago!" she teased.

CHAPTER THIRTY-SEVEN

The morning's chill had dissipated as the sun warmed the air and it was apparent the day would be even warmer than normal for this time of year. Shy Dove had been working on a new weave pattern and was concentrating on the design to make sure she did not confuse the warp and weft. She hated having to take the weave out to start over. Her attention returned to her surroundings as she became aware of a commotion. People were gathering in the center of the village and she noticed that two men had arrived. At first she did not recognize the newcomers and her curiosity was piqued but that was soon replaced with dismay as their features came into focus.

"Nooo, it can't be," she cried out softly. "It's too soon. Broken Wing isn't supposed to be here for two more months."

Her mother startled her as she came up behind Shy Dove.

"What's all the commotion, Shy Dove?"

Shy Dove pointed to the crowd.

"It's Eagle Feather and Broken Wing. They've come back earlier than expected, haven't they, Mother? I thought it would be at least two months before they returned."

"I'd thought so, too," Singing Song replied.

"This doesn't mean that the wedding will be sooner, will it?" Shy Dove asked hoping the worry in her voice was not apparent.

"No, Shy Dove. The wedding will still take place in the summer after the next Maiden Blossoming Ceremony. We'd known that Broken Wing would be spending time with us before the wedding but we hadn't expected him to be here so soon."

Her mother sounded as confused as Shy Dove was which she thought might be a good thing. At least she shouldn't have to be worried about the wedding being sooner. She and Running Deer had been able to store most of what they would need but were still not ready. Running Deer had been training a puppy to carry supplies to help them on their journey. They had named him Shadow as he followed Running Deer everywhere.

"Come with me, Shy Dove. We should greet Eagle Feather and Broken Wing. Have you seen your father?"

The last thing Shy Dove wanted to do was have to greet Broken Wing but knew she couldn't refuse.

"I haven't seen him since breakfast. Should I try to find him and tell him they are here?" she asked hoping this would delay her facing Broken Wing and perhaps she could find Running Deer to let him know he had arrived earlier than expected. They would have much to discuss about when they would leave. They had hoped to be gone before Eagle Feather and Broken Wing returned.

"No, we should just go to greet them. I'm sure your father will find out soon enough and we don't want to show any disrespect to Eagle Feather and Broken Wing."

As they made their way to the crowd, Shy Dove looked around to see if she could spot Running Deer. They had nearly reached them when she spotted him at the fringes of the group. He looked in her direction and the expression on his face worried her. She hoped that no one else had seen the look of hatred he'd had as he watched Broken Wing. As usual, Broken Wing's arrogance was apparent as he appeared to both simultaneously expect and be dismissive of being the center of attention as though those giving it were not worthy of his presence. She and Running Deer exchanged worried glances and she smiled hoping to reassure him. Her attention was brought back as she heard her mother speak to her.

"Shy Dove, come, we need to make our greeting."

"Yes, Mother, I'm right behind you."

"Eagle Feather, Broken Wing, we are happy to see you return to our village," Singing Song turned to include Shy Dove in her greeting.

"Yes, welcome back to our village," Shy Dove directed her greeting to Eagle Feather.

"Thank you, Singing Song and Shy Dove. Our trading mission was more successful than we'd thought it would be so we were able to return earlier than expected. Broken Wing was anxious to return to prepare for the wedding, weren't you, Broken Wing?" he looked pointedly at Broken Wing as though to challenge him to disagree.

"Yes, Father, I was happy to have the trading go well and get back sooner. I'm very anxious to have the ceremony and begin married life," he leered in Shy Dove's direction.

She felt her repulsion again at the thought of being Broken Wing's wife but did her best to hide it. She looked in Running Deer's direction, worried that he might have heard Broken Wing and do something foolish. She could not see him anywhere in the crowd and was relieved that he was not there to hear Broken Wing's remark.

"Shy Dove is looking forward to the ceremony as well, aren't you, Shy Dove?" Singing Song was looking at Shy Dove with an expression that suggested she should have said something sooner in response to Broken Wing's remark.

Shy Dove struggled to think of something to say, not wanting to insult either her mother or Eagle Feather but was having diffi-culty to get any enthusiasm in her response.

"Yes, Mother, I have been thinking of how happy I will be to be a wife," she managed to get out. It was true, but she was not thinking of Broken Wing as she said the words. Her mother and Eagle Feather appeared to be happy with her response. Broken Wing did not seem to care whether she was sincere or not. His body language told her that he thought that she should be grateful to have him as her future husband.

Turtle Dove arrived and Shy Dove was relieved to have the attention taken from her as everyone turned at her greeting.

"Eagle Feather, Broken Wing, welcome back to our village. We were not expecting you so soon. Our apologies for not having a celebration ready for you but we will prepare for a feast this evening. How long will you be staying with us?"

"I will only be here a day or two and was hoping you might have food I could trade for before leaving. Broken Wing will stay with you now until the marriage ceremony. Our trading mission went very well so we were able to return sooner. I thought it best to have him here so that he and Shy Dove can become better acquainted and prepare for the ceremony. Broken Wing also needs to learn more of your village's customs since he will be living here with you after the wedding."

Once again Shy Dove had to lower her face to not betray her feelings. She was having all she could do to not run away to find Running Deer and tell him they should leave immediately even though they were not quite ready.

"Mother, why don't I go back to our house to start preparing for the feast? I can begin grinding corn for corn cakes if that would be alright?" she looked at Singing Song and Turtle Dove for their approval.

"Yes, Shy Dove, that is a very good idea," Singing Song replied and Turtle Dove nodded her approval.

Relieved to be able to leave, Shy Dove headed back toward

their house looking for Running Deer but not seeing him anywhere. She was startled by his voice whispering her name as she arrived at her house. He had hidden on the side where he could not be seen by anyone at the center of the village where everyone was gathered. She looked back to see if anyone was looking their way before going to meet him.

"Why are they here so soon?" Running Deer asked, the worry in his voice obvious.

"Eagle Feather said they had finished sooner than expected and they wanted to have Broken Wing here earlier to prepare for the wedding and to learn our customs," she replied. "I came back to grind corn for corn cakes so I could get away. Seeing Broken Wing look at me as he does made me feel unclean. Turtle Dove wants to have a feast tonight to welcome them back. Running Deer, can we leave sooner? I don't want to spend any more time with him than I must and I am afraid I will do something to displease him and that would embarrass and anger my parents."

"I wish we could, Shy Dove. I would leave tonight with you but we are not ready yet and Shadow is not ready. He needs a little more time to learn how to work with the travois to carry our supplies. Now that I know they are not going to have the ceremony sooner, I feel much better. I don't want to leave any sooner than necessary as we don't know what to expect as we go farther away. It will take us many days, maybe even an entire moon cycle to reach far enough away to not have anyone find us and make us return. It's better that we wait. You can do that, Shy Dove. You must—for us. To have the future together that we've dreamed of."

Shy Dove knew he was right and as long as they were still able to plan their departure together, she could wait.

"You're right, Running Deer," she smiled at him. "I can wait as long as I know we will be together. It will mean that we will have to be even more careful, though. There will be eyes

watching us. I should get in the house and begin grinding the corn. Mother will ask me why I don't have more done if she returns. I don't want her to know I've been speaking with you or she will ask why."

She kissed him lightly on the lips and hurried back inside her house to find the supplies for grinding the corn.

CHAPTER THIRTY-EIGHT

Sharon woke with a feeling of foreboding. She sensed the danger Shy Dove and Running Deer would be facing trying to prepare for their journey while Broken Wing was in their village. *It was just a dream*, she told herself but was not convinced. It had the texture of being real. She realized her body was tense from the feelings of dread she'd felt as she dreamed and shared Shy Dove's repulsion of Broken Wing. She lay in bed for longer than usual running it all through her mind and then got up to add it to her dream journal. Even after going out to the patio to soak up the morning sun, which was warming the temperature more each day as her time in Arizona hurried past, she felt chilled.

The phone rang breaking into her reverie. The noise of the ring was for once a relief and she was surprised to see Joseph's name on the caller ID.

"Joseph, good morning. What a nice surprise to hear from you," she said instead of just a hello.

She heard him chuckle as he said, "I'm guessing you either have caller ID or haven't told me about your psychic abilities."

"Well, you never know. After a visit to Sedona, I may have picked up some of the vortex energy," she replied.

"Sedona, eh? Have you been there recently?" he asked.

Sharon was confused as she felt almost as though she had betrayed him somehow.

"Yes, it was an impulse trip. Cabin fever, I guess. I wasn't even intending to go there but had to get out and just started driving. When I got past Phoenix, I realized I'd been wanting to go to Sedona but had been so busy with getting the house in order and settling in that I'd put it off and so figured, what the heck? *Very* unlike me. I think this place is growing on me in a good way."

"Well, good for you!" Joseph replied. "How's the gourd class going?"

"It's been a lot of fun and I've made a new friend. I think I may have mentioned that to you earlier," she said, feeling somewhat childlike as though she was reporting to an adult rather than a contemporary and wanting to take back the words as soon as she said them.

"Good for you," Joseph said. "The more you can get out and meet people, the more it will feel like home to you instead of just a vacation get-away."

Sharon was relieved that he'd taken her words in the spirit she'd intended.

"It feels like home already," she said, "but I know exactly what you mean and I'm hoping to get out more. I've never been one to have a lot of friends or be very socially outgoing but it's nice to have another woman to commiserate with."

She debated mentioning Hal but for some reason, didn't want to reveal that to Joseph although she couldn't put her finger on why.

"Have those tools helped?"

"Oh, yes, thank you so much for dropping those by. I need to get a few more and want to set up my craft studio. That may be on my agenda for today. How have you been?" she asked realizing she hadn't made her hospitality inquiries.

"Busy finishing up a project but things have slowed down with the economy so have a break before I need to start the next one. I was hoping you might be interested in going out to dinner again. If you're not busy, that is," the comment hanging in the air as a question.

Sharon hesitated just for a second before responding, "I'd love to, Joseph. When would be good for you?"

She realized that second's hesitation was about Hal. It wasn't as though they were an item, though, and neither of them had made any commitment to each other. And Joseph was a friend, she reminded herself. There hadn't been anything romantic between them. They'd gone from being professional associates to friends, but that's all it was. Why was she worried about accepting a dinner invitation? Friends…yes, even friends of the opposite sex…could go to dinner without it being anything more, she chided herself after she and Joseph had concluded their arrangements to meet the next night.

She finished her coffee and put it out of her mind as she made good on her plan to organize her craft room. She was anxious to work on that week's project but wanted to take the few extra minutes to get everything organized. It had been a while since she'd had to do homework but still felt that obligation to get it done on time. She surveyed her efforts and nodded in approval and gave herself an A+ for all she'd done.

As she was taking her bubble bath before bed, she sighed with pleasure at how her life was shaping up. Her morning's foreboding had been replaced with the feeling of contentment that was becoming the routine rather than the exception of her daily life. All of the stress of her work life and Tom's illness had finally left and she hugged herself as the happiness of being who and where she was permeated every inch of her body.

CHAPTER THIRTY-NINE

Shy Dove was busy grinding the corn when her parents returned.

"Thank you for offering to do this, Shy Dove. I'm pleased you are accepting your responsibilities so willingly. Broken Wing will be lucky to have you as his wife," Singing Song told her when she arrived.

Shy Dove's shoulders tensed but she smiled as she said, "Thank you, Mother. I'm happy to do this for you and Father. I wouldn't want to bring shame on either of you or have Eagle Feather be unhappy that he had made the wedding arrangements with you."

"You are a good daughter. We are always proud of you," her father told her as his face beamed with pride.

"Thank you, Father," she smiled back at him.

"We will need more corn," Singing Song said as she looked appraisingly at what Shy Dove had finished. "Let me help you. More hands will get the job done and this is hard work."

Shy Dove knew her mother's comment was not intended to criticize her efforts so was not offended.

"How much do you think we will need, Mother? Is there anything else I should do to help?"

"Turtle Dove has asked all the women to help so we will only need to make the corn cakes but if we are to get them done for the feast tonight, we will need to work most of the day," Singing Song replied.

Even though it was hard work, Shy Dove was relieved that she could spend most of the day in their house. The less time she would have to spend with Broken Wing, the happier she would be.

"Where will Broken Wing be staying before the wedding?" she asked as it suddenly occurred to her that she had not thought about that before.

"He will be a guest at Turtle Dove's home. She and Leaping Frog will be teaching him about our ways and preparing him for the wedding."

"Will she have time for that as well as the next Maiden Blossoming Ceremony?"

"Yes, there are only two girls who will be taking part in the ceremony this year so it will not take as much of her time and Leaping Frog will do most of the training for Broken Wing."

"Will I have to go for more preparations for the wedding as well?" Shy Dove asked, worried that it would mean having to be with Broken Wing.

"I will be able to teach you most of what you will need to know but we will need to make your wedding gifts. I hadn't planned to start those now but Broken Wing's arrival has reminded me that the time will be upon us soon so we should start tomorrow."

"Of course, Mother, I am happy to be with you. Turtle Dove can be scary when she is angry," Shy Dove added.

Singing Song smiled as she admonished Shy Dove. "Be respectful of your elders, Shy Dove."

Shy Dove smiled back as she replied, "Of course, Mother. But I am much happier to be with you."

The village gathered as the day came to an end. Tumbleweed and dry branches had been gathered for a bonfire and the smell of meat cooking filled the air. There was an assortment of meat, stews, and corn cakes for everyone to share. Although they had had little time to prepare, the women of the village had been able to put together a feast that everyone would enjoy and impress their guests. Even Turtle Dove looked pleased with the display of food.

Broken Wing and Eagle Feather were seated in a place of honor and Turtle Dove hovered over them, bringing them plates of food and drinks. Shy Dove reminded herself that she must appear to be happy for the occasion as part of the reason for their being here was her upcoming marriage. It meant, though, that her family would have to be seated near them. She made sure that she would be seated on the far side of her parents and with as much distance between her and Broken Wing as she could be without attracting attention. She looked around for Running Deer and saw him approaching with his family. His face was expressionless but she knew he must be having difficulty keeping it so. She knew he had seen her but had not acknowledged her presence. She turned away as she did not want to betray her feelings. She saw Squash Blossom and Sky Lark arriving, each carrying bowls of food.

"Mother, would it be alright if I go to help Squash Blossom and Sky Lark?"

Singing Song looked in their direction. "Yes, but make sure you come back to sit with us. It would be disrespectful to sit with them during the feast."

Shy Dove was disappointed as she had hoped she would be able to use that as an excuse to sit with them but had another idea and asked, "May they come to sit with us instead?"

Singing Song considered her request and then replied, "Yes, as long as it is alright with their parents and you must all remember to be polite and act as young women, not children."

"We will, Mother, I promise," Shy Dove kissed her mother's cheek and ran in their direction, happy to be away from the oppressive presence of Broken Wing.

"Squash Blossom, Sky Lark, can I help you?" she called out to them.

The girls smiled as they saw Shy Dove running toward them.

"This is so exciting, Shy Dove. You must be so happy about your wedding!" Sky Lark replied.

Shy Dove took one of the bowls Sky Lark had been carrying.

"Mother said you can both sit with us. Would you, please? I am nervous to be around Broken Wing and it would help to have you there to talk to." She hoped they would believe her nervousness was about the upcoming wedding although they all knew that Broken Wing could be violent when he became angry and that it often did not take much to set him off.

Sky Lark and Squash Blossom exchanged glances. Shy Dove was worried that they would refuse but their curiosity and excitement of having a feast to break the monotony of their daily routines got the better of them.

"I will need to ask my parents but I think they will agree," Squash Blossom replied.

"Mine, too," Sky Lark said.

After getting their parents' approval, the girls rejoined Singing Song, Black Bear and Little Bear. Shy Dove felt much better with having their company to deflect the attention that was being placed on her and it meant she would not have to communicate with Broken Wing if she was with them.

The crowd was growing and soon all the members of the village had gathered. The mood was joyous as there had not been a reason to gather for a feast in quite some time and the interruption of the monotony of the winter was a welcome diversion.

Much to her relief, the evening passed without incident and everyone returned to their homes at the end of the evening, their bellies full and spirits revived by the gathering. Shy Dove felt that perhaps her worries were unfounded and if this was an indication, she would be able to pass the time between now and when she and Running Deer could finish their preparations to leave without the fear she'd felt when Eagle Feather and Broken Wing first arrived.

CHAPTER FORTY

The aroma of something delicious wafted out as Joseph opened the door.

"Come on in. It's good to see you," Joseph said as he stood aside to let her in.

Without thinking Sharon gave him the one-cheek hug that had been her typical greeting of those she knew socially.

"Whatever that is you have cooking, I don't even have to taste it to know it's going to be delicious. What are the spices you've used? Oh, and hello, thanks for inviting me." She smiled as she realized she'd relinquished her social graces to the intoxication of the aroma.

"I don't do a lot of cooking but this chicken recipe is my specialty. The secret is in the marinade," he winked at her.

"Is this one of those secret recipes that you have locked in a vault or do you ever share it?"

"Why don't you ask me after you've had some. It may smell better than it tastes," he answered.

"It's a deal but I can't imagine it possibly could."

"How have you been? You still thinking you made the right decision to be a Southwest snowbird?" he asked.

"It's one of the best decisions I've ever made in my life," she answered without hesitation. "The climate and the vibe of this area has always suited me and I've known for years it would be the right move for me. Nothing's changed that."

"That's good to hear. I would have hated for you to go to all the trouble of building a house here only to find out you miss being back East."

"Are you kidding? Not in the least. Snow and cold were always something I just endured because I didn't feel I had a choice otherwise and had been looking forward to this. I know I shouldn't have been wishing my life away but there were times when I truly was counting down how long it would be before I could finally get here."

"Excellent. What can I get you to drink? I don't have a stocked liquor cabinet but I do have some beer or I'd put on a pot of coffee just before you got here that should be done now…"

"That would be perfect," Sharon interrupted before he could go on with the choice of beverages. "If I don't have at least one cup of coffee in the afternoon or evening, I'll be falling asleep by 8. I know it's an addiction but not one I'm willing to give up. Could be worse," she smiled.

"How do you take it?"

"Extra cream and I have my own stevia," she said somewhat embarrassed. "I know most people don't care for the taste but I've gotten used to it and would rather use that than the other artificial sweeteners."

"Whatever makes you happy, makes no difference to me," he smiled reassuringly. "Come on out to the kitchen and keep me company while I get the rest of dinner finished up. I hope you're hungry because I've got plenty."

"I didn't realize just how hungry I was until I smelled that chicken and now I'm famished."

"It won't be much longer but I can get you started with the salad."

"Not unless you're going to have some, too," she answered. "I can wait until you're able to eat with me."

"You sure?" he asked.

"Absolutely," she answered. "How's your new job going?" she asked, trying to take the focus in a different direction.

"The usual headaches with supplies not getting in on time, demanding owner, all the things that make being a contractor fun," he smiled.

"There must be something you like about it to keep you doing it all these years. And you're very good at it. Even with having to do it long distance, this was the easiest house build I've ever had and you're the biggest reason for that," she told him.

"That's what made it so easy," he winked at her to let her know he was teasing. "Now if I could just convince all the other homeowners to move out of state while the build was going on, I'd be a happy camper."

Sharon pretended to be offended. "I think it had a lot more to do with your professionalism, Joseph. Not all contractors would do as well as you to make sure things were done right if the owners weren't around. I always felt like you treated the job as though it was your own house you were building."

"Thanks, Sharon, and you're right, that is how I treat the jobs. When I turn the keys over, I want to feel like it's a house I would be proud to live in. It's what I've built my reputation on and it seems to work. Even during the slow times I've always had work and I think that's part of it."

"I think you're right. A contractor with a good word-of-mouth reputation is worth a lot more than a glitzy ad campaign."

Joseph finished up the side dishes for dinner and Sharon started to help him take them to the dining table.

"No, no," he protested. "You're my guest. You just take a seat and I'll have this all on the table—no problem."

She did as he asked even though it was hard for her to be

waited on but true to his word, he soon had all the food on the table.

"Did you ever wait tables? That was quite impressive how you managed all those," she asked.

"I did a little in high school to make some extra money, but decided I wasn't cut out for a career in the restaurant business," he answered.

They did the usual dinner small-talk and Sharon realized she'd eaten more than she intended but the chicken had tasted just as good as it smelled.

"The verdict is in, in case you didn't notice from all I ate, but if you are willing to share that recipe, I would love to have it. That is some of the best chicken I think I've ever eaten," she said appreciatively.

"Thanks--you've got it! I'll make a copy for you before you go," he answered. "I'm glad you liked it. Let me clear some of these dishes and then we can go sit in the living room where it's a little more comfortable."

"Can I help you?" she asked, knowing the answer.

"Nope. Just sit and relax. This won't take long."

He led the way into the living room and turned on the gas fireplace which lent a warm glow to the room.

"So tell me about this gourd class you're taking. What are you making?"

Sharon told him about the project and described the techniques she'd learned. "I'd dabbled with this hobby back home but was self-taught and it's made a real difference having the hands-on instruction. I'd always been a little afraid of the resin technique but now I've got ideas for several more projects once I finish this one. And meeting Donna has been great. It's nice to have a gal friend and we get each other," Sharon finished up feeling as though she was beginning to border on gushing in her enthusiasm.

"I think that's great," Joseph responded with a smile and the sincerity in his voice reassured Sharon that he was not patronizing her. "Tell me about your trip to Sedona."

Sharon hesitated just a moment and felt butterflies in her stomach. Was that about Hal and, if so, why did she feel that she shouldn't mention him? That was being silly, wasn't it? Why would Joseph care if she'd met someone? All those thoughts flew through her mind in a nano-second.

"Well, like I'd mentioned, it was all on a whim. I'd had a bad dream and just started driving to clear my head and before I knew it, I was well on my way in that direction so decided to keep going. I've never done anything like that before—I didn't have anything more than the clothes on my back but thought, what the heck? Be impulsive for once in your life, Sharon, and I have to tell you it felt good," she smiled still reveling in that feeling of having done something wild and crazy. For her, it had been.

Joseph smiled back at her. "Good for you! And what did you do once you got there?"

"I decided I'd like to hike the trail at Bell Rock so bought a few supplies and change of clothes because it was too late to go by then and knew I'd have to stay at least the night. I'd been there before so checked into the hotel I'd used then that's within walking distance. I met this really nice guy the next morning in the breakfast room and we hiked up the trail together and then the next day we drove over to the Grand Canyon. I'd never been there that time of year and although the weather is a lot nicer later in the season, there sure wasn't the problem of fighting any crowds!"

Joseph hadn't said anything but his expression made her wonder if she should have not said anything about Hal and decided she wouldn't tell him about their meetings in Tucson.

"Are you sure you should have trusted someone that quickly?" he asked with concern in his voice.

"You sound like Donna," she tried to be off-handed in her

response but she also felt annoyance. She was, after all, an adult and in charge of her own life or so she thought. "She was upset with me about trusting someone and cautioned me about the perils of potential serial killers."

"I'm sorry, Sharon. It's really none of my business but as a friend I don't want anything to happen to you."

"I do understand where you're both coming from but as a friend perhaps you could also trust me enough to give me credit for being capable to make decisions about who I can be with."

She was beginning to think her intuition about not mentioning this was justified. Who she was with was really none of his business after all.

"You're absolutely right. I apologize if I offended you and I don't want this evening to end on a sour note."

"Me either," she smiled to let him know she wasn't going to stay angry. "I value your friendship, Joseph, and want to get to know you better. I'm venturing into new territory with my life since Tom passed and trying to be independent. This is the first time in my life that I've done a lot of things and been my own person. It's a little scary for me but I'm finding I like being my own boss and don't want to fall back into the routine of letting others influence my decisions about how I live my life. I guess I overreacted."

Joseph was silent a moment. "No, I'm the one who did. That's something I always did with Susan and the kids—being overprotective, that is. I guess I just fell back into old patterns. I can't explain why I feel that way about you, too, but there's something there that makes me want to look out for you. It's meant with good intentions but it's not my place even as a friend."

Sharon studied his face, her own emotions confused at his words.

"Old habits are hard to break," was all she could come up with in response. "Let's agree we can stay friends and clear the air now that we have some of the boundary lines established." She smiled to reassure him she was ready to move on.

"Yes, ma'am," he smiled back at her. "Why don't I go find that recipe and make you a copy?"

"Good idea!" she responded, relieved to change subjects.

She stayed another half hour, mostly to not have the argument hang over them before leaving.

"Thanks for dinner and the recipe. Next time it's my treat!"

"That's good to hear that you're considering a next time."

"Of course. That's what friends do," she smiled.

"Have a good rest of the night, Sharon."

"You bet—it's been a good one already," she answered and headed home still trying to process all that had happened. She realized that it had struck a nerve she wasn't aware was so raw. It was true that Tom had been overprotective at times and she had often resented it, but this was something more. Something older. It was lurking in the corners of her memory but just out of reach and she finally gave up trying to figure it out. She decided she wasn't going to lose any sleep over trying to psychoanalyze what had triggered her responses to his remarks, at least not tonight. They were still friends which was the main priority, and the rest could sort itself out later.

CHAPTER FORTY-ONE

It had been easier than Shy Dove had feared to avoid Broken Wing over the next few days with all the activity in the village—people trading goods with Eagle Feather and celebrations every evening made it easy to blend into the background--but once Eagle Feather left, she could no longer remain distant without drawing attention. She had purposely kept away from Running Deer during this time but he had spent little time in the village. She was sure this was to have as little chance as possible of having a confrontation with Broken Wing. Their futures depended on maintaining a semblance of civility so as not to arouse any suspicions. He had used the excuse that he needed to hunt to have food for the evening feasts but Shy Dove knew that he had spent far more time away from the village than was necessary. In spite of his youth, Running Deer had become one of the best hunters in the village. He had taken Shadow with him and Shy Dove suspected that Running Deer was using the time to train the puppy to carry small packs so he would be ready to carry heavier ones once they left. They had first thought they could have Shadow use a travois for their supplies but realized that would leave a trail that would be easy to spot for even an inexperienced tracker, so Shy Dove had sewn bags with several pockets that could be tied to the dog. They were small to accommodate his size but she would be making larger ones for when he reached his adult growth and could carry heavier loads.

Shy Dove was deep in thought about how to construct the larger bags to accommodate the most supplies possible without making it too heavy for Shadow. In addition to slowing him down if the load was too much for him, she did not want to injure him. She didn't notice that she had walked right into the path that Broken Wing was taking to Turtle Dove's home.

"Watch where you're going, wife," he said with a noticeable tone of derision.

Startled, Shy Dove looked up to see Broken Wing's face looking down at her with an unmistakable expression of distaste. She lowered her head so that he would not see her equally matched expression hoping he would think this was instead a mark of subservience toward him.

"I'm sorry, Broken Wing, I was thinking about my weaving project and did not realize you were there."

"I am here and it would be best for you to be aware of my presence. A good wife learns that serving her husband is her purpose in life. And bearing him sons," he gave her an appraising look that told her that was all he was really interested in.

She restrained herself from replying that she would never bear him sons because he would never have the opportunity. She kept her face lowered and made her voice take on a humble tone as she replied, "Of course, Broken Wing. I understand my responsibilities as a wife."

He studied her for a moment as though making sure she was not mocking him before responding, "Be sure that you do," and continuing on his way to Turtle Dove's home.

Shy Dove let out the breath she had been holding and took a quick look at his retreating back feeling all the hatred inside her directed toward him. Fearing he might turn around and see her, she turned and ran toward her house, tears rolling down her cheeks as her frustration at her situation overflowed.

We must hurry with our preparations, she thought to herself. I cannot possibly marry that arrogant excuse for a man.

She resolved to find Running Deer later that day to check on their progress and see if she could convince him to leave even earlier. Whatever it would take to help make that happen, she would do as she did not think she could maintain her false attempts to convince Broken Wing she was happy to become his wife over the next several months before the planned wedding ceremony. Feeling somewhat better thinking about seeing Running Deer again, she slowed to a walk, wiped away her tears and resumed thinking of the pack she would make for Shadow.

Running Deer found her instead not long after as she was weaving outside her home.

"Good morning, Shy Dove, how are you today?" he asked in a voice meant to carry inside her house in case anyone was there to overhear his approach.

She looked up, startled at first as she had been concentrating on the weave pattern and had not heard him approach. His hunting training had taught him how to move with no sound. He nodded his head in the direction of her house letting her know that she should not say anything she did not want to be over-heard. She nodded in response letting him know she understood.

"Hello, Running Deer, how are you today? And how are you Shadow?" she beckoned to the dog who first looked up at Running Deer and when he nodded his permission, then came over to Shy Dove and licked her face making her laugh as she scratched under his ears and around his neck.

"I think he is doing very well," she laughed. He has grown so much since you first got him, Running Deer. He must be nearly full-grown by now."

"He has grown into a big dog and will be a lot of help to me

with carrying back meat from hunts so that I can take even larger loads. Have you thought about that pack I asked if you could make for him?" Running Deer's eyes met hers and once again understanding passed between them. She would now be able to make the pack without having to worry about being asked why she was doing so.

"I was thinking about that this morning. How many pockets do you think I should sew into it and how big should they be?" she asked following his lead.

"I don't think he will be growing much more although he may get heavier. Can you make the ties long enough so that they can be adjusted but the pockets can hang down to the bottom of his stomach so they won't drag or be in the way when he lays down?"

"Of course, let me get a string to measure how long that will be and I can begin working on it right away. Do you want all the pockets to be the same size or should I have some big and some small?"

"Yes, some big and some small would be perfect," he responded. "I have some deerskin I have cured that I can give you. Do you think you could come by my house later to see if it would work?"

"I will ask my mother, but I think that would be okay. I have already finished the chores she asked me to do. Let me go ask her now," she began to get up to go inside her house when her mother came out.

"Hello, Running Deer and hello, Shadow," Singing Song greeted them.

Shadow once again looked up at Running Deer for permission to go to Singing Song. Running Deer nodded and he trotted over to Singing Song to receive more neck scratches.

"You have trained him well, Running Deer," Singing Song told him.

"It was easy to do. He is a very smart dog and eager to

learn. I have asked Shy Dove if she could make a pack for him to carry supplies and bring back meat from hunts. I have some leather at my house that I wanted to show her to see if it would work. Would that be alright?" he asked.

Singing Song looked at Shy Dove but did not see anything to be suspicious of in her expression.

"Yes, that would be alright," she replied.

Shy Dove made sure not to let her joy show on her face as she asked, "Would it be alright to go now, Mother? I have finished all my chores and I could use some time to move around a bit. My legs were becoming stiff from sitting at the loom."

"Just don't be too long," Singing Song replied and headed back into the house.

Shy Dove's legs were a little stiff and she stretched as she got up, happy to be with Running Deer and away from the loom for a while, being sure to take the string she had used to measure Shadow with her.

"That was very clever of you, Running Deer," she told him as they walked toward his house. "I was trying to think of how I would explain making the pack to Mother."

"Sometimes it's easier to not arouse suspicion by having your deception be visible," he replied.

She looked at him wondering how he had become so wise.

"That makes a lot of sense," she replied. "How is Shadow doing with the training?"

"He is very smart and is a strong dog so has had no problem at all. I want to get him used to heavier loads, though, as I don't think we will have much time. We will have to leave earlier even though we're not as ready as I would like. You're right that we don't have to have as much as I thought at first but we have enough to get us started."

"How much longer do you think we'll need to wait, Running Deer? I don't think I can be civil to Broken Wing for much

longer," she shivered in disgust thinking of her conversation with him that morning.

"Has he been bothering you, Shy Dove?" he asked and his expression worried her.

"Not really," she answered hoping to assure him she was fine. "I have mostly been able to avoid him but now that Eagle Feather is gone, it won't be as easy. I almost walked into him this morning as I did not see him at first. I was thinking about how to make the pack and all of a sudden he was just there on the path. He was his usual unpleasant self but I'm okay."

Running Deer's scowl worried her and she thought her response had upset him.

"Please do not do anything, Running Deer," she begged. "We must put up with him for now. Just remember that soon we will be away from him and will be able to be together—forever."

His expression changed and he smiled at her, his love for her showing on his face.

"I can't wait."

CHAPTER FORTY-TWO

*S*haron appraised her house one more time, wanting everything to be perfect. The flowers were in full bloom and just seeing the array of vivid hues of blues, orange, red, and yellow with a touch of white here and there to contrast made her smile. The fruit trees were doing well and the irrigation system was working just as advertised.

"I am truly blessed," she thought and felt gratitude for her life and how she was living it. It hadn't been easy getting to this point but the challenges along the way were what had brought her to where and whom she was.

It was almost time for Hal to arrive and she was ready. She'd done her prep work earlier so that all she would have to do was serve it and had some cheese and crackers on hand to nosh on before the meal. She didn't want to have him come through the door and rush straight to dinner. He might enjoy some time to transition from the trip and it would be an opportunity to break the ice after he arrived. Not that that seemed to be a problem between them.

The doorbell rang and she checked her watch—still half an hour before the time Hal was expected to arrive. Her brow furrowed as she walked toward the door wondering who it might be and was pleasantly surprised to see Hal standing there. *Thank goodness I got an early start,* she thought as she opened the door.

"Welcome to my humble abode," she smiled as she let him in. "Did you have any trouble finding it?"

"Nope. You gave great directions," he returned her smile. "It's a gorgeous home from what little I've seen."

"Well, let me give you the tour. Can I get you something to drink first? I made some sun tea earlier or there's beer, water, coffee…"

"Sun tea. I haven't had that in years," he answered.

"Do you like it plain or sweetened?"

"Plain would be great."

"Coming right up. The kitchen's right over here as you can see," she smiled, realizing that with her open concept house the kitchen was in plain sight.

"What's with the greenhouse and all these plants inside?" he asked.

"There is a gray water recapture system that irrigates the planters and this way I can have some vegetables along with flowers inside the house and don't have to worry about any bugs or critters getting into them. And it's on a timer so that when I'm not here, the backup watering system can kick in. I'm considering coming back in November or maybe even October depending on how early it starts getting cold in Maine so will get more benefit out of it than I did this year but this was a learning experience to make sure the system worked and so far I'm pleased with it."

He nodded in approval. "Sounds like you've thought it all through."

"It all sounded good on paper but you know how it is sometimes when it comes to putting it into practice."

"I do indeed," he replied.

She got them both a glass of tea and they continued their tour. She explained the process she was using to decorate her current gourd project and then suggested they go out to the patio.

"No bedroom?" he asked in a teasing tone.

Sharon blushed in spite of herself. She'd debated earlier whether to show him the bedroom as part of the house tour and had decided that might be best to avoid.

Hal laughed as he saw her response. "I'm just teasing you, Sharon. I promised to take it slow and I'll be true to my word. A perfect gentleman," he assured her.

She rolled her eyes as she tried to regain her composure.

"Uh huh, a perfect gentleman asking a lady where her bedroom is?" she half-joked in response.

"I'm sorry, I really didn't mean to make you uncomfortable. Forgive me?"

She took her time responding not wanting to be too eager to let him off the hook.

"This time," she answered smiling, "but I may have to put you on probation."

"Probation, huh? Sounds serious," he pretended to be taking this seriously, too.

"Could be. We'll have to see how you behave the rest of the night."

"Yes, ma'am. I'll be good, promise, cross my heart," and he did so. "Boy scout honor," he added and held his hand up in the familiar three-finger salute.

Sharon was enjoying their light-hearted banter. It was good to be flirting again and she began to relax, her earlier nervousness melting away.

"Come on, then, I guess I can trust you—for now," she smiled. "The patio is out here."

"I like what you've done with it," Hal complimented. "It's relaxing and not too girly."

"I mean that in a good way," he quickly added as he saw Sharon's expression.

She broke out laughing. "I owed you one," she teased. "I know what you mean…and I'm not offended," she added. "I'm glad you like it. Have a seat and I'll be right back with the cheese and crackers. I thought we could just relax before eating dinner…unless you're starving and I can get that started right away?"

"Cheese and crackers would be great," he answered.

She returned with the appetizers and they chatted amiably as she answered his questions about the gardens and the features of the house. Sharon checked her watch and was surprised to find that an hour and a half had already passed.

"Oh my goodness, I had no idea it had gotten so late," she exclaimed. "I'd better get dinner out. It won't take long--I have it nearly all done."

"Can I help you with anything?" Hal asked.

"If you could bring in the dishes, that would be great," she replied. "I was planning to have dinner inside but if you'd like to eat out here, that would be okay, too. It's still warm."

"Inside is fine. That way we won't have to bring out any more dishes."

The dinner turned out as she'd hoped and Hal at least seemed to enjoy it, if having second helpings was a guide. He helped her clean up and accepted her offer for coffee in the living room. He offered to start a fire and she was glad she'd taken him up on it as the ambience of the fire's glow helped even more as they sat side by side on her couch, music playing softly in the background.

"There's nothing as relaxing and hypnotic as a fire."

"I know just what you mean," Hal agreed. He turned her face toward his and gently kissed her lips. And then more deeply as she responded to his touch. Hal broke the embrace and looked into her eyes, still cupping her cheek with his hand.

"You're in control, Sharon. I won't push you into something you're not ready for."

"My body is saying yes," she smiled, "but my emotions are giving *me* mixed signals, so I can understand why you might not know how fast to go." She hesitated, trying to decide how she wanted to handle this. "It's just that it's been so long since I've been in this situation. I know I keep saying that, but it's what's confusing me. It hasn't been that long since Tom passed and a part of me feels that I'm being disloyal to his memory."

"I understand and that's why I want to let you be ready at your own speed. It won't be easy, but I can wait. I know we haven't known each other long, but I know you're worth waiting for."

"Thank you, Hal. I really appreciate that. I have to admit I'm afraid you'll think I'm acting like a teenager, giving mixed signals."

"Not at all," he assured her. He kissed her again lightly this time.

Sharon could sense Ms. Judgmental hovering in the background waiting to pounce if she made the wrong move. But what was the wrong move for her? She didn't feel any closer to an answer. Best to sleep on it and not make a decision in the heat of the moment, though.

Hal stayed another hour before checking his watch and saying he should head back to Tucson.

"Thank you for dinner, great companionship, and the house tour," he told her as she walked him to the door. "I'll call you tomorrow. I can't wait to see you again."

"It's been my pleasure," she answered. "And I want to see you soon, too."

He smiled and bent to kiss her.

"We'll talk tomorrow then."

"Absolutely," she responded.

She watched as he pulled down the driveway and headed to bed, not realizing she was smiling. It had been a wonderful night and she'd already decided that she didn't need the night to sleep on it. She was ready.

CHAPTER FORTY-THREE

Shy Dove was concentrating on the leather Running Deer had given her to determine the best layout before cutting any of the pieces. She didn't want to waste any of the material and now that they were planning to leave earlier, there wouldn't be time to redo it if she did. She jumped as she heard Broken Wing's voice behind her.

"What are you doing, Shy Dove?" he asked in a tone that did not sound friendly.

She looked around to see him staring at her.

"Shouldn't you be weaving blankets instead of whatever it is you're doing? If you expect to be a wife of mine, you will need to earn your keep and those few blankets you made while my father and I were gone are not enough."

Her body tensed and she resisted the urge to tell him to mind his own business, she was not his wife yet—nor would she ever be if she and Running Deer were successful. Not if, she thought, when they were successful because they must be.

"Running Deer asked me to make a pack for Shadow that he could use when they are hunting," she answered as civilly as she

could manage. "My mother gave me permission to make it, so I am working on that now. I have another blanket nearly done and will work on that as soon as I cut the pieces for the pack."

He moved so quickly she did not anticipate his actions as he grabbed her arm and pulled her to her feet.

"Do not argue with me or disobey me, Shy Dove," he snarled, his face distorted making him even uglier to her than she had ever thought of him. "No wife of mine will be allowed to talk back to me." He dragged her by her arm to her loom and pushed her down to the ground. "This is where you should be, not doing favors for the likes of Running Deer. Favors will not make me rich. Now get back to your weaving. If you have time when you're done, you can work on Running Deer's pack, but making me blankets to trade comes first. Do you understand?"

She fought back her tears. There was no way she would give him the satisfaction of knowing he'd made her cry or that she was submitting to him.

"I understand you very well, Broken Wing," she replied but her meaning was clear that she was not agreeing to his intent. "I will speak to my mother about this. I am not your wife now and it is my parents I obey, not you."

She met his eyes rather than lowering her head, further letting him know that he had not bullied her as he had meant to do. He stared back at her for a moment longer before turning and stalking off toward Turtle Dove's house.

It was only then that Shy Dove let the tears fall. She would speak to her mother about this, but she was afraid that Singing Song would take Broken Wing's side in order not to make trouble. Shy Dove knew that her mother did not want anything to happen to upset the wedding plans. Maybe her father would be a better choice to speak with. In the meantime, though, she was determined not to do anything to please Broken Wing and she did not care if he came back and found her working on the pack--

that was what she was going to do. When she returned to the leather, it all fell into place and she instantly saw how she should cut the pieces from the fabric. She was more hopeful and thanked the Earth Mother, feeling this was a sign that everything would be alright and that being with Running Deer was her destiny.

CHAPTER FORTY-FOUR

"Good for you, Shy Dove," Sharon said aloud as she opened her eyes. *But watch out for Broken Wing—he doesn't like being challenged,* she thought and realized she *hadn't* spoken that aloud, as though the threat from the dream world she'd been living in was a real and present danger.

Is that what I've been doing? she thought.

It's just too coincidental that they're coming to me chronologically like I'm watching a movie of Shy Dove and Running Deer's life, she reasoned.

She entered this latest dream into her journal and was still musing about its possible implications when the phone's ringing brought her out of her reverie.

"Hello, Donna," she answered as she noted the caller ID name of Donna Mackenzie.

"Good morning, yourself," Donna greeted her. "Sorry, I know I should have waited until a little more respectable hour to call but I've got a dead cat here."

"You've *what?!*" Sharon asked afraid of what Donna's response might be.

"Not literally. Sorry that lost in translation—as in curiosity killed the cat," Donna reassured her.

"Ohhh, thank goodness," Sharon breathed easier. "You'll have to forgive me. My brain isn't firing on all cylinders yet. I just woke up and haven't had my coffee boost."

"Well, go get that and give me a call back when you're fully awake."

"Will do, give me about an hour so I can shower and get dressed, too."

"Whenever you're ready. I've got nothing on my calendar for today so will be right here," Donna answered.

After a long shower, Sharon felt more like herself. She'd thought about how much she wanted to share with Donna about her dinner with Hal as she knew that was the reason she'd called. There really wasn't that much to share, though. He'd been a perfect gentleman and it had been a lovely evening—nothing that exciting or titillating to tell. That was somewhat of a relief, though. There was nothing she felt she had to hide and could be completely honest—this time, she added. That might not be the case the next time, though, she thought to herself and smiled at the possibility.

She returned Donna's call and after telling her about her evening with Hal, turned the conversation to their gourd projects. Donna seemed disappointed not to have had more juicy tidbits but didn't press the issue, for which Sharon was grateful.

"All this talk about the projects has gotten me motivated to work on it, so think I'll let you go for now," Sharon told Donna. "If I don't hear from you before then, I'll see you at class Monday. Oh, wait, not this Monday. I'd forgotten we won't have a class this week. The next Monday then?"

"Sounds good," Donna answered. "Want to meet me for dinner before class?"

"Sure—how about that same restaurant we ate at last time? It's close so we don't have to worry about finding another parking space," Sharon replied.

"Perfect. I'll meet you there…about five o'clock?"

"That should work. See you then," Sharon hung up anxious to get to the gourd project as she hadn't been saying that just to get Donna off the phone.

She'd decided to try a resin inlay which she'd avoided in the past both because it was a more complex technique and because the fumes from the resin had always bothered Tom. She donned her respirator, turned on the fan and opened a window, and was just about to mix the resin compound when the phone rang again.

Annoyed, Sharon looked at the caller ID to decide if she would answer or let it go to voicemail. Her stomach did a flip-flop as she saw it was Hal.

"Good morning," she answered trying to sound casual.

"Not without you with me," he answered and groaned audibly. "Forget I said that….*please*! Could I possibly sound any more smarmy?" he asked and she could tell he was smiling.

"No, no I don't think you could," she answered laughing.

"It just came out of my mouth before I could stop myself," he replied laughing along with her.

"Let's start over then and pretend it never happened."

"Okay. Good morning, Sharon. How are you today?"

"I'm doing well, Hal. How are you?"

"That's almost as bad. We sound like we're business associates, not in a relationship."

"Is that what this is? I mean, is that how you feel about what this is?" she asked.

"I do and I hope you feel that way, too."

She thought for a moment before responding. "I do. It's a little scary but in a good way."

"I know what you mean. I've dated a lot more than you have recently but this feels different."

"That makes me feel better. My feelings are nearly healed but still a little raw. I wasn't expecting to be dating so soon so this is all confusing to me," she told him.

"I promise I won't take advantage of you, Sharon," Hal reassured her again.

"Well then, glad that's settled." The seriousness in his voice made her a little edgy and she found herself wanting to change the subject. "So, what's on your agenda for today?"

"Have a little business to take care of but nothing that will take that long. How about you?"

"I had just started working on my gourd project. I'd been putting it off because I was afraid of messing up the resin. I finally realized that was just being silly. If I mess up, I just start again and I can practice on some scrap pieces to make sure I have it mixed right. Worrying about it isn't going to get it done or help me learn how to do it."

"Good attitude!" Hal told her. "I'll let you go then. I just wanted to hear your voice."

"I'm glad you called," Sharon told him, deciding not to take him to task for crossing into smarm territory.

"Me, too. Talk to you later?" It was a question.

"I'd like that. How about I call you this evening after dinner?"

"Can't wait. Talk to you later."

She hung up, putting the phone back on the table and staring at it for a few seconds as though trying to stay connected with Hal.

Silly woman! she heard Ms. Judgmental. *Acting like a schoolgirl. You're going to get hurt if you're not careful.*

Maybe, Sharon answered, *but I'll never know if I don't take a chance. Isn't that what this move is about? Living life on different terms? On* my *terms,* she emphasized.

Ms. Judgmental was silent but the silence was its own response as the disapproval was palpable.

Sharon chose to ignore it and returned to her gourd project, determined to not let that best her either.

CHAPTER FORTY-FIVE

The hide Running Deer had was perfect for the carrier and Shy Dove was anxious to begin sewing it together. She'd used an old blanket to make a pattern so she wouldn't waste the hide and after a few changes had come up with what she thought would work best. Humming to herself as she became absorbed in her work, she didn't hear Broken Wing come up behind her.

"What is that you're making?" he asked, his tone demanding.

Shy Dove startled and jabbed her finger with the needle making a drop of blood rise to the surface. Without thinking she put her finger in her mouth before responding to Broken Wing which gave her a little extra time to think of a response. Running Deer's words about telling the truth to hide a deception came back to her.

"I am making the pack for Shadow. As I told you before, Running Deer needs a way to carry more meat back from his hunts and wants to train Shadow to do that for him. He asked if I would make a pack with pockets and that is what I am doing now."

She tried to hide the annoyance she felt and hoped it did not come through. As much as she would like to let Broken Wing know that she did not like him or feel a need to obey him, it would be far too dangerous to do so for many reasons.

Broken Wing did not immediately respond but looked over the pieces that were laid out as though trying to assemble them in his mind. He nodded his head in approval as it came together.

"That is very clever, Shy Dove. Did you come up with the design?" he asked.

She watched him warily, not sure if his compliment held hidden meanings.

"Running Deer told me what he wanted and I made some suggestions for changes, so not all by myself, no," she responded.

His face darkened at the mention of Running Deer and she held her breath waiting for his anger to explode but he quickly hid his displeasure.

"I look forward to seeing it when it is finished. This could be a valuable item for trading." He nodded his head at her in dismissal and walked back toward Turtle Dove's and his--at least until their marriage—home.

Shy Dove let out her breath audibly and fingers shaking, tried to resume her work.

"Stop and breathe," she whispered to calm herself, "or you will poke your finger with the needle again and have blood all over the hide." After taking a few deep, slow breaths she felt better and her fingers had stopped shaking. Absorbed in her work once again, the pieces began to take shape as she had envisioned them and she sat back to admire her work.

"I think this will work well," she said aloud and felt excitement return as she realized how much easier it would make their journey and hoped that Running Deer was right that they could leave sooner. "The sooner, the better," she thought and went

back to her sewing, resolved to finish the pack before the day was done.

CHAPTER FORTY-SIX

The gourd had turned out quite well if she did say so herself. The resin had been tricky to work with but after a few practice runs, she'd found the right combination to create the consistency she needed. It would have to harden before she could go on to the next step of sanding it and her stomach was complaining in rumbling growls that she could almost feel as well as hear now that her attention was not focused on the gourd. She stretched her arms and arched her back and heard the familiar but satisfying pop as her spine realigned itself. She made a sandwich and took it out to the patio to enjoy the sunshine feeling a sense of peace and accomplishment. She let out a sigh as she thought about how great it was to finally have what she'd been dreaming about for years—the time to do a hobby, not dealing with cold temperatures and snow, being financially secure—life was good! Her thoughts went to Tom and realized she felt more at peace with that as well. She still missed him but she knew she'd turned a corner in her grieving process and was ready to let him be a memory of a different phase of her life and was not feeling the guilt of going on without him.

"I'll always love you, Tom. I'm glad we had our time together," she said, her voice almost a whisper.

She looked around at the desert landscape, now changing from its winter brown with hints of spring's soft shades of green breaking through in the vegetation. She sighed again, contentment filling her every pore.

"Life can't get much better than this," she said as she raised her glass of water in salute.

Her mind immediately went to Hal and she wondered if the Universe was telling her it could. She smiled at that thought and realized she was very much looking forward to their call later.

"What to do? What to do?" she said as her thoughts rolled from one possibility to another as to how to spend her afternoon. She felt almost decadent at the idea of having the luxury of not *having* to do anything if she chose not to. This was exactly what she'd hoped retirement would be. She smiled as she gathered up her now empty dishes and returned them to the kitchen and their new spot in the dishwasher. She looked around the house deciding whether it needed a touch-up but it passed muster. The book she'd left on the coffee table the night before grabbed her attention and the decision of what to do was made. Her next challenge of the day was deciding where to spend her afternoon reading. It was not late enough in the year that it would be too hot outside even at this time of day, and the sunshine beckoned her to take advantage of it. She hesitated at the dishwasher debating whether to take her glass back out to refill with water or to take a clean one before awareness....or Ms. Judgmental?...convinced her that she was being silly and she took a clean one from the cupboard.

Hedonist! she heard in her head and giggled in spite of herself not sure if it was Ms. Judgmental she was laughing at or herself for even thinking that.

She settled in on the comfy chaise lounge and put up the sun umbrella to provide shade, applied a liberal amount of sunscreen on her exposed skin, and wiped her hands on the napkin she'd brought with her. The story was good but the warmth and quiet, broken only by the sound of insects and an occasional bird, soon lulled her into a deep relaxation and her eyes insisted upon closing in spite of her best efforts to keep them open. Her head began to nod and she surrendered to her body's demand for sleep.

CHAPTER FORTY-SEVEN

*T*he following month had passed quickly for Shy Dove. She'd finished the pack for Shadow and Running Deer was already using it to train the puppy who was now full-grown. Shadow was a quick learner and had adapted to the contraption with only a passing curiosity. Once he had sniffed the pack and discovered it was not something he could eat, he'd allowed Running Deer to fasten it to him without resistance and had learned to carry heavy loads which were added a little at a time to get the canine used to the feel of it on his body and adapt his gait to compensate for the added bulk.

Shy Dove had another project she was working on which she had kept secret from Running Deer. She'd found a spot where she could work away from the village unseen by prying eyes. While Running Deer was tall and lean, but muscular from hunting, Broken Wing was several inches shorter and had a barrel shaped chest making him broader through his torso. Shy Dove knew that if anyone had seen what she was making they would realize that the clothing she was making would not have been for Broken Wing. Even though they would not be able to have a marriage ceremony at their village, Shy Dove had decided that *she would make them both wedding garments and that once they had arrived at their final destination, they could have their own ceremony. The deer skins had been softened and the fur scraped so that the leather was supple and smooth, soft against the skin. She'd managed to save a number of beads and shells traded for bits of cloth she'd woven. She had told her mother that she was going to use them for her wedding dress—another of those truths within lies. She was pleased with how the garments had turned out. The breeches for Running Deer had been easy as she did not plan to adorn them in any way and she was now working on the tunic. She would have liked it to be more decorative but it took much more of the tiny beads than she had first realized to create the designs she'd had in mind. Her brow was furrowed deep in thought with the tunic laid out on the ground in front of her, rearranging the beads in her mind to create the final pattern before sewing them on and once again did not hear Broken Wing as he approached her. She jumped as she heard his voice behind her and snatched up the tunic to try to keep him from seeing it.*

"What is that you are making, Shy Dove?" he asked in a demanding tone that let her know she would have to answer carefully to not arouse suspicion.

She composed her face before turning around and looking up at him. The sun was behind him and she squinted her eyes against the glare, making it that much more difficult to read the expression on his face.

"It is supposed to be a surprise, Broken Wing," she answered hoping she could avoid having to show him the tunic.

"A surprise? For who? And why are you hiding out here with it?" he pressed.

"It is a wedding tunic," she answered, again hoping he would misinterpret her evasiveness and think it was because the surprise was for him. "I was trying to make sure you did not see it," she said in a voice that was calmer than she felt. Her insides

were clenched in fear that he would see how nervous she was in spite of her even tone.

He looked into her eyes without saying anything more and she thought he had believed her. Just as she was about to relax, he grabbed her hair and pulled her up at the same time snatching the tunic away from her as she'd without thinking raised her arm to try to remove his hand from her hair and in doing so loosened her hold on it. He released her with a little shove away from him and shook out the garment to inspect it. His eyes took in the design but she could see what he was thinking and as though in confirmation of her thoughts, held the tunic up against his body. It was obvious that the garment would not fit his broad frame.

His eyes narrowed and he threw the tunic back at her and it landed on the ground before she could catch it. She began to stoop down to pick it up and her hair fell forward covering her eyes so that she felt rather than saw as his hand came down and slapped her hard enough to make her fall to the ground on top of the tunic. Her ear rang from the force of the blow and she raised her hand to cover it instinctively. He bent down and grabbed it away with one hand tight around her wrist and struck the other side of her face with his other hand making her cheek sting and black dots appear before her eyes as she blinked both in surprise and pain.

"You thought you could fool me?" he yelled as he yanked her to her feet and began to shake her hard enough to make her teeth chatter together. "This is for Running Deer, isn't it?" he continued to rant and his voice was even louder.

She tried to pull away from him to escape but his hold on her wrists was too strong. She began to fear for her life and was about to scream for help when suddenly he released his hold. Blinking and shaking her hair out of her eyes, she was surprised to see he was no longer directly in front of her. She blinked again and saw Running Deer holding Broken Wing with his left hand

and raising his right fist to punch him. Broken Wing was as star-tled as Shy Dove by Running Deer's sudden appearance and had not had time to begin any defense before feeling Running Deer's fist shatter into the side of his face and falling to the ground clutching his face in pain.

"Are you alright, Shy Dove?" Running Deer asked as he left Broken Wing to check on her.

"I'm fine, Running Deer," she answered but her attention was diverted to a sudden movement behind him as Broken Wing lurched to grab Running Deer. She did not have time to cry out but he had seen her eyes move in that direction and was able to step aside taking Shy Dove with him.

The momentum of his movement carried Broken Wing forward into the empty space that had been occupied by Running Deer and Shy Dove and he stumbled but did not fall. He whirled around to face them, hatred obvious on his face. Shy Dove moved closer to Running Deer for protection as he gathered her in his arms and gently moved her behind him standing taller as he did so. She could feel the strength in his body as he straightened and prepared himself for further battle with Broken Wing if it was necessary.

"Go now, Broken Wing," he said between clenched teeth. "Leave before I injure you even more. And if you ever lay a hand on Shy Dove again, I will kill you." His tone left no doubt that he meant what he said.

"You will regret this, Running Deer," Broken Wing threat-ened as he glared back at him, but turned and walked back toward the village.

Running Deer and Shy Dove watched as he walked away until he was out of sight before Running Deer turned and held Shy Dove in his arms as she began to sob and shake violently as the shock of what had just happened overtook her. He kissed the top of her head and held her tight—and safe—in his arms letting her emotions run their course.

"What are we going to do, Running Deer?" she asked as she looked up at him, tears still running down her cheeks, but her sobbing had stopped.

"It will depend on what Broken Wing does," he answered. "He may not wish to admit that he struck you or that I was able to get the better of him. And if he holds his tongue, we will have a little more time but we can't delay leaving much longer."

"We're ready, though, aren't we?" she asked. "Even if we don't have as much as you would like, we have enough to get us started, don't we?" she asked hopefully. "I don't want anything to happen to you because of this."

"Don't worry, Shy Dove. I can protect myself and I will always protect you," he answered and the confidence in his tone reassured her.

"I believe you, Running Deer, but Broken Wing is a horrible man and I don't trust him."

"We will be alright," he said, his voice again sounding confident and reassuring. He held her closer and kissed her gently and her fears melted in the safety of his embrace.

CHAPTER FORTY-EIGHT

*S*haron woke as a shiver that had nothing to do with the temperature passed over her.

"Be careful, you two," she said aloud.

It's just a dream she heard in her head.

"Is it?" she responded. *Or, should I say* was *it?* she asked herself contemplating the possibility.

She'd known for some time that the dreams had a different quality, a sense of remembrance and the visceral response she'd had to many of them reinforced the feeling that they were more than figments of her imagination. She looked out at the desert thinking about how this place had drawn her.

A homing pigeon returning to its roost? she wondered.

Not quite.

She smiled in spite of herself at that comparison.

The prodigal daughter returning might be a better description and she startled a little as soon as she had the thought.

A Freudian slip?

The thought that she and Shy Dove were one and the same had occurred to her before but she'd dismissed it.

Why?

That would be silly! Obviously Ms. Judgmental's opinion.

Would it really be that silly? Sharon asked herself. *You believe in reincarnation—always have. Why wouldn't it be possible for you to have been Shy Dove? You know you've always been drawn to this area and felt it was home. It makes perfect sense you've had a past life experience here.*

It was one thing to believe in it, she thought, *but quite another to be reliving it through my dreams!*

She shook herself out of her reverie wanting to write it down before she'd forgotten the details of the dream. It was too important to forget and there was an urgency about getting it down, to keep the story in its right order. She couldn't say why but knew there was a reason not to dismiss it.

After transcribing it to her laptop, she felt her body relax even though she hadn't been aware of the tension she'd been holding. She'd never done it before, but this time she got her flash drive and backed it up.

Now you're getting a little paranoid, she chided herself.

No, not me, Ms. Judgmental, she replied.

Either way she decided she needed a change of venue to try to shake the cobwebs from her mind and the sense of restlessness she now felt. She had to get out of the house and around people, anything to help connect her more to the here and now. She grabbed her purse and keys and headed into town. The grocery store was usually the last thing on her list of things she'd voluntarily want to do but today was an exception.

Returning an hour later with the couple of items she'd had on her list in addition to a few impulse items, it hadn't been a complete waste of time and she did feel more grounded. She also had Hal's phone call to look forward to and smiled at the prospect of that connection. As the image of his handsome face and movie star smile appeared in her mind, her stomach did a flip and her hand went to cover it. She wasn't sure if it was to hold the feeling in or hide it. It did feel a little silly at her age to be having that kind of reaction.

Why fight it? she asked and hearing no reason why she should—even Ms. Judgmental was silent for once—she concluded that was a good sign. *Why, indeed!*

She'd just finished clearing up the remains of her dinner when the phone rang and Hal's number showed up in the caller ID display. She smiled and felt a tingle go through her even though she'd been expecting his call.

"Hi, Hal," she answered the ring.

"Hi, Sharon. Are you finished with your dinner?" he asked.

"Just finished getting the kitchen cleaned up so it's perfect timing," she responded.

"How was your day? Anything exciting happen?" he asked and she could sense the smile on his face.

She hesitated just for a moment, thinking of her dream. She still wasn't ready to share them with anyone for a number of reasons, though.

"Well, I did finally have success with the gourd project," she answered feeling grateful she'd come up with something other than her dream to talk about.

"Good for you!" he answered and she didn't doubt the sincerity of his compliment. "I'm looking forward to seeing it. I don't think I've ever seen something like that. Or maybe I have and just didn't pay attention. I confess I don't know a lot about that craft."

"I'll be happy to show you once it's finished. Maybe I could bring it with me when I come to my next gourd class. I have a question for the instructor about it anyway and could drop by your place after class if you're going to be home."

She regretted the offer almost as soon as she'd spoken it, realizing that it would be late for a drive back home by the time she was done with class and then spending time with Hal.

"That's a great idea!" he answered. "You could stay the night if you didn't want to drive back home that late," he suggested as though reading her mind. "I have a guest room you could use," he added, "if it's too soon. I don't want you to feel I'm expecting you to be sharing mine, even though I wouldn't mind if you did….share my room, that is," he explained before she had a chance to respond.

"Thank you, Hal. Both for the offer and respecting my feelings," she answered. "How about if I bring an overnight bag and we'll see how it goes as to whether I use the guest room or yours?"

"Sounds like a great plan," he replied. "And I mean it, Sharon. I won't rush you. This feels like the real deal and I don't want to blow my chance with you."

"It feels real to me, too, Hal," she answered.

There was a brief moment of silence….and promise….that hung between them but before it could become awkward Sharon broke the silence.

"That was the excitement of my day. How about yours?" Not entirely true considering her dream, but that was okay.

"No real excitement here. Made a few business calls and enjoyed the sunshine."

They chatted for a few more minutes before saying goodbye. She clicked the phone off and plugged it in the charger before heading to the couch to try once more to read the book she hadn't been able to focus on earlier.

CHAPTER FORTY-NINE

"*What was that all about?" Running Deer asked after they were sure that Broken Wing was not returning.*

Shy Dove had no way of keeping the surprise a secret without lying to him so had to tell him the reason for the altercation.

"I was making you a wedding outfit and had been coming here to work on it so no one would question why it was not the right size," she answered and showed him the tunic. "I had hoped to be able to surprise you with it once we were safely away from the village and could have our own ceremony. Broken Wing sneaked up behind me before I heard him and could hide what I was doing. I didn't say anything but he must have seen the expression on my face when he asked if it was for you because he knew it would not fit him."

Running Deer looked at the tunic admiring the work that Shy Dove had put into the beading, fingering the suppleness of the leather.

"I know it was silly. If we are alone, there is no place else you could wear it, but I wanted our joining to be special," she

looked into his eyes and he could see how much this meant to her.

"It isn't silly, Shy Dove," he told her. "I am honored that you would do this for me." He held her in his arms, reassuring her.

"Come, we must return to the village to find out what trouble Broken Wing may be up to. He is not going to let this go," Running Deer told her echoing what she'd already been thinking.

"I know," she answered. "Perhaps we should go separately?" she questioned.

"I'm not sure if it will matter," he answered. "I think I should be with you to answer any questions and I can let your parents know that I came upon him trying to harm you."

"But how am I going to explain the wedding garments?" she asked.

"That's a good point."

He thought for a moment before saying, "Let me take them to the cave and hide them. Do you think you can lie about what happened?"

She looked doubtfully at him considering.

"What would I say happened?"

"Say that you were out looking for plants to use for dyeing your yarns. No, that wouldn't work," he corrected himself as soon as the words were out. "It's too early," he said almost to himself as he thought through whether the story would be believed.

"What if I told them I had made a mistake about the size? That it really was for Broken Wing? My skills are not that good yet and I could easily have not cut the garment correctly. If it was to be a surprise, I would not have been able to check the fit. I can tell them he did not give me a chance to explain and I was trying to keep it a secret to surprise him. I would need to take it back with me, though."

Running Deer considered her story and nodded in agreement but seemed reluctant to give up the tunic that was meant for him.

"You're right, Shy Dove. That's a much better story and I think they would believe you."

"Don't worry, Running Deer. I will make sure I have it when we leave," she reassured him reading the expression on his face. "And I will make sure I take out the extra material I will need to fit Broken Wing's ugly body," she said with so much distaste that it made Running Deer chuckle.

Shy Dove's lip twitched in response and then broke into a wide grin.

"Come on, let's go before we have everyone coming to look for us," Running Deer said as he picked up Shy Dove's sewing basket and handed the tunic to her.

They returned to the village ten minutes later but nothing seemed amiss. Shy Dove looked at Running Deer with a worried expression, her brows furrowed together.

"Do you think Broken Wing has not told anyone?" she asked. "I had expected to have people looking for us."

Running Deer's expression matched hers. "So did I," he replied. "Perhaps he did not want to admit that I had gotten the better of him."

They continued to Shy Dove's house where her mother was outside preparing corn cakes and her father was repairing the handle of a knife. They both looked up and smiled as the couple approached them. By this time Shy Dove's face had returned to its natural color and there was no visible trace of Broken Wing's attack on her.

Running Deer stopped and returned Shy Dove's sewing basket back to her and his voice so low she could barely hear him tell her not to say anything yet about Broken Wing's attack.

"It might be a good idea to tell them you were working on the wedding garments in case he does say something later. He never gave you the chance to explain so it would be his word

against yours as to who it was for," he went on quietly. "They will be more likely to believe you if you say something first."

Running Deer turned and smiled and waved to her parents as they watched their interaction. They returned the gesture seeming less anxious about what was happening.

"Hello, Singing Song and Black Bear," he called to them. "I came upon Shy Dove as I was returning from scouting for deer and offered to carry her basket for her."

They looked questioningly at Shy Dove.

"I've been working on a wedding outfit," she told them, "and have been going out away from the village as I wanted it to be a surprise," purposely avoiding saying it was for Broken Wing. She knew her skill as a liar would only go so far and would be harder to convince her parents that she was telling the truth.

"Oh," her mother said, the relief apparent in her voice. "Thank you, Running Deer. Would you like to join us? It's been a long while since you've spent time with us."

"Thank you for the offer, but I should be getting back to my house. My mother will be worried if I stay out too long," he excused himself. It was unlikely that his mother would be worried as she had long ago realized that Running Deer was no longer a child. It was, however, the best reason for not accepting Singing Song's invitation as Running Deer knew that she would not argue with the explanation. He wanted to find out where Broken Wing was and whether he had said anything to anyone else about what had happened.

"Thank you for walking back with me, Running Deer," Shy Dove smiled at him as he turned to walk away.

"You're welcome, Shy Dove. I'm always happy to help a friend," his voice held no hint of his true feelings for her but his eyes told her she was much more than a friend.

"May we see the outfit you are making?" Singing Song's

question returned her attention to her parents and Shy Dove walked the remaining distance to their house.

"I think I may have the size wrong," she said as she unfolded the tunic for her mother to inspect. "I didn't want to ask Broken Wing for one of his shirts to try to copy as I was afraid he would ask why I needed it," she said, keeping her face down so her mother would not be able to read her expression and see that she was not being truthful. She'd hoped to be able to just put the tunic back where she kept her personal belongings but that was not an option now. "Do you know how I can fix it? I saw Broken Wing earlier and I realized I have not made it big enough to fit around his chest."

Her mother reached out for the garment and considered its construction.

"You're doing a beautiful job with the beadwork, Shy Dove," she told her and her mother's approval brought a sense of pride at her accomplishment. She'd thought she was doing a good job but hearing her mother's praise confirmed it.

"I think we can add a piece to the front without affecting the beadwork," she said after a moment's consideration. She picked up a stick that was nearby and began to draw how it could be done in the ground. "You see if it is shaped like this," and she drew an upside down V, "you can add enough fabric to make more room. It will mean that you will have to cut the front of the shirt to sew it in but you can add decoration to make it look as though it was your intention to do that rather than to fix a mistake. I don't think it will take a lot but do you have more of this leather?"

"No, I used it all for the pants and the tunic," Shy Dove told her.

"I think I have something you can use and maybe that is even better," Singing Song told her, holding the tunic up inspecting it and in her mind envisioning how it would look with the piece added in. "Yes, I think that would work," she at last said, having

decided the best approach. "Come inside and I'll show you the piece I have in mind."

Shy Dove followed her into the house, relieved at not having returned to find herself in trouble but hating the idea that she would have to alter the tunic and came upon an idea to save it.

"Mother, do you think it might be better to just start over? Perhaps we could save this to trade later. It seems a shame to have to cut it," she reasoned, hoping her mother would agree. She could keep the tunic safe for Running Deer and the chances it would be necessary to trade it before they were able to leave were slight.

"You may be right, Shy Dove," she answered. "It would be a shame to cut this and it would be a good trading piece. The work you've done is very good. Are you sure you wouldn't mind making another and do you have enough beads for another one?"

"I've been trading some small pieces of my weaving and saving up," she answered. "It wouldn't be quite as fancy but I could add some feathers instead. Do you think that would be acceptable?"

"I'm sure we can find something," her mother smiled at her. "Come, let's find the material I have and get a new piece started. We still have plenty of time."

Shy Dove did not respond but her eyes watered and she felt a lump in her throat at the thought that soon she would be leaving her family never to see them again. Her mother had no way of knowing that time was not something they had plenty of.

CHAPTER FIFTY

*S*haron sat reflecting on this latest entry in her dream journal. What would she do if she were in that situation? They were so young but then she realized that for that time, it would not have been unusual to be starting married life and taking on those responsibilities at that age. She sighed and shut down her laptop bringing herself back to this world. The sun was shining and the air, though cool now, promised to be hot by day's end. The gourd project was ready for the next step in the process but she decided that might be a project better left for later in the day when she would want to be inside. Now might be a better time to get outside and get some exercise and fresh air. She cleaned up the breakfast dishes and was about to head out when the phone rang. Her pulse quickened as her thoughts went to Hal but it was Joseph's number that was on the caller ID display.

"Good morning, Joseph."

"Hey, Sharon, how are you?" he replied. "Was thinking it had been a while since I'd heard from you and wanted to make sure you were okay."

"Thank you, that's really nice of you to be thinking of me," she said with sincerity, touched that he was concerned about her welfare. "I'm doing fine—was just about to go outside to get some fresh air while it's still cool."

"Good idea. Looks like it's going to be a hot one today," he confirmed her earlier suspicion.

"That's what I was thinking. So, how have you been? Business keeping you out of trouble?"

"These days getting into trouble isn't much of a worry for me," he answered and she could feel the smile in his voice. "Was thinking it might be nice to get together for dinner and catch up on how you're doing. Are you busy tonight?"

She hesitated for a second as she considered the offer. There wasn't any reason why she should feel like she was cheating on Hal. She and Joseph were friends after all, not romantically inclined.

"That sounds great!" she answered. "What time and where would be good for you?"

"How about I pick you up at 6 and we go to Dos Pollos?"

"Sounds good! I'll be ready!"

"See you then."

Sharon clicked off the phone and tapped it against her chin considering her feelings about the dinner testing whether there was anything more than the prospect of dinner with a friend. *No, just friendship vibes,* she decided and put the phone in her pocket to take outside with her. The plants on the patio needed watering before the sun became too strong and it was time to fertilize again. Her gardening chores done, she looked around and nodded in approval. The plants had filled in and the bright colors cheered her. Her body was still craving movement, though, and she decided to walk to burn off some of the energy that felt pent up. One regret of being where she lived was the lack of a good area to take a long walk without going off into the desert or walking along the road both of which could prove treacherous for different reasons. She didn't feel confident yet to be heading off into the desert alone but cars were not expecting pedestrian traffic and the road had curves and dips that could make visibility an issue. She considered her options with some frustration. She remembered that back in Maine she'd sometimes walked the length of her driveway doing laps rather than walking through the subdivision. Boring but still had the end result of getting exercise.

Better than nothing, she resigned herself to doing the same here for the moment and headed down her driveway thinking that the same ten laps might be a good goal for today. As she walked, her thoughts went back to Shy Dove and Running Deer and wondering how they would make their escape and would they be successful? So much could go wrong and she found herself worrying about them and then feeling silly.

"It's just a dream," she heard Ms. Judgmental chiding her.

"It's a dream now," she answered, "but it was real then."

When was then? she rolled that thought around as she walked. There was nothing about the dreams that could narrow down the time other than that it was sure to be before this part of the country had been settled by the advancing invasion of Americans heading West.

The phone ringing brought her out of her reverie.

"Good morning, gorgeous," Hal responded to her hello.

She blushed in spite of herself.

"Good morning, handsome," she answered. "You're sounding chipper this morning."

"Chipper?" he teased. "Been a long time since I heard that used in a sentence unless it was referring to a machine that shreds wood."

"Showing my age, am I?" she asked, her tone joking.

"Not at all from what I've seen. What's on your agenda today?"

"Decided to go for a little walk to burn off some energy but thought just walking up and down the driveway would be the safest route. I'm not quite up to wandering around in the desert alone. Gets a little boring, though."

"I can imagine," he answered. "What are you doing once you're finished? I'm guessing you're not planning to spend the entire day walking."

"Thought I'd get back to the gourd project this afternoon when it's too hot to be outside. Can't believe I'm saying that since being warm was the reason I moved out here for the winter, but I haven't acclimated yet even if it is a dry heat."

"Give it another year."

"I'm definitely planning to do that!" she replied. "Have plans to go to dinner tonight with a friend."

"Oh?" he questioned.

A red flag went up in her head at his tone but she dismissed it thinking she must have read more into the question than was intended.

"I think I may have mentioned the builder for my house— Joseph Ramos? Tom and I had gotten to know him personally while the house was being built and he's been really helpful since I've moved out," she said in what she hoped was a matter-of-fact tone of voice to let him know friends was all there was to it.

"Ahhh. That's really nice of him to do that," he answered but Sharon still wasn't sure whether the red flag could be brought down yet.

"It made a big difference to me when I first moved out to know that I had at least one person here that I knew. It was a bit scary to do this on my own."

She could feel a shift in the energy as though Hal had relaxed.

"I understand. It must have been hard for you especially thinking that Tom was going to be with you. Sounds like you were leaving your comfort zone to go through with coming here. Some women might have just sold the house instead."

"I thought about it but this place and being here was too much of a dream unfulfilled and I don't think I ever would have been happy with myself if I hadn't. And now I'm really glad I did…for a lot of reasons," she said hoping to reassure him further.

"Me, too," he answered and she relaxed as well.

They chatted for a few more minutes and Sharon felt much better when they hung up. All was still well in her world but there was a niggling sense of discomfort that she'd felt like she needed to explain herself to Hal. It was still early in the relationship and they were feeling each other out but trust was something that was too important to be called into question. She made a mental note to be aware of any signs that this was going to be an issue. It *was* nice to have Hal in her life but she had no intention of being in a relationship if it meant giving up her freedom and her very self now that she had tasted what it was like to be on her own and enjoying it with the knowledge that she could do it.

Sharon spent the afternoon engrossed in her gourd project which was turning out quite nicely if she did say so herself and had it not been for her having set her alarm to let her know it was time to get ready for dinner with Joseph, she might have continued on into the night. It was with a mixture of regret and anticipation that she turned off the alarm. Had it not also been for the grumbling reminder from her stomach that she'd only had a light lunch and was more than ready for nourishment, she might have called Joseph to take a rain check. She stretched and felt the pop in her lower spine from having been bent over all afternoon. Thinking about a quick shower under hot water to relax the muscles helped to motivate her even further. An hour later, showered, dressed and light make-up applied, she was glad she hadn't canceled. The gourd would still be there tomorrow.

"You look great!" Joseph complimented her. "I think Arizona agrees with you," he smiled as he looked her over.

"Thanks and I couldn't agree more," Sharon smiled in return.

She might have felt flustered with the attention but the compliment was sincere and his appraising look held no lechery to make her uncomfortable.

"Hope you're hungry. I missed lunch today and could eat a javelina!"

"Me, too!" Sharon replied. "I didn't miss lunch but it was more of a snack than a meal. I got so wrapped up in working on my gourd project, I didn't realize how hungry I was getting until I stopped."

Joseph held his truck door open for her and held his other hand at her elbow as she climbed in. The trip to town passed by quickly as they chatted about their respective day. The fragrant aroma as they entered Dos Pollos triggered a response from her stomach. If it was possible for a stomach to have emotions, she would have labeled this as irritable. Her hand went to her stomach as though to comfort and reassure it not to worry, that food was on its way. They found an empty table and seated themselves as Mary nodded in their direction in acknowledgment that she would be right there to take their order.

"So, are you settling in okay? Made any new friends?"

His tone was light but there was a slight edge that caught Sharon's attention.

"Just the two I've already told you about," she replied, keeping her tone light as well. "I did tell you about Donna, didn't I? She's the gal I met at the gourd class."

Joseph nodded.

"And the guy I met in Sedona. His name is Hal. I'm not sure where it's going but it's been nice to have a little romance in my life again," she said, meeting Joseph's eyes but not reading any reaction although she thought she saw his eyes flicker briefly.

"Other than that, I've been staying pretty close to home so haven't been out to meet anyone else."

Sharon realized she felt a mixture of needing to apologize for….no, it wasn't that….to *justify*….that felt more like it….her relationship with Hal and a bit of defiance. *What was that about?* she wondered to herself.

"It must be confusing for you," he answered, picking up on her hesitation. "I'm guessing you might be feeling conflicted about having feelings for someone even though Tom is gone."

"Yeah, that's just it," she replied, letting out her breath. "I feel a bit disloyal that I'm seeing someone so soon but on the other hand, I feel like I did most of my grieving before he died. The last few months were rough. We knew he was terminal and even though there was that hope that the doctors were wrong, I realize there was a part of me that was preparing….and griev-ing….for when he died. And really it went back even longer. Things had changed a lot earlier before we found out what was wrong. Tom hadn't been feeling like himself and had started to withdraw from me. I know he didn't mean to shut me out. He was just trying to figure out why he wasn't himself but at the time, I didn't know what was going on and felt it as a rejection. I knew he loved me, but things weren't the same," she looked into Joseph's eyes to find some reassurance that he understood.

He nodded and she felt he did understand.

"Just be careful," he said and although she could have taken his words as interference in her personal life, after their last conversation she knew they were meant with the concern of a friend.

Still, this was the second person who'd cautioned her. Should she be concerned? She felt Ms. Judgmental's presence waiting for her to make a mistake and the inevitable *I told you so*. That angered her and although she knew there was a bit of petulance in the internal response, she was determined not to let that happen.

The conversation moved on to less dangerous topics and the evening ended on a positive note. Joseph declined the offer to come in when he returned Sharon to her house saying he had an early morning and busy day ahead so needed to make it an early night but she felt relief, followed quickly by guilt after having been treated to dinner and a good time. It had been a long day for her and she was ready to call it a night herself.

CHAPTER FIFTY-ONE

*R*unning Deer returned to his house alert to any signs *that something might be amiss but everything was as it normally would be.* What would he do in Broken Wing's place? *he wondered to himself. Knowing how big of an ego Broken Wing had, he decided that it was more likely that he would keep quiet than to have to admit that Running Deer had gotten the better of him but he would not let it pass. He would be planning his revenge to come at a later time. It made the decision to leave more urgent and he would have liked more time to prepare but he knew it would not be safe to stay much longer. He went over in his mind the inventory of the supplies he and Shy Dove had been storing and realized they would be okay at least to get started. Once they reached a safe distance away and started their life together, he would be able to trade for anything they might need.* Just how far would they have to go to be safe, though? *That question had nagged at him for all the time they had been planning their escape and he still had no good answer. He'd learned a lot about the places they might go from visitors to their village and stories he'd heard from his elders, but they* *might not be able to go to any village or their presence would be reported back. They might not be accepted as outsiders in any case which meant the only option was to be on their own. He wondered if Shy Dove realized what their life might be like and worried if he was being selfish to ask that of her. He couldn't imagine his life without her as his wife but was this too much to ask? What would their life be like living alone without the comfort of friends and family? What would become of any children they might have with no other children to play with? Would that be fair to them? And then what would happen when they grew up? How would they find mates? He pushed those thoughts away, thinking that would be something they could worry about later. The first thing they must do was to get away and then the rest would take care of itself. He would have to trust that the Great Spirit would help them find the answers. He'd been so deep in thought that he hadn't heard Broken Wing following him and startled as he felt a hand grabbing at his shoulder to turn him around.*

"You will regret your actions today, Running Deer," Broken Wing snarled at him, his face mere inches away.

Running Deer brushed Broken Wing's arm away and met his gaze showing no emotion.

"You threaten me, Broken Wing? I was just protecting Shy Dove from a weak little boy who only knows how to pretend to be brave by hurting others."

Broken Wing's head snapped back as though he had been physically slapped although Running Deer had not touched him.

"You will regret this, Running Deer. I promise you," he snarled and turned on his heel and stalked off before Running Deer could respond.

Had Running Deer not already thought about leaving earlier, that sealed the decision. They would have to leave even sooner, though, perhaps even within the next day or two. He went over his plan for their escape one more time trying to think of every contingency and how to handle it. This would be one more thing he would have to trust to the Great Spirit.

"Keep us safe, Great Spirit," he whispered. "We will need all the help we can get."

CHAPTER FIFTY-TWO

Sharon spent the morning finishing the gourd but as noon approached and she hadn't heard from Hal, she wondered if he might have been more upset about her dinner with Joseph than he'd let on. She chided herself for trying to read more into it than was probably the case.

"There's no reason why he has to be the one to call," she reminded herself.

"You're absolutely right," she said aloud. "Lunch first," she reassured her grumbling stomach whose emotional temperature was approaching irritable again, "and then I'll call him."

She felt the butterflies in her stomach as she hit the speed dial for Hal's number and then heard the ring tone and her anxiety level bumped up a notch with the third ring. Debating whether to hang up or leave a message, she was surprised to hear his voice.

"Hey, gorgeous, sorry I didn't answer right away. Was just wrapping up a business call," he answered sounding cheerful.

"Sounds like it was a successful one from the tone of your voice," she said, feeling relieved.

"Could be. Time will tell. How are you this morning? Did you have a good dinner with your builder friend?"

She still didn't notice anything amiss in the inflection in his voice and decided she must have misjudged her concern about Hal's objection to her seeing Joseph.

"It was good. Joseph is a nice guy and he understands how it is to lose a spouse so it's easy to share those feelings with him."

"Mmmmm. Having someone to talk to who's been through it and can relate. I get that."

"Exactly," She hesitated before deciding to go on. "And he let me know that I wasn't being disloyal to Tom by being with you."

There was a beat before Hal answered as though he was processing this information and changing his mind about how he'd been feeling.

"I'm glad to hear that. I suppose hearing it from someone else carried a little more weight than hearing it from me. Someone who could be more objective, that is."

Sharon didn't detect any note of sarcasm in his voice and felt more at ease.

"Yes, I suppose you're right," she answered. "It wasn't that I didn't believe what you were trying to tell me, but you weren't exactly in a position of uninvolvement. Is that a word? Uninvolvement? You know what I mean," she finished in a rush.

He chuckled.

"I don't think it is a word, but yes, I do know what you mean."

"Phew. Sooo, do you think we can say this is resolved and move on?"

"Absolutely, now that you seem to be more comfortable about *us*, I'm all in favor of moving on. What are you doing for dinner? And how would you feel about a sleepover tonight instead of after the gourd class like we talked about earlier?"

"Whoa!" she stuttered. "There's moving on and then there's light speed!"

"Too soon?" he chuckled.

She hesitated.

"How about we play it by ear like we'd talked about earlier, too?"

"So is that a definite maybe?" he asked.

She considered whether she was really ready for this before answering.

"Yes, a definite maybe."

They made plans for meeting at his place at six and Sharon hung up wondering if she had lost her mind encouraged by Ms. Judgmental in that train of thought.

"New place. New life. New me," she said aloud both for her benefit and Ms. Judgmental's.

"Back to your corner, bitch!" She giggled at her audacity, feeling a little silly in spite of her attempt at assertiveness.

"Oh, girl, you have lost it!" she muttered as she went to the bedroom to pack an overnight bag.

CHAPTER FIFTY-THREE

For the next few days both Running Deer and Shy Dove were more cautious than usual about making sure no one saw them leave the village and avoiding each other when others were around. They'd been able to meet at the cave and begin packing everything in anticipation of leaving before the week was out. Running Deer had found a spot where they could meet a few miles away from the village, leaving by separate routes. He would leave at night so no one would see him with their belongings. He had a backpack for himself and would carry the rest in the carrier that Shy Dove had made. Shy Dove had brought the few belongings from her home that she would need a little at a time so as not to arouse any suspicion, including the wedding garments for Running Deer. Once again, she was relieved that she'd suggested making a new outfit for Broken Wing so that she wouldn't have to take apart the one for Running Deer.

"I think we're ready," Running Deer said looking at their supplies for at least the tenth time since they'd met that day.

"We will be fine," Shy Dove reassured him. "You have thought of everything, Running Deer. We have all that we will

need to start our new life together and what we don't have now, we can get or make when we reach our destination."

Not knowing what that destination was didn't worry her. She trusted Running Deer completely and had faith that all would be well. Surely the Great Spirit meant for them to be together.

Running Deer looked up and met her eyes, seeing the trust in them. He wasn't sure if that made him feel better or worse. He loved Shy Dove with every fiber of his being and the thought that she might come to harm because of something he did...or failed to do...was a great responsibility.

"I love you, Shy Dove."

"I love you, too, Running Deer," she smiled up at him.

"Are you sure you want to do this?" he asked. "I would understand if you changed your mind. The journey will be diffi-cult and we can be in danger especially if we are caught."

"I know but it doesn't matter," she reassured him. "I don't want to marry Broken Wing and if there was another way, we wouldn't need to be leaving but this is our only choice."

"You're right. I just wanted to give you the opportunity to change your mind. I don't want you to have any doubts about leaving your family and your friends just to be with me."

"I've thought about it a lot and I know I will miss them but I love you and being with you means more to me."

He took her in his arms and held her close. She could hear the beat of his heart, strong and steady, and feel the warmth of his body. And in his arms she felt safe. No, there was no doubt in her mind that this was what she wanted to do.

CHAPTER FIFTY-FOUR

Sharon's nerves began to get the better of her the closer she got to Tucson. She'd engaged cruise control as soon as she'd gotten on I-10 or, she realized, she'd have been slowing down.

Was this just nerves or intuition making her so jittery? she asked herself waiting for feedback from her body. She didn't have the sense that this was more than nerves. And why should she? She and Tom had been together for 25 years and there had been no infidelity. Being nervous about having sex with someone new—and with the added stress of her age—would be the case for anyone, she reasoned. She'd kept in good shape but even with exercise and a good diet, growing older had taken its natural toll. With Tom it hadn't been an issue as they'd gotten older together and were comfortable with each others' bodies.

She sighed with resignation thinking that she would just have to let it go. If Hal couldn't be comfortable with her body as it was, then there wasn't much future for them and better to find that out now before she really fell for him.

Even more than I already have, she admitted to herself.

She switched the radio to listen to an audiobook to help the miles go by and distract her from her brooding. Not much point getting uptight about it she realized and settled into the story.

After stopping to pick up a bottle of wine, she arrived at Hal's house an hour later. She'd put the overnight bag on the floor of her car on the passenger side and she sat looking at it as though it contained a venomous snake debating whether to take it inside or get it later if things seemed to be going in that direction. Even though the invitation had been made, she felt presumptuous about arriving bag in hand. And not only that, but showing up with it in hand might put some expectations on both of them. Better to leave it in the car and get it if she needed it later. She let out her breath, not realizing until then she'd been holding it, and the relief washed over her.

Now maybe that is something to think about, she considered but then dismissed it.

After checking the mirror in her visor and fluffing up her hair, she took a deep breath and grabbing her purse and the bottle of wine walked up to the door. Taking another deep breath in and slowly letting it out through her mouth to steady her nerves, she rang the doorbell.

Hal's smile as he opened the door to greet her helped to further reassure her.

"Come on in," he said as he stepped aside to let her pass but as she did, stopped her long enough to kiss her lightly on her lips.

She could feel the warmth of his breath and smell his after-shave. She was glad he was a man who knew how to use it sparingly and obviously had good taste. She couldn't place the scent but was sure it was not a drug store item.

"I brought some wine," she held up the bottle for inspection. I don't know if it will go with your menu but took a chance anyway."

"It will be fine. I'm not that much of a wine snob but we can always have it after dinner, too," he smiled to reassure her. "Let's take it in the kitchen and I'll put it in the wine cooler to chill," he said as he took it from her and headed in that direction. "How was the drive?"

"Not bad. I listened to an audiobook to help pass the time," she answered not mentioning that it was also to distract her from her nervousness.

"Great way to pass the time," he agreed. "I got into audiobooks a few years back when I was doing more traveling for my job. Made the driving a lot more pleasant than having to search for a new station every hour or so when I got out of range. That was before I had a car that had satellite radio, but I still prefer the audiobooks."

Sharon accepted Hal's offer for lemonade and pouring a glass for himself, too, they took it out to his back yard to enjoy the afternoon sun. Their conversation flowed easily and she finally relaxed. Hal proved his cooking skills once again at dinner and opened the bottle of wine she'd brought. The evening was cooling which made the decision to sit inside by the light of the fireplace an easy one. Hal's arm was across her shoulders and she settled in comfortably feeling her body mold next to his, his thigh warm against her own. She looked up into his face as he reached over to take the glass of wine out of her hand and put it on the coffee table so that he could kiss her. A gentle but thorough kiss that awakened parts of her body that had long been sleeping. He broke off the embrace searching her face to gauge her response which she did by kissing him again, feeling her body responding as he pulled her closer.

"You sure?" he asked to the unspoken question. "I don't want you to regret this later."

"I'm as sure as I'll ever be," she whispered and then quickly added as she saw the hesitation on his face, "I didn't mean it quite like it sounded. Yes, yes, I'm sure," she said and this time her voice was louder and less timid and he could see the certainty in her eyes.

Sharon woke the next morning confused about her surroundings at first and then the awareness of where she was came over her. She glanced over to see Hal's side of the bed empty but heard him in the kitchen and smelled the aroma of coffee and bacon cooking. She settled back on the pillows looking up at the ceiling, not quite ready to get up but not needing to go back to sleep. Their lovemaking had been gentle and Hal had taken care to put her completely at ease but as her body responded and the passion and sexual tension she hadn't known was there, rose to the surface, she thought perhaps she had surprised him with the intensity of her response. She chuckled at the memory and feeling more confident and alive than she had in a very long time, got out of bed. It was then that she realized she'd never retrieved her overnight bag from the car. Too late now, she would just have to put on the clothes she'd worn last night and get it later. She went into the bathroom and finding the toothpaste Hal kept in a drawer, put a dab on her finger and brushed it on her tongue and with a little water from the tap swished it around in her mouth before making her way to the kitchen.

"Good morning, that smells terrific," she smiled at him.

"Thanks," he smiled back. "I worked up quite an appetite and thought you might have, too."

She blushed in spite of herself but returned his gaze.

"Is there anything I can do to help?"

"Nope, I have everything under control. Hope you like scrambled eggs and bacon. I was going to bring you breakfast in bed so just went ahead and made an executive decision but can whip up something else if you'd rather."

"Scrambled eggs and bacon are perfect!" she said.

She retrieved her bag after breakfast and asked if she could use the shower before changing her clothes.

"Of course," Hal answered. "No need to ask. I'll clean up here."

She had closed her eyes to let the water flow over her body

and hadn't seen Hal come into the shower until he was standing behind her and felt his hands on her waist as he nuzzled her neck. She felt her nipples respond as he gently massaged her breasts and his thumbs rubbed across them. She leaned back against his chest as her breath quickened. He took the soap from her hand and lathered his hands before once again massaging her breasts, teasing her nipples and nibbling on her ear lobe, his breath warm and she noticed the scent of mint toothpaste. He lathered his hands again and slowly made his way down her stomach and over her hips before sliding a finger between her legs and slowly stroking her. Her breath was ragged and her knees were feeling weak but she didn't want it to stop and she willed herself to stay upright. She could feel the obvious signs of his arousal against her and took the soap, lathering her hands this time and reaching behind to return the favor, slowly stroking him and feeling his immediate response. He groaned as she continued to stroke him, then turned to face him.

"There was a time when I might have been okay with continuing this here but that was at least a couple decades ago. How about if we take this back to your bed? I really wouldn't want to have to explain to my daughters how I broke my hip," she teased.

He chuckled. "No, I don't imagine you would," he replied as he reached around to turn off the water before grabbing a towel to dry her off and then quickly did the same for himself. He took her hand and she followed him back to his bed.

He kissed her hard as they lay side by side on the bed and then rolled over on top of her. She gasped as he entered her and his penetrations, slow at first, sped faster and faster, their rhythms matching.

"Now, now," she moaned and she felt Hal shudder as he peaked in unison with her. She opened her eyes just as he leaned down to kiss her, the hint of a smile in the corner of his mouth.

CHAPTER FIFTY-FIVE

he day was sunny and warm. Everything was as it normally was with the exception that this would be Shy Dove's last day with her family and friends. The thought that she would never see them again filled her with sadness but every time she saw Broken Wing and how he looked at her with suspicion and distaste affirmed that she was making the right decision to leave. She had taken the last of her belongings to the cave the day before so that Running Deer could pack them with the rest of their belongings which were nearly ready for his departure that night. He had taken her to the spot where they would meet a couple of miles away from the village and instructed her on how to get there leaving the least amount of tracks. The first part of the trail was one that was used by most of the villagers and would be the least obvious and the second was an arroyo with rocks and other debris from previous flooding, now dry, but that she could step on to leave less evidence of tracks. She was to leave later in the afternoon to arouse the least suspicion and give them some daylight to cover more distance before dark set in making it that much more difficult to track them even if anyone tried to find them before the next day. She'd spent time with Squash Blossom and Sky Lark in the morning and had been able to laugh and gossip with them as they usually did all the while taking in every detail of them to carry with her. Being with her family was much more difficult. Even Little Bear did not annoy her as he usually did in the way of brothers and sisters. She saw him with new eyes, taking in his likeness to their father and seeing the man he would become one day and feeling tears at the corner of her eyes in spite of her resolve not to show any signs of behavior that was out of the norm. Her father, Black Bear, was making handles for knives that he would be trading with Eagle Feather when he returned to the village in another month's time, teasing Little Bear about his squeaks as his voice tried to adjust from childhood to adulthood. Her mother was busy with weaving, her long black hair shining in the sun, and her hands deftly manipulating the yarn through the warp threads. The rug would be beautiful and Shy Dove could see it finished in her mind's eye, having inherited her mother's skill and talent. Her eyes began to water again thinking about not being there to see it completed and thinking about how her family would react when they realized she was gone.

"Are you alright, Shy Dove?" her mother asked, noticing her distress before she could discreetly brush the tears away.

Shy Dove smiled to reassure her.

"I'm fine, Mother. I think I just got something in my eye."

Her mother searched her face but seeing nothing more amiss went back to her weaving.

It was time to leave and she could not delay any longer both because Running Deer was waiting and she did not want to draw any more attention to herself as her emotions were beginning to take over.

"I'd like to take a run for a little while, if that would be okay," she asked, praying her mother or father would not say no so that she would have to find another way to leave.

"Be back before dinner," her mother answered smiling.

"Thank you, Mother," she answered, leaning down to give her a kiss and a hug and then doing the same with her father. She would have liked to do the same for Little Bear but knew she could not without arousing suspicion. Instead she said, "I love you all, even you Little Bear," and stuck her tongue out at him and he returned the gesture adding one of his own smiling as he did so.

Shy Dove looked at each of them in turn one more time before turning and quickening her pace before breaking into a full run as she came to the path that left the village and the world she'd known all her life behind.

Running Deer was kneeling beside Shadow stroking the ruff of his neck. Their packs were on the ground beside him and seeing Shy Dove approaching, he reached down to put on Shadow's carrier before lifting his onto his back. There was another smaller one that Shy Dove would carry. He searched the direction where Shy Dove had approached making sure no one was there to see them leave.

"Did you have any problem leaving?" he asked her after giving her a kiss in greeting.

"Only in my heart," she answered but seeing the expression on Running Deer's face quickly added, "but I don't regret my decision. I will miss my family but I can't stay."

He searched her face again before nodding, having satisfied himself that there was no need to cancel their plans.

"I'm sorry that you have to leave, Shy Dove. If there was another way to be able to stay...."

"It's okay, Running Deer," she interrupted. "I've made my decision. We should go now before anyone comes along and sees us," she said as she looked back to make sure no one had and put her pack on her back.

That settled, they both gave one more look back in the direction of the village each silently saying their good-byes before walking away to a future filled with uncertainty but one they would face together.

CHAPTER FIFTY-SIX

Sharon hummed along with the radio as she drove back to her house. She was still feeling the afterglow of her time with Hal and felt no regrets about what had happened. Even Ms. Judgmental wasn't commenting, which relieved her. The radio was replaced with the connection to her phone and she thumbed the steering wheel to take the call after seeing it was Donna calling.

"Good morning, Donna."

"Well, good morning to you, too," she answered. "Are you in the car?"

"I am, but I'm using the hands-free, so legal," she replied. "What's up?"

"Just calling to see if you might want to meet for lunch or dinner," Donna asked.

"I'm just outside Tucson now so could turn around if you'd like to do lunch," Sharon answered.

"*Reeeally?*" Donna asked but Sharon could hear the question beneath the question and almost see the smile on Donna's face.

"Yes, *reeeally*," she answered chuckling. "Should I just come to your house and we can figure out where to go from there?"

"That works. Think about where you might like to go and I'll do the same and we can compare notes when you get here."

"Sounds good. I should be there in say twenty minutes."

"See you then," Donna said.

Sharon disconnected the call and the radio resumed. She'd have to turn around at the next exit, but traffic was light this time of day so would be no problem and Donna's condo was in a part of town that she was familiar with so no need to program her GPS. She arrived with minutes to spare. Donna greeted her at the door, a Cheshire cat grin on her face.

"So, what have you been up to?" she asked.

"As if you haven't already guessed," Sharon answered one eyebrow raised and looked at Donna reproachfully. "I suppose I could have lied and told you I'd gotten up early to do some shopping but I knew you'd never believe me."

"You're right there," Donna answered smiling. "Come on in and tell me all about it."

"'Fraid not, no kissing and telling from me," Sharon replied. "Hal invited me to dinner. It went well."

"Mmmmm….hmmmm," Donna continued to tease, "I can see that."

"What's that supposed to mean?" Sharon asked but not upset.

"How it went is all over your face," Donna replied.

"Hmmmph," Sharon blushed. "Well, then, nothing more to say. Where are we having lunch?"

Donna's smile broadened even more.

"Okay, okay, I can take a hint, I won't badger you for details," she said but then her face took on a more serious expression. "Just be careful, okay? I don't want to see a friend get hurt."

"I'm a big girl," Sharon answered but seeing Donna's hurt expression at the edgy tone in her voice, went on, "I really do appreciate your concern, but I trust Hal's motives. I don't think he's playing me."

Donna searched Sharon's face and seeing nothing there to not believe her, nodded.

"Okay, I believe you and trust your judgment. Discussion closed. Let's talk about lunch."

253

CHAPTER FIFTY-SEVEN

hey had decided to follow the arroyo to the point where it picked up the trail leading to the village thinking that they could then blend in with the other footprints of people coming and going. Shadow was not the only dog in the village so his prints would blend in as well. It was nearing dark by that time but they decided to continue on to get as much distance as possible between them and the village even if it meant walking all night. Running Deer knew of a spot where they could sleep for a few hours without being seen and they could continue on after resting. Shy Dove's sadness was at least for the moment replaced by a growing excitement of the adventure ahead. The pack was heavy but she hardly noticed. Her eyes became accustomed to the dark. It hadn't been planned because they had left sooner than they'd wanted to, but it was a moonless night, having reached the new moon phase. That was to their advantage as it would make it more difficult to track them should anyone decide to do that. After saying her initial good-byes, Shy Dove had returned one more time after coming up with an idea to ask if she could stay the night with Squash Blossom so that her parents would not miss her right away and perhaps give them until at least the next morning to make their get-away. She hated lying to her parents, but it was imperative that they get as much distance between them and the village as possible.

They were able to make more distance than expected and spent the next afternoon sleeping in a hidden outcropping that Running Deer had further camouflaged by pulling up tumbleweed. Even Shadow did not object to sleeping and seemed relieved to be resting without the burden of the pack he'd been carrying. They'd had a light meal and were soon fast asleep, planning to continue on in the early evening and on through the night at least for the early part of their journey through areas that Running Deer was familiar with from hunting trips. Once they had reached the point where he no longer knew the paths, they would travel by day and if they made it that far without being discovered, he thought they should be safe to travel during daylight hours.

By the end of their second night of traveling and still no sign of anyone following them, Running Deer felt comfortable enough to travel during the day.

"Do you think you could go on if we stopped for an hour or so to eat and rest? I think we can travel during the day now but I know you must be tired from walking all night."

Shy Dove was extremely tired but was encouraged by the idea that they had made it this far safely and could return to a normal routine of traveling by day and sleeping at night. It had made her uneasy to be in the desert at night not only for the possibility of having someone following them but of the night creatures that they might not see until it was too late. She breathed a deep sigh of relief before answering.

"If it means we could rest at night instead, I will walk all day long no matter how tired I am," she smiled to reassure him. "I think Shadow might like that, too."

Running Deer had taken Shadow's pack off and the dog had laid down and was already dozing until he smelled the jerky that

Running Deer took out of his pack. They had not wanted to make a fire to cook fearing that the smoke would give them away and had been eating nothing but jerky and pemmican. Shy Dove longed for hot food but knew that Running Deer was right to insist they wait until they had put more distance between themselves and the village. They had been staying close to the stream so that their water gourds had been easy to replenish and they'd been able to wash away the dust from their travels which helped Shy Dove to re-energize herself after the long night's walk. They each took a nap while the other stayed awake to make sure they did not sleep the day away by accident, exhaustion overtaking them, Shy Dove sleeping first.

While Running Deer was sleeping she went to the stream to wash and let the cool water revive her. The day was cloudless and there was no need to worry that a flash flood would cause any danger. The water was only up to her thighs so not deep enough to swim but she laid down so the water could flow over her body and ease her sore muscles. Even though she'd been running and walking in preparation for the journey, it had not fully prepared her for walking hours on end and her muscles were reminding her that this was not their usual routine. She sighed as she felt her body relaxing and rolled over to her stomach, her hair sticking to her back, holding onto the rock stream bed, and feeling the difference in the sensation before rolling over once more to float weightless as she looked into the deep blue sky. Her mind had wandered and she realized with a start that she was no longer in the same spot as the stream's current had carried her back in the direction they'd come. She quickly got to her feet and made her way back to where she'd left her clothes at the side of the stream to find Running Deer glaring at her. Without thinking she tried to cover her nakedness, not sure whether she was more worried about her modesty or the look on Running Deer's face as he was clearly upset with her. He looked away and handed her her clothes which she took and dabbed at herself before putting them on.

"Running Deer, I'm sorry. I didn't mean to frighten you. I didn't want to wake you before you'd had a chance to get your rest and I was just going to take a quick bath and didn't realize I'd gone so far away with the stream's current," she said in a rush hoping her explanation would soothe his anger.

He put his hands on her cheeks and looked into her face, his eyes still worried but did not shout at her as she'd feared he might.

"You frightened me, Shy Dove," he whispered. "I'd thought someone had come and found us and captured you. Shadow followed you here and at first I could not see you—just your clothes and then thought you might have drowned. I began to panic. The thought of losing you was more than I could bear."

She covered his hands with her own and stood on her toes to kiss him. He hugged her close to him, kissing her deeply before releasing his embrace as he stroked her hair away from her face in spite of it being drenched. He felt his body respond, thinking of her nakedness as she'd approached him in the stream. He had not seen her naked since they'd been children and her body was now very much a woman's body. They had still not made love, being too concerned with getting as far away from the village as they could and being too exhausted by the time they stopped. He hoped that tonight would be different.

CHAPTER FIFTY-EIGHT

Sharon could hardly believe it was the middle of March already. The days were warmer and she spent more time outside in her garden, taking exploratory walks farther away from the house. She'd bought a walking stick hoping the advice she'd been given to use it not just for walking but to make noise by bouncing it with each step to scare away snakes was true. Even so, she made sure to bring her cell phone with her. She'd packed a snack, water, and her phone in her backpack and headed out to an area she'd been to before but wanted to check out again. She'd noticed an outcropping of rocks that had drawn her attention but was too late in the day then to explore. She found the cairns she'd made during her hike the last time so she could find her way again and before long was back to the outcropping. The spot that had interested her was elevated about twenty to thirty feet from the spot where she was now standing but didn't look like it would be a difficult climb either up or down. Perspiring with the heat and exertion, she reached the rock ledge and could see there was an opening behind the brush. Without thinking she turned to scan the area back to where she'd come. She could see her house from this elevation and guessed she had come perhaps a mile away. The sky was the deep blue that always amazed her with its saturation of color. She wasn't sure why she'd turned but the movement felt familiar, as though she'd done this before. The hairs on the nape of her neck and her arms rose at the feeling of déjà vu and she felt butterflies in her stomach when she turned to look back at the opening she'd seen behind the bushes.

There could be animals in there…or snakes…or scorpions! Ms. Judgmental warned.

I'll make noise with my stick and stand to the side before looking in, she answered but without feeling reassured.

She wished she'd put a flashlight in her backpack but it hadn't occurred to her that she might be exploring a cave.

Next time, she said at the same time as the thought that she intended to come back again surprised her and completely forgetting that she could have used the Flashlight feature on her phone.

Taking a deep breath to steady herself, she pounded the stick on the ground several times and poked at the bushes hoping to attract any wildlife that might be inside, praying as she did so that either there would not be any…first and best outcome…or that whatever might be inside would be small and harmless and would leave on its own without noticing her…second outcome, but one she could still live with.

After a minute or two of making noise and waiting to see what would happen without any response, she decided it would be safe to poke her head inside. At first she could not see anything but her eyes adjusted to the darkness after closing them for a minute after she'd crawled just inside the opening. It opened up a few feet from the entrance and the gooseflesh rose again as she could see objects toward the back of the small cave that were clearly man-made behind a pile of rubble that looked like it might have at one time been part of a partial wall. She hesitated, letting it sink in that someone had been here before her. It looked like they'd been there a long time ago, though, as there weren't any signs as she looked around of recent occupation. She was able to stand and although the light was dim, her eyes had adjusted enough that she could make her way without any problem to the back of the cave. Someone had stored supplies here. She found remnants of a gourd that had been stoppered with clay. Animals had chewed through making a hole to get at the contents so that she was not able to tell what might have once been inside. She sat on her haunches looking at the area where the gourd was to see what else might be there, not sure that she wanted to be touching anything for a number of reasons. Her heart skipped a beat and she drew in her breath as the shape she saw in the corner formed itself into a crude loom with a partially finished piece of cloth. It was covered with dust and the colors had faded but being out of the sun and weather had preserved much of it. She stared at it open-mouthed and then closed it with a snap, realizing what she was doing and noticing that her knees were aching from having sat in her crouched position for too long. She stood up and slowly approached the loom, the pattern of the weave eerily familiar. She knew she'd seen it, not in books or a museum. This was the exact pattern she'd seen Shy Dove making in her dreams.

It's just a coincidence, Ms. Judgmental opined but Sharon was not convinced.

Had she not already begun to believe that what she was seeing was her dreams manifesting themselves in reality, what she found next to the loom removed all doubt from her mind. At first it looked like just a rock but it was in a clay dish and she knew it had been intentionally placed there, not just debris that had fallen in from the cave. She picked it up to inspect it more closely, wiping the dust off on the leg of her jeans and could see the hint of green.

Malachite! she said out loud, filled with awe.

CHAPTER FIFTY-NINE

hey made good progress in spite of their fatigue, stopping only to eat a light lunch. The daylight hours were stretching out and gave them extra time to continue but Running Deer noticed that Shy Dove was beginning to slow down and she was looking more at her feet than the direction forward. He didn't think she even realized that she was doing it. Shadow was also panting more and although he could have continued, decided he should look for a spot to camp for the night. That opportunity came not long after he'd become aware of the situation.

"This looks like a good spot to spend the night," he said as he pointed to a stand of trees near the stream.

Shy Dove looked up as though woken from sleep. In fact, she felt as though she had been sleep-walking and shook her head slightly to clear her mind to focus on the place where Running Deer was pointing.

"That would be wonderful," she smiled at Running Deer. "I was hoping you would stop soon. I'm not sure how much farther I could go on. Do you think we could have a small fire tonight?" she asked, the desire palpable in her voice.

Running Deer smiled as he answered, "I think that would be a good idea. It may be cool tonight and it's been several days since we left with no sign of anyone following us. Let's set up our camp and I'll see if I can catch some fish for us to cook for our supper."

Shy Dove brightened at that and felt a burst of energy she didn't know she had left. Her mouth watered just thinking about a hot meal of freshly caught fish and corn cakes. The jerky and pemmican had sustained them but after several days of eating nothing else, she was more than ready for a change of diet.

"Be sure to catch some extra for Shadow," she said as she ruffled the fur on his neck. "He deserves a treat, too."

"Yes, he does," Running Deer replied. "I'm not sure we could have made it this far if we didn't have his help carrying our supplies."

He gave the dog a pat on his head and Shadow responded with a lick of his hand.

"Let's get set up," Running Deer said as he turned to make his way to the trees.

It didn't take them long to find a spot that would give them some shelter but was still close to the water. Shy Dove gathered branches that had fallen and dry brush that could be used for tinder and kindling to make the fire. After getting their bed rolls out so they could also have a place to sit, she found her cooking supplies so that she could make the corn cakes. Running Deer had already gone to the stream to see if he could catch any fish but was having some difficulty keeping Shadow away. Freed from his pack, the dog now thought this was play time and was splashing in the water. Running Deer called out to him to stop but Shadow ignored him and continued looking into the water, snapping at it before lunging his head into the water and emerging with a fish in his mouth and padding back to shore with his trophy. Running Deer and Shy Dove both laughed seeing Shadow's pride at his fishing skills.

"Perhaps you should let Shadow catch our dinner," Shy Dove called out to Running Deer.

"He is a good fisher but I don't think he'd be willing to share," Running Deer chuckled. "At least now I know there are fish here to be caught. Do you have some branches that we can use to cook them?"

"Yes, I saved out some before making the fire," Shy Dove called back and held them up for Running Deer to see.

He nodded and waved in reply before turning back to his task.

Shy Dove hummed to herself as she prepared the batter for the corn cakes and put the griddle nearby to warm when the fire burned down enough to set on the coals. For the first time since they'd left their village, she felt relaxed and confident that they really would be able to have a life together. She looked over at Running Deer concentrating on catching more fish. There were already what looked like two on the ground near him. She smiled to herself thinking about how good they would taste and her mouth watered. Shadow had finished his fish and was busy licking his paw and washing his face. The fire had made enough coals that she could begin to fry the corn cakes and her stomach grumbled as the aroma of the grease and cakes filled her nose. Running Deer had gutted and cleaned the fish and brought them to her to be cooked.

"The corn cakes smell wonderful, Shy Dove," Running Deer told her as he threaded the fish onto the sticks she'd saved. "My stomach is grumbling."

"Mine, too! I've missed not having a hot meal. This is like a feast!"

Running Deer smiled but his eyes searched her face for reassurance.

"Are you still sure we've done the right thing?" he asked.

Her eyes held his as she answered without any hesitation.

"There is no doubt in my mind, Running Deer. I don't

remember when I've been happier," she answered and reached out to touch his hand. "There was no other way. I know that if we could have convinced my parents that we should be wed, we could have stayed but it was not to be. My life married to Broken Wing would have been unbearable. I know there will be hardships but we'll be together to face them and that's all that matters to me."

"I love you, Shy Dove. You are my heart and my soul."

"And you mine."

CHAPTER SIXTY

"*W*here has the time gone?" Sharon asked rhetorically when her daughter, Jess, asked how she was doing.

"I know. I can't believe it's almost time for you to come home again," Jess replied. "Are you sorry to be leaving?"

"Mixed feelings," Sharon replied. "I'll definitely miss the weather as I know how April in Maine can still be wintery at times and I'll miss the people I've gotten to know here."

Sharon had told her daughters about her growing friendship with Donna and Joseph but had only mentioned in passing her friendship. . .relationship?. . .with Hal and was still not sure when to broach the topic. Both girls had considered Tom their father as he was the one who had been their father figure and she was not sure how they would react to having another male love interest in Sharon's life and by extension, theirs.

"It won't be that long before the weather will get better here and you know you wouldn't enjoy being in that much heat for very long," Jessica reminded her.

"So true. I'm hoping I won't be too much of a wuss dealing with the cooler temperatures to get the garden in shape. I was thinking of putting in a small vegetable garden this year. There was just too much going on last year to even think about having one."

"It sounds like you're doing better now. I'm really happy to hear that, Mom. We've been worried about you," Jessica said and Sharon could hear the concern in her voice.

"No need to worry anymore," Sharon replied. "This winter in Arizona was just what I needed to get my feet back underneath me," she reassured her. Changing the subject after a short pause, she asked, "Would you or Mandy be able to pick me up at the airport? I can take a cab if neither of you are available. I wouldn't want to put either of you out and the flight doesn't get in until after 10 PM your time."

"*Mom!*" Jessica interjected. "You wouldn't be putting us out and we can't wait to see you. Text me the flight info and I'll check with Mandy but at least one of us will be there to pick you up."

"Thanks, honey. I'm so looking forward to seeing you both again."

"We've missed you, too."

They said their goodbyes and love yous and Sharon disconnected the call. She really did miss them and realized she was ready to go home even as another part of her wanted to stay.

CHAPTER SIXTY-ONE

"*Let's take a walk," Running Deer suggested. "I want to see if there is a spot on higher ground for a lookout."*

"That's a good idea," Shy Dove agreed. "It might help me wake up a little. After eating all that food I'm feeling sleepy but I don't want to fall asleep yet. Which way should we walk?"

Running Deer pointed to the left and Shy Dove could then see a small hill not too far away.

"Should we take our things with us?" she asked.

"Not yet," he replied, "just in case it's not a good spot. It doesn't look like it's that far and we can come back to get them if it turns out to be right."

They walked at a comfortable pace with Shadow trotting behind them. When they reached the top of the hill, they were still able to see quite a distance beyond the trees and shrubs growing there. The vegetation would hide them but no one would be able to approach without being seen. Running Deer shook his head in approval as he surveyed the area.

"This looks like a good spot. There's a nice flat area there

where we can set up our bedrolls," he said pointing to a spot under a cottonwood tree.

Shy Dove smiled up at him.

"It will be strange to sleep at night again but I'm looking forward to it."

"Me, too," Running Deer smiled back at her. "Let's go get our supplies and set up camp before the sun goes down."

They'd only taken out a few cooking supplies and their bedrolls so it didn't take them long to repack and be on their way. Once they'd set everything up they were able to truly relax.

"Shy Dove, I'm sorry we were not able to have a marriage ceremony with our families and the village but I hope you know I will always consider you my wife."

Shy Dove smiled at him and placed her hand on his cheek.

"It would have been nice to have the ceremony and I wish it could have been so but you will always be my husband. I have a surprise for you that I have been waiting for the right moment to show you. I think this may be the right time."

Running Deer's face showed his curiosity.

"What is it, Shy Dove?"

"I have it in one of my bags. Wait just a moment while I get it but I don't want you to look until I tell you. Do you promise?"

Running Deer smiled and shook his head in agreement.

"I promise."

"Close your eyes and don't open them until I say it's okay," she said as she got up and went to their packs.

It took her a few minutes to find the right one and bring it back.

"You can open your eyes now," she said.

Running Deer opened them to see her standing before him with the most beautiful wedding garments he had ever seen. She was wearing hers and holding out his.

"Shy Dove, you look even more beautiful if that is even possible. And is that mine?"

"Of course," she chided him, "whose else would it be?!"

Running Deer's face reddened in embarrassment.

"It's mine, of course," he replied. "I recognize the beadwork but I thought you were going to have to make it over to fit Broken Wing."

"I convinced my mother that I should make a new one for Broken Wing and could use this one to trade. I know it won't be like the ceremony we would have had in the village, but I wanted to make our joining special and I hoped some miracle would happen so that we could wear them there," her words rushed out, "but then I thought that even if it was just the two of us, we could still have our own ceremony because nothing else matters but our being together forever and we could still wear our wedding clothes for each other. I hope you like them."

"When did you find the time to make them, Shy Dove?" Running Deer asked as he held his in his hands and examined the stitching and the intricate beadwork more closely than he'd been able to do when she'd first shown it to him. "It is truly beautiful!"

It was Shy Dove's turn to feel embarrassed but proud at the same time.

"I hope they fit you," she said. "I had to guess when I started making them several months ago. It looks like you might have grown since then."

"It doesn't matter," he replied. "I'll wear them even if the bottom of the legs come up to my knees and the sleeves are at my elbows," he smiled. "Wait here and I'll be right back to show you."

"Where else would I go?" she teased.

Running Deer returned after just a few minutes and Shy Dove caught her breath as she saw him. She had guessed well as the garments fit him perfectly. He had tied his hair back and he appeared even more handsome than she ever remembered seeing him before. Perhaps it was the pride she could see on his face as he turned for her to see how they fit.

"You couldn't have done better, Shy Dove," he said with a big smile. "Are you ready now to become my wife?"

"I've been ready all my life," she answered.

They spoke the words of the ceremony which they'd heard numerous times over the years and kissed each other hesitantly at first and then embraced with the passion that had been building for so long.

"I will be gentle," Running Deer whispered in her ear.

Shy Dove shivered both from the soft touch of his breath on her ear and in anticipation of their lovemaking. She had been told what to expect as part of her coming of age ceremony but was still nervous.

Running Deer took her hand and led her to their bedrolls which she had put together while he was getting dressed. He held her cheeks in his hands and tenderly kissed her lips before taking her hand as they both knelt on the blankets. He gently laid her back and kissed her again as he stroked her arm, warming her skin with his touch. He tugged up the bottom of her dress to slip his hand under sliding it up her thigh making her shiver but not from being cold. She gasped slightly as her body responded with feelings she had never experienced before. He stopped as she moaned.

"Have I hurt you?" he asked, his eyes wide as he searched her face.

"Not at all. Don't stop," she answered looking into his eyes to reassure him.

He smiled in return and continued to stroke her thigh as she responded to his touch by arching her back and moaning softly. He stopped when she reached down and began to tug at his shirt so that she could pull it over his head and then stroked his bare skin with her hands. He kissed her once more before pulling her dress over her head and caught his breath as he saw her nakedness.

"You are so beautiful, Shy Dove," he whispered into her ear and began kissing her neck. She arched her back in pleasure.

"Take off your leggings so I can feel your body against mine," she whispered.

Running Deer slipped off his leggings and she stroked his body feeling her excitement and anticipation grow with the simple touch of his skin on hers. He rolled over her and spread her legs before slowly entering her, restraining himself from going too deep until he had broken her virginity. She cried out as he pierced the skin and he stopped to give her time to recover.

"Are you okay?" he asked.

"Don't stop," she replied.

Slowly, slowly at first he penetrated giving her time to meet his passion and then faster as her breathing quickened and her hips rose to match his strokes. They cried out in ecstasy as the moment of their orgasm came in unison. Running Deer held her close to him while their breathing regained normalcy and then rolled off beside her drawing her close to him in his arms, kissing the top of her head and stroking her hair. She snuggled against him with her hand on his chest and her legs twined in his as they both fell asleep.

CHAPTER SIXTY-TWO

Shy Dove was instantly awake at the sound of Shadow's low growl. Running Deer put his hand on her shoulder and whispered shhhhhh. He was sitting up and in spite of the dim light, she could tell he was surveying their surroundings to see what had caught Shadow's attention. He pulled on his leggings as quietly as possible and Shy Dove did the same with her tunic. Shadow was still growling and his attention was focused on an area of shrubs about 100 feet away.

Running Deer reached for his knife that he had kept nearby and whispered in Shy Dove's ear, "Stay here. I'm going to see if I can circle around so whatever is in the bushes won't know I'm coming." To Shadow he said, "Stay with Shy Dove."

He crouched low and headed toward the shrubs, circling wide as he did so. Shy Dove stroked Shadow's head and he whimpered in response and licked her other hand. She knew he wanted to be with Running Deer but would obey his order to stay with her.

Running Deer's eyes had needed more time than he'd have liked to adjust but nonetheless, he was thankful for the darkness that the lack of moonlight provided to hide him from whatever or whomever was hiding in the bushes. He had circled around crouching low to not be seen or recognized as human and so that he could approach from behind. He asked the Great Spirit to protect him and even more, to protect Shy Dove. The thought of leaving her alone here if he should be killed filled him with worry. He stopped as he reached the spot where he could now see what was there and, as he feared, it was a human not an animal. The shape shifted and he thought it looked familiar. As though sensing a presence behind him, the shape turned and Running Deer now saw clearly that it was Broken Wing. Their eyes locked and in spite of the darkness, they each knew that they had been seen.

Broken Wing leaped to his feet and charged at Running Deer, yelling as he approached.

"I will kill you!"

"Not if I kill you first," Running Deer said under his breath as he leaped up to meet Broken Wing, his knife ready.

Broken Wing's anger had made him reckless and instead of slowing down, he had run full-speed at Running Deer who stepped aside just as Broken Wing reached him. Broken Wing stumbled forward with his momentum and Running Deer kicked him to the ground from behind. Before Broken Wing had a chance to stand, Running Deer knelt down intending to grab a handful of hair to lift his head and slit his throat but Broken Wing was able to roll his body away first. The two men simultaneously jumped into a crouch facing each other, the hatred clear on their faces.

"I should have killed you the first time you laid your hands on Shy Dove," Running Deer spat at Broken Wing.

"It is only for my father's honor that I'm even bothering to bring her back to the village. Why anyone would want that worthless, homely bitch is more than I can understand. I only agreed to the marriage because my father insisted and convinced me that she could make me a rich man with her weaving skills,"

he taunted. "On the other hand, it would give me great pleasure to just kill you both for having shamed me and my father. I can tell them you both attacked me and I had to kill you defending myself. I can always find someone else to make me rich."

"I will not allow that to happen. You will never be worthy of her and you will never have her." Running Deer replied keeping his voice steady in spite of the anger he felt, not wanting to give Broken Wing the satisfaction of knowing his words had any effect on him.

Before Broken Wing could reply, Running Deer sprung at him and the two men wrestled each other to the ground. Broken Wing was able once again to break free and they jumped to their feet, circling around each other brandishing their knives which they had somehow managed to hold onto during their earlier confrontations. They had worked their way back to the bushes that Broken Wing had been hiding behind and Running Deer looked beyond him as though spotting someone there. Broken Wing turned taking the feint as Running Deer had hoped he would giving him time to rush toward him, his knife ready.

SHY DOVE HEARD the scream of another man and clasped her hand over her mouth to keep from screaming herself. The bushes were rustling and then parted as two men fell through and she could see Running Deer struggling with someone who looked familiar. In the space of a second she knew who it was. She would never forget Broken Wing's face. She gasped as they continued to struggle and then all was quiet and their movements ceased. The two men were still as she held her breath waiting for some movement. Shadow broke free from her hold and ran toward them barking.

"Be still, Shadow."

She began to breathe again when she heard Running Deer's voice. He had rolled off the top of Broken Wing's body and lay on his back breathing hard. Shadow licked his face and then began to growl and bark when he recognized Broken Wing but there was no movement or sound from him. Running Deer got up and headed in her direction with Shadow following on his heels.

"Is he dead?" she asked when Running Deer reached their blanket.

"Yes," he answered, his voice barely audible.

She jumped to her feet and hugged him so tight that he had to pat her on the back and then loosen her arms so he could breathe.

"Has he been following us all this time?" she asked.

"He was a few days behind as it took him a while to pick up our trail. He told me he would kill us both for shaming him. He was by himself so we will be safe now but we can't stay here. We must get as far away from his body as we can."

"Should we bury it so no one will find him?"

"No, we'll leave it for the animals. It's what he deserves."

They finished dressing and gathering their belongings in silence. Before long they were headed north again, neither of them wanting to speak. As dawn approached, Running Deer broke the silence. "I think this looks like a good spot to rest and then if you're able, we should try to put more distance between us for a few hours until we can find a safe place. He said he was alone but I don't want to risk that someone else followed him."

Shy Dove shook her head, too exhausted both physically and mentally to speak.

Two hours later after having had something to eat and drink but too on edge to sleep, they set out again.

CHAPTER SIXTY-THREE

*S*haron lay in bed thinking about the challenges that Shy Dove and Running Deer had faced and how brave they were. They had become real in her mind, not just actors in an ongoing series she had been watching in her dreams over the past months since arriving in Arizona. Could she have done what Shy Dove had at that age? *Did* she*?* she asked herself thinking of herself as having been Shy Dove in a past life especially after having found the cave that mirrored the one she'd dreamed of so many times.

Realizing it was one of those questions that could never be definitively answered, she got up, retrieved her laptop, and wrote down the dream in her journal. There was nothing pressing she needed to do that day so didn't rush and by the time she'd finished her usual morning routine, it was nearly noon.

The rest of the day was spent working on her gourd project. She wanted to have it finished to take to her last class to show her instructor. They'd talked about it in a previous class and the instructor had asked her to bring it in for a show and tell. She hoped it was going to pass muster but even if the others weren't impressed, she liked it and wasn't that really all that mattered?

CHAPTER SIXTY-FOUR

Shy Dove was tending to the vegetables she had planted, humming as she watered them from the stream nearby and pulled the few weeds. It had been four months since their encounter with Broken Wing and no one had found them. They had walked another week before finding what seemed to be a perfect spot with a stream and fertile land and a cave not too far above that provided shelter and safety with a clear view of the surrounding area for miles. Running Deer's hunting skills had kept them fed and there was even enough extra to preserve. They were happy and at peace now that they were able to live their lives together. Shadow lay nearby panting in the heat of the day. Running Deer had left him with her while he went hunting as he did not want to risk alarming whatever animal he might find.

"What do you think, Shadow? Should we go back to the cave and start our supper?"

Shadow barked once in agreement and jumped up to walk with her back to the cave.

"Running Deer should be home soon," she assured him. She knew that Shadow would much rather be roaming with Running

Deer than staying here with her but his presence made her feel safer whenever Running Deer was away.

She made preparations for their supper but still no sign of Running Deer. Hours passed and still he had not returned but it was now dark and would not be safe for her to go out looking for him.

"He must have had to go farther away this time, Shadow, but he should be home soon," she said more for her benefit than his.

She slept fitfully through the night and arose at dawn but Running Deer had still not returned. Her feeling of dread was unbearable. She knew she had to find him. The morning air was chilly and she shivered both with the cold and the anticipation of what she might find.

She'd walked nearly a mile calling to him as she did until her throat was sore and her voice hoarse but still no reply from him. Shadow had run ahead and was barking near a grassy spot where they'd found berries earlier that summer. Looking in that direction, she spotted the remains of a deer carcass that had been torn apart and gnawed upon by what she thought must have been a mountain lion. She could tell the animal had been dragged to this spot as the grass had been flattened leading away from it. She looked to her right and left and turned back in the direction she'd come to make sure the lion was not still there. Not seeing any sign of it, she kept going in the direction from where it had been dragged. About fifty feet away, Running Deer lay motionless. His body was sprawled on the ground face down and a pool of blood surrounded his head and shoulders. Shy Dove froze, her breath hitched and she sank to her knees as her eyes registered what her head and heart did not want to accept. She forced herself up to go to him. Although she knew with a certainty that it was too late, she called his name softly as she turned him gently over and held him in her arms. The cat must have been tracking him as he was butchering the deer and caught him unaware from behind. It had bitten his neck severing his carotid artery. His death had come quickly. Her keening filled the air, startling birds that had been roosting in the trees nearby. Shadow had joined her and his howling mingled with hers.

It felt like an eternity had passed before her wails became sobs and then finally there were no more tears left in her. She gently laid him down and thought about what needed to be done. She didn't want to leave him here in case the lion returned but she didn't know how she could carry him back closer to the cave. She thought perhaps if she could pull the remains of the deer carcass farther from his body, it might be enough to keep the lion or any other animals away while she returned to the cave to get what she would need to bury him. It was then that she remembered that Running Deer must have taken the supplies to make a travois to carry back any meat and that perhaps the mountain lion or whatever it was that had killed Running Deer had interrupted him while he was butchering the deer. She had to coax Shadow away from Running Deer's body but he finally relented so that she could have him with her while she looked around the area to find Running Deer's backpack.

It took her over an hour once she found it and put together the travois and rolled Running Deer's body onto it so that she could return to the cave. Her body and mind were numb as she went through the motions and slowly plodded back with Shadow trotting beside her. The sun was high in the sky and the day had grown hot by the time she was finished digging a grave for him in a spot they had both enjoyed sitting in to watch the sunset. She opened the blanket she had wrapped his body in to look at him one last time. Gently she brushed the hair back from his face, still handsome even in death.

"I will always love you, Running Deer."

She kissed his forehead, his cheeks, and his lips one last time as tears welled in her eyes and rolled down her cheeks. Not wanting to close the blanket around him, knowing that she would never again see him, she sat for a long time gazing at his face as the sobs again overtook her. It was the changing light that broke through her misery and she knew she could no longer put off placing his body in the grave.

Although she'd not eaten all day and her stomach grumbled in protest, she had no interest in food. She curled in a fetal position on their sleeping mat and wrapped the blankets around her with Shadow nestled against her. She'd taken Running Deer's extra shirt with her as though holding it and smelling the faint scent of his body which remained on it could keep away the reality that he was gone. She lay there motionless, her eyes open but unseeing, her mind far away, the grief overtaking her. At some point she fell asleep.

CHAPTER SIXTY-FIVE

Sharon woke with tears streaming down her face. Memories of Tom's death came rushing back and it was some time before she got out of bed feeling emotionally drained. The rest of the day her every movement felt forced as the fugue engulfed her and she was unable to shake the sadness that her dream had brought on. She let the feelings be what they were knowing from experience that the grief would only be exorcised by time and letting them be felt but not knowing whether it was grief about Running Deer or Tom that she felt the most. How was it possible that she could be grieving this way about a person who was only real in her dreams?

The next day she awoke feeling better and no dreams had disturbed her sleep. Today was her class and she looked forward to getting out of the house and seeing Donna again.

She was aware of Donna giving her a closer look when she arrived at class.

"What?" Sharon asked.

"You look different," Donna answered. "I can't quite put my finger on what it is, but are you okay?"

"Just the after-effects of a bad dream," Sharon replied. "It took me by surprise and brought up some old feelings about Tom's passing."

"Ahhh, that would explain it. Anything you want to talk about?"

"No, I think I've worked through it. Just needed to have a good cry and get it all out. My eyes are probably still puffy," Sharon smiled as she answered, hoping that would be enough to stop Donna's questioning. She didn't really mind as she knew Donna meant well but she wasn't ready to tell her the real source of what led to the tears. Not yet, anyway.

"Is this a bad time to ask about what's going on on the Hal front?"

Sharon chuckled.

"Your guess is as good as mine. I'm trying to play it cool and not act like the teenager I feel like. Shouldn't ladies of our age be a bit more respectable?"

"We don't have time for that," Donna replied drily.

"You may have a point there," Sharon said with a smile.

Just then, the instructor came into the room and their attention returned to the task at hand.

CHAPTER SIXTY-SIX

*S*haron smiled as she saw Hal's name on her phone's screen. It had only been a couple days since they'd seen each other so why was she feeling relief?

"You're acting like a teenager," Ms. Judgmental sniffed.

"You're right. Time to get past that," Sharon replied and could almost see the surprised expression that there was no argument this time.

"Hey, how are you?" Sharon asked.

"Missing you. Sorry I didn't call yesterday. Had meetings back-to-back nearly all day long and it was late before I was able to wrap things up so didn't want to disturb you. Wasn't last night your art class?"

Sharon felt a tingle at Hal's response. *Yup, just like a teenager.*

"It was! You remembered."

"I listen," Hal answered and Sharon could see his smile even over the phone line. "How was it?"

"Good. It was nice to see Donna again, too. I'm going to be sorry to have it end next week. I can't believe it's only a couple weeks before I go back to Maine."

"That's something I wanted to talk to you about. What would you think about my coming to see you there? I've never spent any time in Maine and would love to have a local show me around."

"I'd love it and had planned to ask you the same thing the next time we talked," Sharon replied, feeling that tingle again.

"The other thing I wanted to tell you is that I'm not going to be able to take you to the airport. A problem came up on those phone meetings that I'm going to have to handle in person and it means being away when you leave."

"Oh, don't worry about that," Sharon replied trying to hide her disappointment. "I can get a ride and would have had to figure it out for myself anyway if we hadn't met. Knowing you'll be coming to Maine to see me more than makes up for a ride to the airport. When will you have to leave, though? Will we have time to see each other before then?"

"Another reason I was calling. How about tonight? I can come to see you there or bring an overnight bag with you and spend the night at my place. Lady's choice but I hope you'll tell me to bring my overnight bag if I come to see you."

"Decisions, decisions," Sharon teased. "How about you come here and be sure to bring that overnight bag."

"It's a date. See you around 6?" Hal asked.

"Perfect. I'll get something easy to cook on the grill and we can watch the sunset on the patio. Can't wait to see you!"

"Me, too," Hal replied.

"See you tonight," Sharon replied.

She took a quick inventory of her refrigerator to decide what she would need from the grocery store for their dinner which she also needed to plan, she realized. She wanted it to be perfect and then chastised herself. "Don't overthink it. Keep it simple and stop stressing out."

"Good advice," Ms. Judgmental told her. Maybe you aren't being as much of a teenager as I thought."

On that vote of confidence, Sharon dressed and made her way to the grocery store.

285

The doorbell rang promptly at six o'clock and Sharon tried to compose herself before answering the door. She had everything ready for dinner and had kept it simple. It had taken her longer to get herself ready but after trying on and discarding several outfits, finally gave up and settled on casual but accessorized and light makeup. She wanted Hal to know she'd made an effort but wasn't overdoing it.

"Hi, how was the drive?" she asked, stepping aside to let Hal come in.

"A bit more traffic than I was expecting but it kept moving so made good time," he replied and gave her a peck on the cheek.

"Oh, where are my manners? Let me take that and put it in the kitchen," Sharon said as she noticed the bottle of wine Hal had in his left hand and tried not to focus on the overnight bag in his right.

He handed it over and asked, "Where can I put my bag? You're still okay with me staying over?"

"Definitely," she replied. "This way," and led him into the master bedroom.

"Very nice," he said as he looked around and set his bag

down on the luggage rack she had set up earlier that day. "I have to confess I was afraid it might have been a different style of decorating and was one of the reasons why you didn't show it to me the last time I was here."

"Too girly, you mean?" she teased.

"You got me," he smiled back at her.

"I got over that decades ago. I do like girly things, don't get me wrong, but I don't feel the need to go overboard with it. The bathroom is right through that door if you want to put any of your things in there now or we can open up the bottle of wine you brought and sit out on the patio while the grill heats up. I have kebabs already made up and marinating so it won't take long to get dinner ready."

"Sounds good, but first, let me do what I've been dying to do since you opened the door but my hands were full."

He walked toward her and took her in his arms and gave her the kiss she'd been wanting as much as he had. Deep, slow, and gentle. Then moved his way down to her neck, making her shiver in spite of herself.

"Maybe we should just stay here for a little while until it cools off," he murmured in her ear.

"I have a feeling it's going to get hot in here, too," she smiled seductively.

"If I have anything to do with it, you bet it is."

"Dinner can wait then. I'm not sure that I can for much longer. I've been thinking of you all day long."

"And just what have you been thinking?" he asked as his hand went to her breast.

She sucked in her breath and moaned. "I've. . .uh. . ." she moaned again as he continued to rub her nipple. "Been thinking about how good it would feel to have you doing exactly what you're doing right now."

"So I shouldn't stop?" he asked knowing exactly what her answer would be.

"NO, no don't stop. Do it more."

"You don't have to ask twice. In fact, I'm going to do that and a whole lot more," and proceeded to do just that.

Sharon sighed in contentment as they snuggled together with her leg wrapped across his after some of the best lovemaking she'd had in years.

"I don't want to move but my stomach is telling me that I skipped lunch and really doesn't give a flip about the fact that it's so nice just being here with you," she murmured.

"Me, too. Just one more kiss and then we go get that glass of wine and get the grill fired up."

"Just one," she agreed.

A promise they both broke. It was long after dark by the time they finally got to the wine and dinner but by then the temperature was perfect for sitting outside and the sky was filled with the twinkling of stars.

"This is amazing," Hal said as he looked up at the sky. "It's been a while since I've seen the night sky like this without all the ambient light to hide the stars."

"It is amazing. You forget how many stars there really are until you see it like this. It makes me feel so small and insignificant but in a good way if that makes any sense at all and I'm not sure it does," she said.

"I do know what you mean," he replied.

They sat in silence for a while longer taking it all in before heading back inside.

"I'm going to miss you."

"I'm going to miss you, too," Sharon replied. "This. . .meeting you and all of this…was totally unexpected. I never thought I'd be involved with someone again after I lost Tom and I'm a little nervous, truth be told."

"About what?" Hal asked.

"That it's too good to be true."

"I hope I can convince you otherwise. I don't want you to be out of my life once you leave and I hope you mean it when you said you'd like me to come to Maine to see you."

"I do!" she replied. "I wasn't sure if you did but let's settle that right now. When can you come to see me?"

"I've got some business to take care of and won't be able to take you to the airport but I've already told you that. How much time do you need once you get back to be ready for me?"

"How about a week? I'm probably going to regret not making it sooner but this is my first time being away for so long and don't know if I'll need more time to get things back up and running."

"It's a date and if you need any help, I'm more than happy to come sooner. I want you to know this is real, Sharon, not just a dream and not just a fling for me."

She didn't doubt his sincerity.

"I feel the same way and so glad you do."

She'd thought about saying she was relieved but realized how needy and insecure that would have sounded.

"Good job," she told herself in her head both for her benefit and Ms. Judgmental's.

Hal took her hand and led her back to the bedroom where he showed her again how much he enjoyed being with her.

CHAPTER SIXTY-EIGHT

"Can you believe tonight is our last class?" Donna asked when Sharon answered the phone.

"No, it's gone by way too quickly," Sharon replied. "I'm so glad I took it so I got the chance to know you."

"Me, too. But now you're going back to Maine next week and leaving me here all alone," Donna teased. "We should have a farewell party before you do. Do you have time tonight? You could stay over so we don't have to call it a night early. We could do each other's hair and paint our nails…"

They both laughed.

"I'd love that! Maybe skip the hair and nails, though. Thanks so much for asking."

After the class, they went to eat at one of their favorite restaurants and then back to Donna's condo for their final get-together. At least for this year.

"*Soooo*, tell me all about what you've been doing since last week. Have you seen Hal? And yes, I am shamelessly fishing for all the details," Donna teased.

"You are incorrigible," Sharon laughed in spite of herself. "As a matter of fact, he came to my house last week and stayed over. That's as much as I'm going to say, though, as I believe ladies also should not kiss and tell. I'll let it suffice that we had a wonderful dinner, sat outside admiring the stars, and have made plans for him to come to Maine to visit me."

"This sounds serious."

"Maybe. Possibly. I don't know," Sharon hesitated. "I think I want it to be but am still a little worried I'm jumping in too soon and too fast."

"Like I told you before, we don't have the luxury of time at our age," Donna answered. "I get what you're saying, though. Hearts can still get broken if it doesn't work out."

"That's exactly it," Sharon agreed. "I've already been through as much heartache as I think I can handle the past year. This wasn't anything I was expecting, not just this soon, but ever, to be honest. It doesn't feel. . .I don't know if real is the right word. I'm not sure what the right word is. I just know for now I want to keep seeing him and will have to trust that it either works out or I can handle it if it doesn't.

"Sounds like a good way to think about it. And if ever you need someone to talk to, you know I'll be there for you. I may not be able to give you a good hug but there's a sympathetic ear and a good virtual kick in the butt if you need that, too."

Sharon laughed.

"Had to lighten that up," Donna winked. "You know me, humor is my go-to position especially when things get too serious."

"It's one of your endearing qualities," Sharon replied and lifted her wine glass in a toast.

The next morning they had breakfast followed by a leisurely walk and then it was time for Sharon to go home.

"I'm really going to miss seeing you every week, but let's keep up the tradition and call on our regular class night. Maybe we could do a weekly FaceTime?" Sharon suggested.

"Perfect! I'm going to miss you, too. Who knows, though,

maybe I'll meet *my* Mr. Right or even better, Mr. Right for Now, too," Donna rolled her eyes even as she said it and they both broke out in laughter as though they were 14 again.

"*That* is what I'm going to miss most but in the meantime we can come up with ideas for what we'll do when I come back again."

"Great idea! Until then," Donna gave Sharon a big hug and peck on the cheek. "You take care of yourself and call me. Don't think you're going to leave me hanging with the story of Sharon and Hal."

Sharon laughed.

"I promise. But *no details!*" she wagged her finger at Donna.

They both laughed as Sharon got into her car, waved one last time and headed back home.

CHAPTER SIXTY-NINE

Sharon checked the caller ID and smiled to see Hal's name. He'd had to leave earlier than expected and was still not going to make it back in time to take her to the airport.

"Hey, stranger," she teased.

"A stranger already? I've only been gone three days," he replied in mock indignation.

"It feels a lot longer. Just missing you."

"I miss you, too, and it's killing me that I'm not going to be there to take you to the airport."

"Really, don't worry about it. I'm going to ask Joseph Ramos if he would be able to take me."

"Joseph? The same Joseph you had dinner with?"

Was that a hint of jealousy she detected?

"Yes, that one. You're not jealous are you?" she asked, hoping that he knew she was teasing.

"I don't need to be, do I?" he asked.

"No, you don't," she reassured him. "Joseph has been a good friend, that's all. You've got my undivided attention."

"Glad to hear that because you've got mine, too. I've got my reservation booked to come to Maine. I'll email you the itinerary so you'll have. . .oh, sorry, I'm going to have to cut this short. My client just arrived."

"OK. Thanks for calling and good luck with the meeting!"

Sharon disconnected the phone and realized she needed to actually ask Joseph if he'd give her a ride. If not, she'd need to be making alternate arrangements. They'd met for lunch or dinner a few times while she'd been there and he'd offered any help but somehow it felt different to ask him now that she was involved with Hal.

"It's not like you're cheating on him," she admonished herself. "Your relationship with Joseph has been purely platonic," she went on and then wondered why it felt so much like she was trying to convince herself of that. "You're being silly," and with that she finally ended the internal conversation.

She brought up Joseph's name and number from her Contacts list and hit the button. He picked up on the fourth ring just as she was preparing to leave a voicemail.

"Hi, Sharon."

She could hear construction noises in the background.

"Hi, Joseph. Did I catch you at a bad time?"

"Never a bad time to talk to you. What can I do for you?"

"Well, I was hoping you might be able to take me to the airport on Saturday. If you don't have the time, though, just say so and I'll make other arrangements," she added hurriedly.

"No, no, it's no bother. I need to go to Tucson anyway so that's another reason to make the trip. What time do you need to be there?"

"The flight leaves at noon but I can check in online and I don't have any luggage to check in, so should probably get there by 10:30 or 11 at the latest."

"Perfect. How about I pick you up around 9:30 just to be on the safe side?"

“That would be great. Thanks so much for doing this for me.”

“It’s my pleasure. See you then.”

295

The conversation on the ride to the airport was light and upbeat. Although the topics were banal—the weather, traffic, how quickly her time there had gone by--it didn't feel trite. Their relationship had grown into the place where they could have comfortable banter interspersed with silences that didn't make them uneasy.

They arrived at the airport with time to spare and since she only had a carry-on bag, they drove into the passenger drop-off area. Joseph insisted upon helping her retrieve her bag from the back of his truck. He started to hand it to her but as she reached to take it from him, he took her in his arms and gave her a big hug. As he let her go and she looked in his face, it was not his but Running Deer's that she saw and the surprise must have registered on her face.

"I'm sorry, I shouldn't have done that," Joseph's face flushed with embarrassment and he backed away from her.

"No, no, it's not that. You just took me by surprise," she smiled and put her hand on his arm to reassure him.

"I'm going to miss you. I didn't realize that until your call asking me to bring you to the airport."

"Joseph, I. . .I don't know what to say," she stammered.

"You don't need to say anything," he replied. "I'm really sorry. I shouldn't have done that. It was purely impulse and now I've put you in a bad spot."

Her mind was going in different directions. *Should I tell him I'm in a relationship? Is that even what this is about? Maybe he just means this as a friend and you're making a whole lot more out of this.*

"No, it's okay. Really," she smiled to try to lighten the tension that had built up between them. "You've been such a great friend to me at a time when I really needed that. I can't thank you enough for all you've done for me this winter. It's always hard to leave friends but I'm sure we'll see each other again when I get back next winter."

"You bet," he smiled. "I'm counting on it. But now, I really need to let you go to catch your plane and I should get out of the drop-off lane before they give me a ticket. Have a safe flight!"

"Thanks!"

She turned and walked into the terminal still rattled about the hug and seeing Running Deer's face. She hadn't had any more dreams since the one in which he'd died. Was this some sort of an omen? A sign that she wasn't meant to be with Hal? Was she letting her imagination run away with her?

"Get a grip," Ms. Judgmental's voice came through loud and clear.

"Maybe for once she's right," Sharon thought as she squared her shoulders and walked to her gate putting aside for now all the possibilities awaiting her.

Thank you for reading my book and if you liked it, I hope you will leave a review.

To get the latest information on new releases, excerpts and more, be sure to sign up for Marsha's newsletter.

Coming in January 2022

Deja Vu Dreams

Book 2 of The Arizona Series

In book 2 of the series, Sharon returns to Maine for the summer and breaks the news of her romance with Hal Jackson to her daughters. As she'd feared, her younger daughter, Amanda, is extremely upset by the news and isn't afraid to let it be known when Hal comes to visit Sharon. The tension continues in spite of Sharon's best efforts to smooth things over but holds out hope that once she's back in Arizona, it will resolve itself. Or will she find that Joseph Ramos is really the better man to have in her life?

During her time in Maine, her dreams of the Native American couple had stopped but upon returning to Arizona, they pick up where they'd left off.

Will Sharon and Shy Dove finally find their happily ever after?

ABOUT THE AUTHOR

After retiring from her day job of nearly 33 years, Marsha DeFilippo has embarked on a new career of writing books. She is also
a lifelong avid crafter and has yet to try a craft she doesn't like.
She spends her winters in Arizona and the remainder of the year
in Maine.

Visit her site
https://www.marshadefilippo.com